A figure staggered out of the smoke

It was Wilson. Sergeant Pierce stopped in midstride and turned around. Wilson was coming, but not fast enough. As the sergeant watched, the medic stumbled and fell. Pierce started running back.

Two gunships came charging in side by side, their rotor blades almost touching. Their noses blazed fire and 2.75-inch high-explosive rockets lanced out from the pods on their pylons.

Below, the forest was coming apart. The rockets, miniguns and thumper rounds peppered the jungle, shredding the foliage and dropping trees as if they were matchsticks.

Pierce was oblivious to the destruction around him. He was also unaware of the wound he'd taken, a small piece of shrapnel in the shoulder. He was totally oblivious to everything except the need to keep running toward the hovering gunship.

Suddenly, Wilson seemed to weigh a ton. Pierce felt his strength rapidly leaving him. His energy reserves were all but drained. He was moving solely now on stubborn willpower. Pierce decided that as long as he was alive, he would keep on running.

Knox Gordon

HATCHET

A GOLD EAGLE BOOK FROM
WORLDWIDE ®

TORONTO · NEW YORK · LONDON · PARIS
AMSTERDAM · STOCKHOLM · HAMBURG
ATHENS · MILAN · TOKYO · SYDNEY

First edition November 1991

ISBN 0-373-62114-0

Special thanks and acknowledgment to
Michael Kasner for his contribution to this work.

HATCHET

1

April 15, 1968, Nha Trang, RVN

It was a typical early April morning on the coast of
Vietnam. It was only a little past 0900, but even with
the fresh sea breeze the air was already so hot and thick
that you could feel it on your skin.

Coming in low over the bay, a camouflage-painted
C-130 transport plane, her flaps down, lined up with
the end of the runway at the Nha Trang Air Force Base,
Republic of Vietnam. The turboprop transport touched
down on the tarmac with a brief puff of smoke from
her tires and rolled a few yards before the pilot threw
the props into reverse. The turbines screamed as the
plane slowed against the reverse thrust. Halfway down
the runway, the C-130 pilot turned onto the taxiway
and shut down the two inboard turbines. A second
later the rear ramp door slowly opened and a man
stepped out onto the tarmac with a loaded duffel bag
in each hand.

He walked a few steps before he abruptly stopped
and grounded the two heavy duffel bags. The brand-
new set of jungle fatigues with full-color insignia fitted the man's six-foot athletic build as if they had been
tailored for him. Although newly issued, his jungle
boots had been spit-shined. The famous green beret of

the U.S. Special Forces with captain's bars pinned over the Fifth Group flash covered his close-cropped brown hair as his light blue eyes slowly scanned his surroundings.

It was all so familiar to him: that strange smell that pervaded all of Southeast Asia, the sweltering heat and the jungle fatigue jacket already sticking to his back. He didn't have his in-country tan and his fatigues hadn't been washed yet so they still gave off that smell peculiar to new Army uniforms, although the man barely noticed. He could hardly believe that it had been eleven long months since he had DEROS'ed to go back to the World. Even with that all behind him now, he felt as if he had never left. Captain Mike Reese, United States Special Forces, was home.

Reese had been in Nha Trang before. Less than a year earlier he had flown out from this same air base at the end of his first tour. He still marveled at the tropical beauty of the coastal town. Even though he knew better, Nha Trang looked as if there couldn't possibly be a war going on anywhere in the vicinity. It looked more like the setting for the next Beach Blanket Bingo movie, not a place where people were dying just a few miles away.

Even Camp Alpha, the in-country replacement center at Long Bien Junction outside of Saigon, looked more warlike than Nha Trang. Outside the perimeter fence of the air base the late-afternoon sun glinted off slow-breaking waves in a picture-postcard bay. Motorcycle pedicabs putt-putted down a broad boulevard lined with stately palm trees, and sea gulls slowly circled over the gleaming white beaches. Reese grinned and slowly shook his head. What a place to fight a war!

Nha Trang was the third-largest city in Vietnam and had once been known as the Jewel of the South China Sea. The French had turned the town into a world-class seaside resort, and even with the destruction it had suffered in the abortive Tet Offensive earlier that year, it was still one of the most beautiful spots in all of Southeast Asia in the spring of 1968.

Nha Trang was situated along a gently curving bay on the eastern side of a spit formed by the mouth of the Cua Be River. Inland, across the river, the verdant green of the jungle-covered Dong Bo Mountains formed a perfect backdrop for the clear water of the sheltered bay. The broad stretches of white sand resembled the beaches of Hawaii before World War II. Modern hotels and French colonial villas lined the beachfront coastal highway that wound past the rugged coastline south to Phan Rang and north to Hue. Because of the constant breezes off the South China Sea, the climate was milder and considerably cooler than it was just a few miles inland.

It was small wonder that the Fifth Special Forces Group had located their headquarters in Nha Trang. Those guys had real brains under those funny little green hats. The town was also home to the First Field Force Vietnam Headquarters as well as the First Logistical Command's huge supply and maintenance center, Camp John F. McDermott. Also, the U.S. Air Force had built a plush stateside-style air base right on the edge of the bay. The Zoomies always knew where the good beaches were.

Reese squared the green beret on his head, picked up his bags and followed the rest of the passengers across the hot tarmac to the white building with the sign reading Nha Trang AFB Passenger Terminal.

At the Army passenger representatives' booth in the terminal, the captain dropped his bags on the concrete floor. "How do I get a ride over to SFOB?" he asked the scrawny SP/4 behind the counter.

The man dropped his *Playboy* magazine and yelled across the room, "Hey, Walker! Another customer for ya!"

A PFC in rumpled fatigues slowly roused himself from his chair and sauntered over. "You need a ride, sir?"

Reese handed him his duffel bags. "Fifth Group."

"No sweat, sir. Just follow me."

On the short ride along the road through the middle of Camp John F. McDermott, the sprawling four-hundred-acre Army support base south of the airfield, Reese was surprised to see how much the camp had grown in his absence. It had been named after the first American killed there, but now no one could tell by looking that the war had ever passed this way.

Camp John F. McDermott, or CJFM, was just as finished as many stateside Army posts. White head-quarters buildings, huge warehouses, maintenance shops with tin roofs and rows of barracks buildings linked by wooden sidewalks crowded the flat expanse of sand. A little piece of America had been trans-planted to Vietnam. As they turned down the road to the Fifth Group Special Forces Operating Base—SFOB—Reese saw that the REMFs were building even more stateside-type facilities.

SFOB, however, looked more like what one expected of a Vietnam outpost. None of its buildings were painted, while well-built defensive positions flanked the main gate and the armed guards on duty looked more than ready for war. The driver stopped at the main gate and handed Reese his bags.

The captain shouldered them and, after asking directions to his destination, walked through the Special Forces headquarters complex. By the time he had gone ten yards he was sweating like an FNG. The back of his fatigue jacket was soaked.

Unlike Camp Alpha, the Nha Trang air base or Camp McDermott, this was Reese's home turf. SFOB was the home base of Reese's fraternity, Fifth Group, U.S. Special Forces, the proud men who wore the green beret with the yellow and red stripes on the black flash. As a member of this most elite group of fighting men, Reese felt most at home when he was among his brothers-in-arms.

A slight shift in the wind assaulted him with the familiar odor of human waste burning in diesel fuel as he passed the nearby latrine. An old Vietnamese papa-san wearing a set of cast-off U.S. khakies slowly stirred the nasty concoction in the cutoff fifty-five-gallon oil drum. The blazing fire sent a coil of thick, greasy smoke and shimmering heat waves into the already humid air.

Reese couldn't see how the old man could breathe. The Army probably used more diesel fuel to burn its shit than it did to run its trucks, he thought. Even when fuel had been rationed during his last tour there had always been enough to burn shit.

Beyond the latrine Reese saw his destination—the wooden tropical hut that housed the officer assignment clerk. A small sign over the screen door to the building read S-1 Officer Assignments. Reese paused to square the green beret on his head. Unlike the rest of his gear, it was the only thing that wasn't brand-new. It was the same slightly battered, sun-faded beret he'd worn on his last tour in an A-camp down in the Delta.

As Reese opened the door and stepped into the building, a voice sang out loud and clear, "This fuckin' Army's all right!"

The Special Forces officer smiled to himself as his eyes adjusted to the dim light. A young soldier was standing with his back to him, both arms over his head as if he were delivering a papal benediction to the masses outside Saint Peter's in Rome.

"You got that shit right," Reese said. He grinned broadly when the soldier jumped and spun around to see who had walked in on his solemn pronouncement.

"Sorry 'bout that, sir," the soldier said nervously. "I didn't know you were there."

"No sweat," Reese answered, noticing the half flash on the green beret on the Spec Five's desk, a "Candy Stripe." The embroidered cloth bar in the yellow, red and black colors of the Fifth Group flash meant the man wasn't Special Forces-qualified. He was an REMF staff specialist assigned to SFOB to take care of ash-and-trash administrative duties in order to free a Green

Beret for field duty. Things had really changed in the SF since Reese had last been in-country.

"Can I help you, sir?"

"I think so," Reese said with a grin. "I'm Captain Mike Reese. I understand you have an assignment for me."

"Yes, sir." The clerk was all business now as he checked his roster of incoming officer replacements, thankful to have escaped an ass-chewing. "Ah, sir, it says here you were supposed to report directly to B-40 in Can Tho."

Things had definitely gone to hell in the SF during the year he'd been gone. "My orders read that I'm supposed to report here," he said, handing a copy to the clerk.

The man shook his head. "It's those goddamn REMFs at Camp Alpha, sir. I can't get it through their heads that our people don't need to check in with us here like they were fucking legs or something."

The clerk didn't wear the winged parachute badge of airborne status on his fatigue jacket, but he had soaked up the airborne soldier's prejudice against their non-airborne-qualified comrades. "What's the rush, anyway?" Reese asked. "And where am I going?"

"A-410 down in the Delta, sir, at Ban Phoc. Their CO got greased a couple of weeks ago, and the XO's been running his ass off trying to keep them going."

"Who was their old CO?"

"Captain Jack Fields."

Reese was silent for a moment. Fields had been a good man. The SF was such a small fraternity that almost everyone knew everyone else. Every time a Special Forces man was killed anywhere in-country, it was almost like a death in the family.

"What is A-410?" he asked.

"Mike Force," the clerk answered. "Mostly Nungs, but they've got a platoon of Cambodes, too."

Reese was pleased. He had always wanted to command one of the hard-hitting Mobile Strike Force companies. His first tour had been as an adviser to a CIDG battalion at a strategic hamlet deep in the Delta. It had been a good assignment, but with limited action. Too much of his time had been spent running a training program for the CIDG troops and trying to teach the South Vietnamese LLDB—the Luc Luong Dac Biet, their Special Forces—how to operate in the field. The Mike Force units were all well trained, and he wouldn't have to argue with the South Vietnamese officers before he did something; the Mike Force units were under direct U.S. command with no LLDB presence.

He smiled. "Outfuckingstanding. How soon can you get me down there?"

The clerk glanced at his watch and reached for the phone on his desk. "I think I can get you out with the 281st today, sir," he said. "I'll have them save a seat on the ash-and-trash run for you."

"Great." Reese reached down for his bags. "Do I need to check in with anyone else around here?"

"No, sir. Like I said, you were expected at B-40, so you'll need to see them sooner or later."

IT WAS A SHORT jeep ride across the compound to the airfield used by the 281st Assault Helicopter Company, the Wolfpack, one of the two assault helicopter companies that supported SF operations throughout Vietnam. The Huey's rotor was already spinning when Reese walked up to the chopper. "You going south?" he asked the pilot.

"You got it, buddy. Where you going?"

"Ban Phoc, Four Corp."

"Hop in."

Reese barely had time to strap himself into the canvas seat in the back before the pilot pulled pitch and lifted off. The chopper banked south as it climbed, and Reese settled back to watch the countryside rush past several thousand feet below him.

The long flight south from Nha Trang was a welcome reacquaintance with the country for Reese. Vietnam was stunningly beautiful from the air. The patchwork of dense jungle and half-flooded rice paddies around little villages looked like something out of the glossy pages of a *National Geographic* magazine.

At one point they flew over a piece of jungle that had obviously been hit by a B-52 Arc Light strike. Only an Arc Light could make holes that big in the jungle in such a perfectly straight line. But even the pattern of raw red craters where the bombs had torn up the jungle had a picturesque quality to it.

All too soon the flight was over. The pilot turned back and pointed forward. "There it is," he shouted over the beat of the rotors. "Ban Phoc."

2

Special Forces Camp A-410, Ban Phoc

Reese unbuckled his seat belt and moved forward between the pilot's and copilot's armored seats to have a better look at his new home.

The A-410 camp looked much the same as any of dozens of similar so-called CIDG fighting camps he'd seen up and down the Vietnam-Cambodia border. The outer perimeter was shaped like a five-pointed star, with the barbed wire obstacles and the sandbagged fighting bunkers for the platoons constructed within the points. Inside the outer perimeter was a five-sided inner boundary of trenches and final defensive fighting positions. A spindly wooden tower stood in the center of the camp next to the half-buried command bunker. He could see the welcome sight of six well-protected 81 mm mortar pits as well as a pair of 106 mm recoilless rifles for heavy weaponry. Ban Phoc had been built to dish it out as well as take it.

The small PSP-covered helicopter landing area was right outside the inner ring of wire in one of the points of the star. A short, stocky, well-tanned man, naked to the waist, stood at the edge of the pad, shielding his eyes from the whirling red dust as the helicopter touched down.

The pilot kept his turbines spinning as Reese grabbed his gear and jumped down. "Thanks!" he yelled.

"No sweat, sir." The warrant officer pilot shot him a thumbs-up.

Crouched over to clear the spinning rotor blades, Reese ran to the edge of the landing pad. The man waiting for him reached for his duffel bags. "Sergeant Torres, sir, radioman," he said, introducing himself. "Welcome to Ban Phoc."

Reese handed him one of the bags. "Mike Reese," he said, shaking the man's hand. "Glad to be here."

"If you'll follow me, sir," Torres said, "I'll take you to meet the rest of the team."

Reese glanced around as he followed the sergeant to the half-buried rectangle of the operations center and command bunker. Ban Phoc had the raw look of a remote Special Forces outpost, and it also looked well kept. The wire obstacles were tight, the sandbagged weapons positions on the inner perimeter looked recently rebuilt and the grounds were clean.

A-410 might have been without a CO for the past several weeks, but someone was sure as hell keeping a close eye on things, and he was very glad to see it. Reese had half expected to find a camp that desperately needed work. This was going to make things a lot easier for him as the new team commander.

"Here we are, sir," Torres said, ducking into the sunken steps to the bunker. "Watch your head."

Reese noted the heavy wooden beam above and read the sign posted there: Camp Bum Fuck. Home of A-

410, The Mushroom Detachment. He chuckled. "Mushroom Detachment?"

"Yes, sir." Torres grinned over his shoulder. "'Cause they keep us in the dark and feed us bullshit."

As Reese stepped inside, a man wearing a master sergeant's stripes on his jungle fatigue jacket sleeves stood up from the chair in front of the radios. "Sorry I wasn't at the pad to meet you, sir," he greeted Reese. In his late thirties and not as tall as Reese at six feet, he had a solid build and a face that showed American Indian ancestry. "I was on the horn to the B-40 S-3 at Can Tho."

"That's all right, Sergeant," Reese said, extending his hand. "I'm Mike Reese."

"Master Sergeant Ray Pierce," the man said, taking his hand. "I'm the team NCO. Of course you've met Sergeant Torres."

"Yes, I have."

"Everyone else is out in the field right now," Pierce explained. "Since Tet we've been doubling up on our patrols to keep those VC bastards in line."

Reese laughed. "It's a dirty job, but someone's got to do it."

"Ain't that the fucking truth," Pierce said with a smile. "Would you care for a cup of coffee or a beer, Captain?"

"Coffee, please."

"How do you take it?"

"Barefoot."

While Pierce ducked into the back room, Reese sat down in one of the folding metal chairs around the rough wooden table in the middle of the room. Like everything else he had seen in the camp so far, the command bunker was a bit primitive. Sheets of raw plywood covered the sandbagged walls and sheets of PSP landing strip mat served as flooring. The low ceiling consisted of more PSP mats supported by closely set, massive wooden beams. It was all well kept.

A weapons rack by the door held polished M-16 rifles and a generous supply of loaded magazines, the radios were free of dust and the acetate-covered operations map on the wall looked up-to-date. From where he sat Reese could see a patrol area outlined in red grease pencil with the day's date written above it. Reese could tell a lot about a unit just by seeing where they lived and worked, and so far he liked what he was seeing. But, of course, he expected no less from one of the SF's elite Mobile Strike Force units.

Sergeant Pierce returned with two brown plastic mess hall cups of coffee and handed one to Reese. "I'm sure glad to see you, Captain. We've been without a team leader for a couple of weeks now."

"So I understand," Reese said. "I knew Captain Fields. I'm sorry to hear he was killed."

Pierce sipped his coffee. "Yeah, he was a good CO. We got in some pretty heavy shit when we went after the VC who were pulling back from Saigon after Tet, and he was killed in a night ambush. We got ours that night, too." Pierce shook his head at the memory. "But that doesn't make up for it."

"It never does," Reese said.

"What do you want to see first, sir?" Pierce asked, all business again.

"How about giving me a brief rundown on the camp and anything you've got going on now?"

The sergeant stepped over to the wall map. "We're a four-platoon Mike Force company," he explained, "with three Nung platoons and one Cambode, organized into three rifle platoons and one heavy weapons. First platoon is a Nung LRRP and the weapons platoon is Nung as well as the team security detachment. Our TO&E strength is 185 Cidge and twelve U.S. Now that you're on board we're up to full strength on U.S. and only short a dozen Cidge.

"As far as ongoing operations, Lieutenant Santelli, the XO, is out right now with one of the Nung platoons sweeping this area." He pointed to the red-marked area on the map. "They're due back before dark. I've got two platoons on standby in case they step in some shit and one platoon pulling routine maintenance."

"Have you had much activity in the area lately?"

"No sir," Pierce said. "Since the enemy pulled back across the border after Tet, it's been real quiet. Maybe too quiet."

"What do you think's going on?"

Pierce shrugged. "I don't know, but they've been too goddamn quiet lately for my taste. I like my zips out in the open where I can see 'em."

Reese laughed. "That makes two of us. What does Can Tho say?"

"They're thinking a lot like me," Pierce admitted. "They think it's much too quiet, too. That's why the LT's out right now. He's looking for the little bastards."

"What kind of man is this Santelli?"

"Well, sir," Pierce said with a grin, "just between you and me, Jack Santelli's one of the best LTs I've seen in a long time. He's OCS and he's still a little too hard-charging for his own good, but he's a real good man to have in a firefight. He keeps his head and gets the job done."

"Somebody's been keeping this camp in good shape."

"I've been taking care of the camp and letting the lieutenant run around in the woods, sir." Pierce looked pleased by the compliment. "He likes it that way."

"I'll keep that in mind when I pull him back to start running the camp again."

"You'll have to drag him kicking and screaming, sir," Pierce warned him. "That man really likes to get his buckle in the dirt."

"There'll still be time enough for that, but the XO is supposed to be running this camp so I can use you in the field."

"Yes, sir."

"Who else is on the team?"

"Well, you met Torres," Pierce said, nodding at the man sitting behind the radios. "The rest of them are up there." He pointed at a unit status board with the names of the A-team written in with black grease pencil.

Reese scanned the names for any he recognized. "Kowalski. How many tours does he have in?"

Pierce thought for a moment. "I think he's on his third."

"Uh-huh." Reese nodded.

"He's a good intel sergeant," Pierce said. "He can find Charlie just by stepping outside and sniffing the air. He's out with the LT looking for 'em today."

"Who's Rohm?"

Pierce grinned. "Another old-timer like me. A hell of a mortar man. I knew him in Korea and Oki."

"Who were you with in Korea?"

"First Rangers," Pierce answered proudly, pointing at the red-and-black Ranger scroll on his right shoulder. "I made the drop at Musan-Ni."

Many of the older Special Forces NCOs were Korean War Ranger or Airborne veterans, and they were proud of their little-publicized combat jumps in that forgotten war.

"How long have you been in the SF, Sarge?"

"I came in with Bull Simons when he was forming the White Star Project in Laos with the Meo tribesmen. Later I helped him put the Eighth together in Panama before going to Oki, and when that got a little too boring, I got myself assigned to Fifth Group."

"You've been around," Reese commented.

"Damn straight, sir." Pierce grinned. "But I've only got nine more months of this shit to do before this Indian can finally hang up his war bonnet, sit back and take life easy for a change."

Reese smiled knowingly. "Good luck, Sarge."

"If you want, sir," Pierce said, "I can show you to your quarters in the team house and let B-40 know you're here. They may want to see you right away."

"Fine," Reese said, draining the last of the coffee and getting to his feet. "I could use a little cleanup before I meet the rest of the team."

Pierce picked up one of Reese's bags and led him to the low tropical hut next to the bunker. A four-foot-high double layer of sandbags surrounded the walls, and a single layer of bags lay over the tin roof. "You get much mortar fire around here?" Reese asked.

"Enough that the sandbags come in real handy sometimes," Pierce admitted.

"I hope the hell they give me a night or two off so I can get caught up on my sleep before they start that shit."

"I'll ask Kowalski what it looks like when he gets back, sir," Pierce said. "Maybe he can get them to knock it off for a night or two."

"Do that, please," Reese said, laughing.

REESE LOOKED around the small room in the back of the team house. All signs of its previous occupant, Captain Fields, had been removed and the room swept clean. It wasn't much as far as quarters went—a wall locker, two footlockers, a metal bunk frame and an Army mattress—but it would be his home for the next several months at least.

He immediately started putting his gear away, laying aside some dirty laundry until he could find out who performed that chore for the team. Reese had very little with him except for his recent issue of uniforms and field gear. All he had brought with him from the States was a pair of well-used boots, his personal weapons, his fighting knife, a large jar of instant iced tea and his toilet kit. It was best to travel light when you were in the SF.

After getting his gear squared away, he threw his poncho liner on top of his bunk and lay down for a short nap. If anything happened that required his attention, Pierce knew where he was.

As tired as he was with jet lag, Reese didn't fall asleep right away. Too much had happened in a very short time. It had only been a little over a day and a half since his Braniff 707 had touched down at Long Bien after a twenty-two-hour flight from Travis Air Force Base in California.

So far it looked as if the gods of war were with him for a change. Pierce seemed to be a typical SF senior NCO—functioning well. First impressions could be deceiving, but he felt he had lucked out this time.

He had been sweating out this assignment ever since he'd talked with the Infantry Branch Assignment Team at Fort Benning, Georgia, his last duty station. He'd been finishing up the nine-month infantry officers' advanced course when the team came down from the Pentagon to talk to the student officers about their next assignments. For the most part, the advanced course had been a complete waste of Reese's time. He had been ready to get back to what he knew best—running an A-team in Nam, but the Assignments Team had had other ideas.

Reese had been commissioned through the ROTC at the University of Washington. Since he'd been a Distinguished Military Graduate, he'd been given a regular Army commission rather than a commission as a reserve officer. While the Army brass at the Pentagon didn't mind their regular officers doing one tour in Special Forces, they didn't like to see them become too attached to the glamorous green beret.

When the team asked Reese what he wanted to do on his next assignment, he told them he wanted to return to Fifth Group in Vietnam and take over another SF A-team. The major in charge of the team had quickly thumbed through his 201 file and announced that Reese was due for a tour as a staff officer at Battalion or a higher level—as part of his career development, as the major put it.

Reese had looked the major straight in the eye and told him exactly what he could do with his staff job. He added that if he didn't receive orders sending him back to Fifth Group Special Forces, he would resign his commission immediately. Reese didn't mind fighting a war, but he wasn't about to fight it as a staff REMF behind a desk in an air-conditioned office.

The Army was short of regular officers. The assignments major had had no choice but to give Reese the assignment he wanted. The man reluctantly filled out the order forms to send him back to Vietnam.

Reese knew the old saying about getting your heart's desire. This time, though, it looked as if it had worked for him.

3

Special Forces Camp A-410, Ban Phoc

Reese couldn't sleep right away that afternoon. Usually he could doze off anywhere, even standing up. As a professional soldier, he had learned long ago that sleep was even more necessary than food and water. But he was thinking about why he was back in Vietnam so soon after his first tour rather than cooling it at some easy job back at a stateside Army post and driving around town in his little green sports car.

He had tried to convince himself he had come back so soon because he felt more comfortable in Vietnam than he did in his own country. There was a great deal of truth in that. He hadn't liked what he'd seen back in the World on his month-long leave in California before he had reported to Fort Benning. The stateside, peacetime Army bullshit at Benning had driven him crazy. Even so, there was far more to it than just that.

When he was being completely honest with himself, he recognized that the real reason he was back in Nam again so soon was primarily because of his wife, Judy. It had been far easier for him to run back to the war than it had been to stay in the States and try to deal with her.

When he had gone back to his wife in California after his first tour, he had discovered that in only one year's time their marriage had turned into something he didn't even recognize. From almost the first minute he was home, Judy had made it perfectly clear she was extremely unhappy with both him and his chosen profession. She had liked being the wife of an Army officer during his European tour, when she had been with him and had enjoyed a long German holiday. She hadn't liked having an absent husband while he'd been in Nam. Now that he was back home she didn't like his new Vietnam-born attitude toward life.

She had no appreciation for what he'd been through there, and she didn't want to listen to anything he had to say about it. She told him she found war stories boring. As far as she was concerned, Vietnam had turned him into a humorless, cold-blooded bastard. He wasn't any fun to be around anymore. She couldn't understand why he wanted to stay home and watch television instead of going to the frequent parties with her social set. When he did go out with her, she couldn't understand why he drank so much and got obnoxious when her friends asked him about the war.

"But, Mike," Judy had protested one night after he'd blown up at some stupid bitch who had asked him how it felt to kill people, "they're just curious. You're the only military man they know."

"It's still a stupid question!" he had said. "How would she have liked it if I had asked her how it felt to lose her virginity?"

"That's not really the same!" Judy had snapped back. "Most women lose their virginity sooner or later, but not all men go out and kill people."

He had ended the argument by calling her friends a bunch of stupid, fucking, draft-dodging cowards, and told her that if they wanted to know what the war was like, they could damn well go to Nam and see for themselves. She had refused to sleep with him for the next week.

By the time he'd finally gotten back into bed with her, she had decided she wanted him out of the Army so he could work with her father selling real estate in California. He'd refused to even consider the idea, so she'd threatened to divorce him. Reese had thought her talk about divorce had been only that—just talk. But the talking had continued for the rest of his leave and, when it came time for him to leave for Fort Benning for the advanced course, she refused to go to Georgia with him.

At first he'd tried to patch things up with long-distance phone calls. After several months of trying to make peace with her while still staying in the Army, he gave up. And when it came time to decide about his next assignment, he volunteered to go back to something he knew he could handle—Vietnam.

"Damned woman," he muttered as he tried to get comfortable on the narrow Army-issue cot. "Why the fuck couldn't she just leave well enough alone? God-damn it, anyway!"

There had been a time when he'd loved that woman more than anything in the world, except maybe the

Army. But now he wondered how long it had been since he had felt any real love for her. The constant fighting had made her the enemy. Altogether he wasn't sure how he felt about her anymore. Maybe the old Army saying was right: if the Army had wanted him to have a wife, they would have issued him one.

REESE WOKE rested after his short nap. He put on a fresh set of jungle fatigues and polished jungle boots before returning to the command bunker. He knew his new team was checking him out just as thoroughly as he was evaluating them.

Sergeant Pierce looked up from the radio message he was reading when Reese stepped into the bunker. "The LT's on his way back in, sir," he said, handing him the message form. "And this just came in for you."

The message told him to report to his B-team headquarters at Can Tho in the morning. The B-40 commander was sending a chopper to pick him up at 0900.

A Special Forces B-team was the headquarters for the A-teams under its control and, in this case, B-40 controlled all the Mike Force units in the IV Corps AO, the delta region to the south of Saigon. He was supposed to meet the commander, be briefed on the operations in their AO and sign over the A-team's property books. It was all routine Army bullshit. Even in the elite Special Forces there was still a certain amount of it that had to be endured.

"They're coming up to the wire now, sir," Pierce said. "You want to go down to meet them?"

"Sure, let's go."

Outside, the sun was setting over the Plain of Reeds. There was still enough light to allow Reese to make out the column of camouflaged figures approaching across the open ground for the main gate of the camp. Even so close to home the lieutenant was taking no chances. His flank security was out on both sides and a drag team watched their backtrail. Reese noted that Pierce had posted several extra squads of Nungs along the perimeter in case Charlie hoped to catch the camp's defenses off guard.

Santelli might only be a first lieutenant, but as Pierce had said, the man knew how to handle himself in the woods. That much was apparent from watching his patrol formation. Reese walked down to meet his executive officer.

First Lieutenant Jack Santelli was hot, tired and desperately needed to take a leak when he spotted the tall figure of the captain in fresh fatigues and shiny boots at the perimeter gate.

Aw, shit, Santelli thought, meeting the new team leader was just what he needed right now. He straightened the sun-faded, tiger-striped boonie hat on his head and tried to brush some of the dried red mud from the front of his camouflaged uniform while rubbing the toes of his well-worn boots on the backs of his pant legs. He knew it was ridiculous to try to look neat after a three-day patrol, but old habits died hard.

Jack Santelli was an oddity in Special Forces—an Italian kid from the Bronx. Most SF men, both officers and NCOs, were from the rural areas of America, particularly from the old Confederate states of the Deep South. Few men from the big cities ever found their way into an organization that spent most of its time in the jungles of Southeast Asia and Latin America or the deep, dark forests of Europe. But then Santelli wasn't your average guy from the Bronx, either.

On his graduation from high school, Santelli had turned his back on the family fruit and vegetable business and immediately enlisted in the Army. After basic training and AIT, he'd been chosen to go to Officers' Candidate School at Fort Benning. Santelli had done well in OCS. He had immediately signed up for Airborne training and the Ranger School after receiving his commission as an infantry second lieutenant. With the coveted Ranger tab sewn onto his uniform, he had looked around the army and decided he wanted to add the famous green beret to his list of military accomplishments. He was accepted at the John F. Kennedy Special Warfare School at Fort Bragg in North Carolina.

Following that graduation, Santelli was sent immediately to Vietnam and made executive officer of A-410. Like all soldiers new to combat, he'd been a little apprehensive at first about how he'd do on combat missions. Within a few weeks, however, he'd discovered he liked field duty more than he did staying behind and running the base camp.

He had wondered how he'd react the first time he came under enemy fire. When he finally found out during the third week he was in-country, he was surprised and pleased to find that he reacted exactly as he'd been trained to do. In fact, when the brief fire-fight was over and he saw the bodies of the VC his ambush team had killed, he decided this was what he wanted to do more than anything else in the world.

Now, though, Santelli was more than a little resentful about having to turn over his temporary command of A-410 to the new team leader. He had enjoyed commanding such a large unit. And second, he was afraid the new commander would put him back doing his normal job as the team's executive officer, the man in charge of bullshit paperwork and other noncombat functions. Being a good XO was vital to the team's mission, but it kept him from playing in the woods with Charlie.

The new team leader was a tall, well-built man with pale blue eyes. He stood with the casual yet alert stance of a man who was very sure of himself. Even though he must have just flown in today, he was wearing a fresh set of fatigues and his boots were polished. Santelli saw the sun-faded green beret on the man's head, so he knew the captain wasn't a complete cherry. More than likely the man had been in Nam before. Santelli sure as hell hoped so. He didn't feel like breaking in some FNG captain.

Although saluting in the field was usually a big no-no, Santelli felt it was appropriate here. "Lieutenant Jack Santelli, sir."

Reese returned Santelli's sharp, Airborne-style salute with one of his own. "Mike Reese," he said, extending his hand. "Glad to meet you. Make any contact?"

Santelli shook his hand firmly. He liked this guy's directness. "'Fraid not this time, sir. They're all hiding across the fence."

"Come on in and give me a rundown on your patrol," Reese said. "We've got a cold one waiting for you."

Santelli turned to the Chinese Nung interpreter at his side and told him to let the men stand down. Then he himself followed his new commander back to the bunker. Sergeant Pierce awaited him with the promised beer. He took a quick gulp, dumped his weapons and rucksack and excused himself to go back outside to take a quick leak.

When Santelli came back he found the other Americans from his patrol crowded into the bunker. Sergeant Gil Kowalski was talking with Reese as if they were old friends. Since Special Forces was such a small family, it wasn't too surprising that Reese would know someone on the team.

Reese looked up and motioned Santelli over to the map. "Brief me on the patrol."

"Well, sir," Santelli began, taking another deep drink from his beer, "we cleared the wire at 0400 on the thirteenth and initially moved out to the west." He pointed at the map. "Then, once we were outside the mortar fan, we dodged a klick to the south and holed up till first light."

The Special Forces trained its men to give detailed after-action reports. Santelli quickly warmed to his topic and described the three days he and his men had spent in the woods in a fruitless search for traces of their elusive enemy.

"Basically," he said in conclusion. "We dryholed. We found diddly squat."

"Where do you think they are?" Reese asked, scanning the map.

Santelli shrugged. "My money says they're cooling it across the fence in Cambodia. They're just waiting for us to get slack again and then they're going to sneak over here and zap our asses."

"I would agree with that, sir," Sergeant Kowalski, the team's intelligence sergeant, spoke up. "Everything we've been getting indicates they're licking their wounds from Tet and resupplying as fast as they can."

"For what purpose?" Reese asked him.

Kowalski shrugged. "Beats the shit outta me sir. But they're going to start giving someone a rough time before too long."

"How about us?"

"I don't know about that," Kowalski said, rubbing his hand absentmindedly over his close-cropped dark hair. "We're in their road if they want to move on Saigon again, but I don't think we're a prime target. There's been no recon activity against us that we've been able to detect so far. They know we're here, sure, but nothing we've seen indicates they're going to come after us anytime soon."

Reese looked around the room at the other men. "Any of you want to add anything to this?"

There was silence, and Reese turned back to his lieutenant. "Write up your mission, Jack, and I'll take the patrol report to Can Tho with me when I report to the B-team CO in the morning."

"Yes, sir," Santelli said.

"Now to the real matter at hand," Reese said. "As soon as you've gotten some chow, I want to start going over the property books with you. I've got to sign for them in the morning, and I don't need any surprises."

Santelli nodded. Back to the base camp bullshit, he thought. "Yes, sir."

4

MACV-SOG Headquarters, Tan Son Nhut Air Base

CIA agent Dick Clifford slipped the aerial reconnaissance photographs back into their classified folder with the photo analysts' report and laid it on his desk. Taking a sip of the cold black coffee in his mug, he stared out his second-story window in the MACV-SOG Headquarters building at the edge of Tan Son Nhut and watched the sun set over the sprawling air force base and the outskirts of Saigon.

Clifford was a sharp-featured, tall, thin man with close-cropped black hair and dark eyes. His pale skin testified to a life spent inside the dim corridors of the MACV-SOG building. Most people recognized MACV as the acronym for Military Assistance Command, Vietnam, and to those outside the organization SOG stood for Studies and Observations Group, a harmless data-gathering, think tank. Actually, SOG signified Special Operations Group, the deepest, secret level of the war in Vietnam.

SOG had been formed in January 1964 to oversee the clandestine military operations of the war. Unlike the widely publicized "conventional" unconventional war fought in South Vietnam by the Special Forces units, SOG's activities were known only to those on a strict need-to-know basis. These missions included strategic reconnaissance, intelligence-gathering, raiding the enemy's home bases, POW rescue, rescuing downed pilots and aircrew, training and controlling agents in North Vietnam, forming resistance groups, kidnapping or assassinating key enemy personal and sabotage missions, all performed outside the borders of South Vietnam. Burma, Cambodia, Laos, North Vietnam and three provinces of Red China were all within SOG's area of operations.

Given the political limitations imposed upon the American forces in Southeast Asia, the most important of the SOG missions were the cross-border reconnaissance and intelligence-gathering operations known as Operation Shining Brass. If the United States couldn't take the war to the enemy in the supposedly neutral nations along South Vietnam's western border, at least they had to know what the enemy was doing there.

Supervised by MACV, SOG took its orders directly from the special assistant for counterinsurgency and special activities of the Joint Chiefs of Staff at the Pentagon. SOG operational personnel were drawn from the elite units of all the services, most of them from Army Special Forces assigned to the Special Operations Augmentation unit of Fifth Group, U.S. Special Forces.

These men fought their secret battles deep in enemy territory, far from the highly publicized helicopter war shown around the world on the six o'clock news. Their war was classified at the highest possible level, and so were the dates when they died; the where, how and why of their deaths were also kept secret. Not even their wives or families were told that their loved ones had fallen in Laos, Cambodia or North Vietnam on a SOG "black" operation.

A large number of CIA, DIA and other civilian agents worked within the military organization. Clifford's assignment was to evaluate the intelligence information gathered by the SOG RTs—the recon teams—and the far-flung CIA field agent network. Most of the civilians were in headquarters jobs like Clifford's while others worked on the operational planning for the SOG missions or on the logistics of equipping and transporting the forces. All told, MACV-SOG was a closely guarded secret war within a war. Now that war was about to heat up again.

The SR-71 spy plane recon photos in Clifford's folder were about to send another SOG unit across the border into Cambodia for a closer look at a suspected enemy buildup. Bits and pieces of field agent information had been coming into Clifford's office for weeks, indicating the North Vietnamese were planning to launch another Tet-style attack into South Vietnam. Also, reports from several SOG recon teams confirmed the photographic evidence that the NVA were massing their forces again in Cambodia.

In Clifford's mind all this information pointed to only one thing. So far, though, no one at MACV Headquarters seemed very concerned about it. Clifford's reports countered their public claims that Tet had been a decisive victory for the Allied forces in

South Vietnam and the enemy was on the run. However, it didn't mean the North Vietnamese forces had been completely crushed or had been rendered ineffective in combat.

True, the NVA had been run out of South Vietnam at the end of Tet and tens of thousands of them had been killed in the fighting. There was even a widely publicized mopping-up operation going on in the countryside around Saigon at the moment that was adding even more of the enemy to the body count. But there were still tens of thousands more North Vietnamese regulars poised just beyond the borders of the "neutral" nations of Laos and Cambodia. They were sitting there, patiently waiting their turn to be thrown into the meat grinder of the Vietnam War.

Clifford's main job was to make predictions based on the intelligence information that passed over his desk. The problem was that his hunches based on that information weren't enough to be taken seriously at MACV Headquarters. He needed concrete evidence to get Westmoreland's staff off their asses.

To do that he first had to convince his boss, Colonel Stewart A. Marshall, that the North Vietnamese threat was real and that he needed to send someone into Cambodia to find out exactly what they were up to. As was always the case, convincing the colonel of the necessity of an operation was the hardest part of Clifford's job.

The CIA agent couldn't figure out why a man like Marshall was running MACV-SOG operations. Most SOG personnel were freethinking military radicals who loved the strange, wild life of clandestine operations. Marshall, on the other hand, was a throwback to the Napoleonic era when the infantry wore pretty red coats and advanced in neat, straight lines. The colonel was totally out of step in SOG's war where small teams wearing enemy uniforms and armed with foreign weapons operated deep behind enemy lines in nations that claimed neutrality in this wide-ranging conflict.

To top it off, Marshall didn't like having anything to do with the CIA, either. As far as he was concerned, spies were about as welcome in his Army as whores in a nunnery. He felt that it wasn't gentlemanly to spy on one's enemy. If he were sitting in Westmoreland's office, the CIA, the DIA and all of the other dozen spook organizations in Nam would be completely run out of the country. In fact, if Marshall had had Westy's job, MACV-SOG would probably be disbanded, as well.

Many things about the war in Vietnam were as equally stupid as having someone like Marshall in charge of SOG operations. Clifford dreaded every time he had to go into the crusty old bastard's office and try to talk him into authorizing a mission whose importance should have been immediately obvious to any schoolboy with half a brain. This time, though, Clifford thought grimly, he shouldn't have too much trouble convincing the colonel. His photographs showed hundreds of NVA vehicles coming down from the North along the roads of the Ho Chi Minh Trail in Cambodia.

More new vehicles were rumbling down into the Parrot's Beak every day, and they sure as hell weren't carrying Peace Corps volunteers. Something big was going down, and he had to find out what it was before it was too late to stop it.

Clifford was typical of many of the CIA men of his generation. The son of a wealthy East Coast family, he had majored in foreign relations at Georgetown University, intending to go into the diplomatic service when he graduated. Kennedy's presidency had changed his plans. Like so many American college students at that time, he got caught up in the youthful President's stirring "Ask Not What Your Country Can Do for You" inaugural speech.

After the Cuban Missile Crisis, the Berlin Wall, the Bay of Pigs and the President's assassination, he decided that what he could do for his country was help guard her from communism. He had never considered a career in the military, but the life of a CIA agent appealed to him. To Clifford the intelligence service represented the cutting edge of the forces fighting for freedom and democracy.

Following his graduation from college, he enrolled in extensive training at the CIA's headquarters in Langley, Virginia, at the infamous farm, going on from there to specialize in intelligence analysis and evaluation. Despite his initial hopes for an assignment in Europe, preferably in Berlin, his first job for the Company was his present assignment at SOG. And if he couldn't figure out how to get his boss off his ass, it would probably be his last.

Clifford reluctantly drained his coffee, scooped up the recon photo folder and headed for the door. There

was no point in putting this off any longer; it wasn't
going to improve with age. Halting outside the colonel's closed door, he knocked twice and waited to be
invited to enter.

The colonel liked the CIA personnel on his staff to
halt the military regulation three paces in front of his
oak desk and stand at attention until he offered them
a seat. "Sir," Clifford said, halting, "I think we've got
a situation here that needs to be looked at."

"Have a seat," Marshall said.

A tanker by trade, Colonel Stewart A. Marshall had
roamed Europe as a second lieutenant in the command hatch of an M-4 Sherman tank with an armored
battalion in Patton's Third Army. In Korea he had
commanded a company of M-46 Pershings against the
Russian-built T-34 tanks of the North Koreans. Marshall certainly understood fire and maneuver, particularly when it came to deploying armored forces.

Only a whim of the capricious gods of war could
have given a tanker like Marshall an assignment as the
operations officer for the dirtiest war being fought in
Nam, MACV-SOG clandestine operations. In a country covered with jungle and rice paddies, there was little use for tankers. But if General Creighton Abrams,
himself a tanker, could be chosen as Westmoreland's
replacement, Marshall felt he could take care of his
part of the war, as well.

"What seems to be the problem?" Marshall asked.

Clifford laid the photos on his desk. "I just received these from the latest Blackbird run over the
roads leading into the Parrot's Beak."

He pointed out the NVA trucks that the SR-71 spy plane had photographed on the Ho Chi Minh Trail. "I think they're doing a major buildup in the Parrot's Beak, sir. I'd like to send a Hatchet Force in to do a thorough recon of the area. I don't want to let them slip another one in on us like they did during Tet."

Marshall looked up at the CIA agent, somewhat amused. "Don't you think you're overreacting, Clifford? We see this all the time, and it doesn't look like an indicator to me."

It was on the tip of Clifford's tongue to remind the colonel that the SOG intel reports had accurately predicted the Tet Offensive right down to the exact date as well as most of the targets for the surprise attack. But he knew better than to remind his boss of that.

Despite all the frustrations that came from having to work with Marshall, he liked his job and really didn't want to be sent to Bumfuck, Ethiopia, for his next assignment. Even though the colonel would never make his brigadier's star, he still had powerful connections in Washington.

Clifford took a deep breath. "Sir," he said carefully and patiently, "this is definitely not a normal NVA resupply pattern. There are too many trucks in too short a period of time. I've got field reports describing hundreds of vehicles moving into this area over the past two weeks. Something big is going on in there. I really think we need to take a closer look."

Marshall was silent as he looked at the photos again and thumbed through Clifford's agent report summaries. "Okay," he finally said. "Who do we have to send in to take care of this?"

Caught off guard, Clifford stared at his superior. He quickly recovered himself for the hardest part. All of the SOG recon teams and Hatchet Force units were tied up right now on other equally important missions. He was going to have to go outside the organization for the necessary people.

"There's no one on hand right now," he said thoughtfully. "I'm going to have to borrow someone from Fifth Group to handle it." He paused to gauge Marshall's reaction.

The colonel frowned and leaned back in his chair. "You know I don't like to have outsiders involved in our operations. We can't afford any leaks."

This was so typical of Marshall. He hated clandestine operations, but he was scared to death the press would get their hands on information about SOG's activities and that it would reflect badly on him.

"I'll get Fifth Group's recommendation on a team," Clifford offered encouragingly. "That way, if there's a compromise, it'll be their problem, not ours."

Marshall smiled. That would cover his ass at MACV Headquarters if anything went wrong on the mission. "Do it."

"Yes, sir," Clifford replied as he stuffed the photos and reports back into the folder. "I'll get right on it."

Clifford strolled back to his office. He had anticipated this particular problem and had already coordinated the mission through Fifth Group headquarters in Nha Trang. They had given him a Mike Force unit in

the Delta, A-410 at Ban Phoc, one with a first-class
Nung recon platoon. From what Fifth Group had said,
they could do as good a job as any of the usual SOG
teams.

5

April 16, Camp A-410, Ban Phoc

Mike Reese was up early the next morning. After a quick shave and a wash, he put on a clean uniform and a pair of spit-shined jump boots. Instead of the normal tiger-striped uniforms the A-team wore around the camp, he dressed in a set of OD-507s, standard jungle fatigues with full-color insignia, to meet his B-team commander. Then he headed over to the operations bunker to get his morning coffee and to take a look at the night's radio messages and reports.

Sergeant Torres had the early radio watch and looked up when Reese came down the stairs. "Morning, Captain," he greeted him with a smile. "Coffee's ready."

"Thanks. Where's the pot?"

"In the back. There should be a cup lying around somewhere that's not too dirty."

Reese came back with his coffee and picked up the clipboard. "Anything of real interest in here?"

"No, sir," the radioman answered. "Just routine bullshit." It was common practice to transmit routine radio traffic during the evening hours to free the frequencies for tactical communications during the day.

"Anything going on?"

"No, sir," Torres said with a shake of his head. "It's as quiet as the night before payday all over the Delta. There were a couple of minor incidents, but nothing to get excited about. It's almost too quiet." He frowned. "I like it better when something's going on."

"Me, too. That way I know where the little bastards are."

Torres laughed. "You got that shit right, sir!"

Tony Torres was a product of the Hispanic barrios of East Los Angeles. Only the unflagging efforts of his widowed mother had kept him out of real trouble with the law during his turbulent high school years. He had finally stepped beyond her protection, though, when he was caught dealing grass. The judge had offered him the choice of going into the Army or doing hard time. He had wisely chosen the first option. After completing his GED in infantry AIT, he went on to work his way through Airborne school and into the Special Forces.

The SF had given him a good place to work out the hostilities he still harbored from his L.A. street days. Because his opponents in Nam shot back, he had also quickly acquired the discipline he needed to back up his natural combativeness. He was halfway through his tour now and was enjoying himself so much that he was thinking of extending his service when the time came.

Reese finished reading the night's messages at the same time that he finished his coffee. Putting the cup back, he headed for the door. "I'm expecting a chopper from Can Tho to pick me up at about 0800 hours," he told the radioman. "Give me a yell when they call in."

"Will do, sir."

Outside, Reese looked out over the camp. In the fighting positions on the outer perimeter the Mike Force strikers were changing to the daytime guard. The men just coming off duty headed for the mess hall or crawled back to their bunks to catch up on their sleep. Reese wasn't much of a breakfast man, but he decided to check in at the mess hall and see what was on the menu. There really wasn't much point in his getting started on anything until he got back from his meeting.

In the mess hall he found several other team members he hadn't met the day before. Sergeant Pierce was eating breakfast with Staff Sergeant "Doc" Hayes, the senior medic; Staff Sergeant Frank Baker, the team's demo man; and SFC Vic Hotchkiss, the light weapons specialist. Reese took some toast and another cup of coffee and joined the group at the table.

He was still talking with his NCOs when the runner came to tell him the chopper was inbound.

THE B-TEAM BASE at Can Tho was a larger version of A-410's camp: the same five-pointed star defensive positions, the same red dirt and the same half-buried bunkers. The main difference was its artillery, a battery of 105 mm howitzers, the tangled antenna farm above the commo center and the big chopper pad inside the wire.

A first lieutenant was waiting for him with a jeep when Reese's Huey slick touched down. He noted the vehicle's Fifth Group bumper markings. "Hop in, sir," the lieutenant said, saluting him smartly. "The major's waiting to see you."

Reese returned the salute and was whisked directly off to the team commander's office where Major Jim Nolan, the B-40 commander, was waiting for him.

"We're going to have to cut the introductions short," the major said pleasantly after shaking hands with Reese. "There's a man from MACV-SOG waiting to see you."

Reese frowned. "What's going on, sir?"

"Your Mike Force company has been loaned to SOG for an operation," Nolan replied. "Their man is waiting in the briefing room to give you the details."

The thin man waiting for him in the small room across the hall had spook written all over him. The Hawaiian shirt, the tan chino jeans and the aviator sunglasses told it all. The Colt Python .357 Magnum he wore in the agent-style shoulder holster was another CIA favorite. Reese wondered if all the Company people bought their shirts, sunglasses and .357 holsters at the same store in Langley, Virginia. This spook, however, was a little skinnier than most of them and wasn't sporting a poolside tan. He must be a real back alley spook.

"Dick Clifford," the man said, coming forward with his hand extended.

Reese introduced himself.

"Sorry to break into your time with Major Nolan, Captain," Clifford said. "But I've got a hot one here, and we need to get you moving on it."

"Why me?" Reese asked. "My unit's Mike Force."

Clifford looked at Reese, his eyes unreadable behind the shades. "That may be, but until further notice, Captain, you've been opconned to SOG."

He handed Reese a piece of paper without the usual military letterhead. "Here are the opcon orders signed by Colonel Stewart Marshall, MACV-SOG operations officer."

Reese glanced down at the paper. This could prove to be real interesting. "Okay," he said, handing the paper back. "What's the score?"

Clifford uncovered a big map on the wall. He tapped an area where the piece of Cambodia jutted down into the heart of South Vietnam. "I'm sending your people into the Parrot's Beak."

Reese stared at the map. Oh, shit, he thought instinctively.

REESE HIT the ground running as the Huey's skids touched down on the small PSP landing pad at Ban Phoc. Sergeant Pierce and Lieutenant Santelli were both waiting for him. "We've got a mission!" Reese yelled over the beat of the rotors as the slick lifted off. "How soon can you get the recon platoon ready?"

"Depends on where we're going!" Santelli yelled back.

"How about Cambodia?"

"Outfuckingstanding!" Santelli exclaimed. "In that case we can leave at first light tomorrow."

"Good," Reese said, turning toward the bunker. "That's what I told the man. Get the team together and I'll give you the mission."

When the men had assembled in the bunker, Reese pinned up a map on the operations board. "Okay," he said as soon as everyone was accounted for, "here's the drill. Until further notice we've been placed under the operational control of MACV-SOG."

Santelli's face broke out in a wide grin. Although he had enjoyed working with the CIDG Mike Force, he'd wanted to find a way to get into the real good stuff, the "black" operations for which SOG was famous. Rumor had it that those guys were always up to their belt buckles in the enemy.

"This briefing is classified top secret," Reese continued, "and is on strict need-to-know basis. Tomorrow morning the recon platoon and a split A-team will be moved by chopper to this location."

He tapped the map at a spot midway up the Parrot's Beak where it protruded into South Vietnam. This piece of Cambodia had long been a major NVA staging area and took its name from its shape.

"From here you'll cross the border into Cambodia and will make a five-day recon of the Ho Chi Minh Trail and any supply dumps you find in the area. The major emphasis will be to do a head count of enemy personnel and vehicles."

"Oh, shit!" Kowalski muttered quietly. The Parrot's Beak was a real hot spot right now, full of North

Vietnamese units licking their wounds and refitting after the ass-kicking they'd received during Tet.

"Santelli?"

"Sir."

"You'll be in charge of this little expedition."

Santelli's grin broadened further.

"I'd go," Reese said, "but B-40 wants me to finish signing the camp over before I get wrapped up in field operations, so you've got it this time."

"Suits me, sir."

Reese glanced at the intel sergeant. "You'll take Sergeant Kowalski as your number two and two other Americans with you. You can ask for volunteers."

Everyone chuckled. Once a man had volunteered for Special Forces, he was considered to have volunteered for anything else that came with the green beret.

"Fine, sir," Santelli answered, looking at the men in the room. "I'll take Larry and Ski."

Reese looked over at Pierce, who nodded briefly. "Do you two have any problems with that?" he asked the men.

Neither did and Reese resumed his briefing. "You'll take one Nung sterile team in full NVA kit, and the rest of you will go as Mike Force."

All of the Nungs in the sterile squad would be armed and outfitted with NVA equipment to avoid looking like U.S. troops. They wore specially made black NVA-style uniforms and carried NVA rucksacks and enemy weapons. About the only thing that would identify them as an American unit would be the small rolls of U.S. C-ration toilet paper they all carried. Even at close range the Vietnamese-speaking Nungs could easily pass themselves off as VC or NVA.

In fact, on many sterile SOG operations the Nungs had walked right into enemy camps, told the North Vietnamese they were a lost VC unit and had gotten directions to the locations of other nearby enemy units. Then they'd blown the shit out of those locations before fading back into the brush.

It was usual practice, however, to use sterile weapons only in areas where U.S forces weren't operating. When Americans heard the distinctive, familiar sound of AK-47s firing in the distance, they were likely to call down artillery or an air strike on that location. This time, however, since they were going into an AO clean of American troops, the Nungs' AKs would work just fine. Nobody would hear them except the enemy.

"Although this is planned for a five-day mission," Reese continued, "everyone will go equipped for seven days."

If something went wrong inside Cambodia, there would be no aerial resupply. The men would have to fight their way out with what they carried in on their backs.

"Now for the details," Reese said. "You'll be lifting out in a four-ship lift with a Light Fire team for escort. You'll make two dummy insertions before you're dropped off at your LZ, and the slicks will go on and make a couple more before they return. If you're lucky, any VC who happen to be in the area will think you're just another airmobile Eagle Flight.

"Once you've determined you're not being watched, make a run for the border here." He tapped the map. "Once across you'll move to this area and use this location as your primary recon base. That night you'll split up into four recon teams and start combing the area."

He handed Santelli a set of aerial photographs. "Specifically you'll recon the areas marked on these photos. You're looking for supply dumps, large base camps and anything else that might indicate a major buildup. Take photos of everything you see but, except for two commo checks at noon and midnight, you'll maintain radio-listening silence. The exception to that is, of course, if your mission is blown. If you make contact, you're to evade and get on the horn ASAP. Also, if you find a good Arc Light target, call that in and then get the hell out of the area.

"At the end of the fourth day, call in a status and your expected PZ. I'll have the same chopper team standing by to make the pickup. If everything goes as planned, you'll be in and out of there without anyone being the wiser.

"Now commo and C and C will be through B-40," Reese continued. "As I said before, two commo checks and listening silence. Pick up the funny books on the way out for the frequencies and call signs. Are there any questions?" Reese looked around the room.

There were none.

"Okay," Reese said, satisfied that everyone knew what was expected of him. As veterans at this sort of thing, they would work out for themselves anything he hadn't covered. "Note the coordinates, brief your troops and start getting it ready. I'll be here if anything comes up."

Sergeant Pierce waited until the bunker was cleared to turn to Reese. "Captain," he said, "you didn't mention anything about SOG having a reaction force on standby for us."

Reese nodded. "I know, Sarge. I asked the SOG briefer about that and he said he can't give us anyone on standby because they're all tied up right now. He thinks there'll be time enough to put a reaction force together if a problem comes up. He also said he doesn't want to risk compromising the mission by placing a bunch of choppers on standby when he doesn't have the people to put in them."

"I don't know if I like that line of reasoning, sir," Pierce said with a frown. "If things get sticky over there, I'd like to be able to get help to them ASAP."

"I agree," Reese said, "but that's the way they want it. He said that if we needed it, he could break loose a Hatchet Force in an hour."

"And it'll take another hour to find the lift ships," Pierce pointed out. "If, that is, there are any available in our AO. It would take another hour after that before we could have the reaction force on the ground. It's too damn long, sir."

"What do you recommend, Sarge?"

"Well, sir," Pierce said slowly, "I've got some friends in the helicopter business, and we could use one of our own Nung platoons as the reaction force."

"Set it up," Reese said, "but don't tell me anything about it until I ask."

Pierce grinned. "You got it, sir!"

6

Camp A-410, Ban Phoc

As soon as Captain Reese's briefing was over, Lieutenant Jack Santelli told Sergeant Kowalski to alert the Nungs in the recon platoon and then started working on his own weapons and equipment. This was something the young officer always enjoyed doing. He could easily have had one of the Nung interpreters keep track of his gear, but he always insisted on cleaning his weapons and packing his rucksack for him.

The first thing he did was choose the weapons he wanted to take. From his wall locker he pulled out his Swedish K, the Karl Gustav M-45 9 mm submachine gun. The K was a simple blowback-type submachine gun, rugged and reliable. With a cyclic rate of six hundred rounds a minute it was quite effective and widely used by all the elite units in Vietnam. The K's 9 mm round wasn't as hard-hitting as the M-16's 5.56 mm round, but it worked well in the short-range combat they'd be facing in the Cambodian jungle.

He took his Canadian Browning Hi-Power pistol as his backup piece. Since it used the same 9 mm ammunition that the K did, he wouldn't have to worry about ammo supply. Lastly he took out the cased, silenced

.22-caliber Ruger Mark 1 semiautomatic pistol with its four-power telescopic sight.

He broke down his weapons for a thorough cleaning, starting with the K. The routine work was part of his mental preparation for combat and helped him get over his premission jitters. Over the past couple of months he had learned that the tenser he was about the mission, the more time he needed to prepare for it.

Santelli realized he was really excited about this mission as he disassembled his K magazines and checked the spring tension of each piece. He forced himself to concentrate on his preparations. Methodically he wiped the dirt and sand off every round of ammunition before reloading thirty 9 mm rounds into each magazine.

He tapped the back side of each against the bottom of his boot to seat the rounds against the back wall of the magazine. Only then did he replace them in his magazine pouches. Then he stripped his Browning Hi-Power pistol next, thoroughly cleaned it and checked all of its magazines, as well. Then he opened the Ruger case and took out the silenced pistol. This would be his ace in the hole. They just might need its quiet-kill capability where they were going. With the scope fitted to the pistol it could take out enemy sentries from as far away as a hundred yards. And if the group ran short of C-rations, it was perfect for silently hunting small game.

As soon as he had checked it over, Santelli went over his hand grenades, six frags and four smoke and two thermite, checking that their pins and fuses were tightly screwed into their bodies. He taped down the spoons with black electrician's tape. That way, even if the pin snagged on something and pulled off, the spoon wouldn't fly off. It would be unhealthy to have a grenade spoon fly off before you wanted it to.

When his weapons were ready, he turned to the rest of his personal gear. First he chose the C-ration meals he would take. He often went short on his field rations to avoid having to hump the extra weight, but this time he took enough to keep him going for two days beyond the scheduled mission time as well as coffee for several days more. He also packed several extra small rolls of toilet paper in a plastic bag with two pairs of extra socks. If there was anything he hated, it was to run out of ass-wipe and dry socks.

Everything went into his NVA-style rucksack with his poncho liner, a bag of blood expander, two sticks of C-4 plastic explosive, a claymore mine, a Prick-77 battery and his extra 9 mm ammunition. His compass, penlight, grease pencils, C-4 stove, malaria pills and salt tablets were already packed in the side pouches. He checked them over, as well.

Lastly he put fresh water in both of his two-quart canteens. Now he was ready to go.

Getting out his writing pad, Santelli started a letter to his father back in the Bronx. He was the first soldier in his family since his ancestors had come over from Italy before World War I, and his father worried about him more than his mother did. He tried to reassure him that he was all right by keeping him informed about what he was doing. He tried to write once a week.

As he sat trying to find something to tell his father about the mission that wasn't classified, he couldn't help thinking about where he was headed again. There were a hundred and one things that could go wrong on a mission like this and, once across the Cambodia border, they wouldn't be able to call for someone to run to their rescue if the shit really hit the fan. On all his previous missions he had always known in the back of his mind that he could call on Tac Air and artillery to help him out if something really went wrong. For all the horsepower behind MACV-SOG operations, there was a limit to what they could do to assist them once they got deep into Cambodia.

He knew they could call in the B-52s for a high-altitude strike if they found a lucrative target, but the close-in gunship and Tac Air support he'd been able to call on when he was operating in South Vietnam wouldn't be there this time. This mission would truly test his abilities as a jungle fighter. This time he would be deep in enemy territory, surviving by his own stealth and cunning alone. The Special Forces had originally been formed as a counterguerrilla force, and to fight guerrillas you had to become a guerrilla yourself.

Not that they would be going up against the old-time VC guerrilla forces, however. The North Vietnamese units in the Parrot's Beak were regulars, hard hats, and he would be playing the VC role against them. Santelli smiled at the thought of seeing if he could out-VC the VC.

He finally put the half-written letter aside. Grabbing his beret, he left the team house and headed to the Nungs' area to talk with the men coming with him the next day.

OF ALL THE LOCAL PEOPLES involved in the Vietnam War, none was more fiercely anti-Communist and loyal to the cause of freedom than the Nung Chinese. Unlike the South Vietnamese who often played both sides of the conflict, or the Montagnards who sometimes just got tired of the war and went home to their wives and pigs, the Nungs were America's most efficient and faithful allies.

The Nung commander, Ninh le Vao, was playing Chinese dominoes in the tropical hut he shared with the other Nung leaders and the interpreters when Santelli entered. Like many Asians, Vao was a compulsive gambler. He was a poor one, though, and lost far more than he won. At his age gambling was one of the few passions left to him. His other great passion was killing Communists.

Vao was in his late forties and had been killing Communists longer than the young American officer had been alive. Every year of his long personal war was etched on his weathered face. Those Americans who said they couldn't tell the age of an Oriental had never met Vao.

He was a veteran of the Chinese Nationalist armies and had fought both the Japanese and Mao's Communists in World War II. After that he had joined up with the French in North Vietnam to fight Ho Chi

Minh's Communist Vietminh. Now, at an age when most soldiers had long since been retired, the wiry old Nung was still fighting Communists as a striker in a Special Forces Mike company.

"*Trung Uy!*" Vao said, looking up. "You have come at a most auspicious time. I am winning back all the money that I lose to these sharks this month."

Santelli pulled up a chair to the makeshift wooden table. He had never learned to play the complicated game, but he found it interesting to watch.

"See, *Trung Uy,*" Vao said, gathering up all the piaster notes in the middle of the table. "Luck favors me today. We will have a good mission tomorrow."

"That's what I wanted to talk to you about," Santelli said. "I need to go over the personnel going out with us tomorrow."

Now Vao was all business; killing Communists always came before gambling. "I have alerted the First Platoon, *Trung Uy.* Two men are on leave, but I have picked good men from the other platoons to replace them. Whiskey and Kent are going as your interpreters. Also I am sending one of the Khmer interpreters if you need to speak with any Cambodians."

"Good idea," Santelli said, mentally kicking himself for not having thought of that possibility himself. Old Vao didn't forget anything.

"Lam Noc will lead the sterile team," Vao continued. "He is a fearless man, and all of his men speak the northern dialect perfectly."

"One thing about Lam Noc, though," Santelli said. "You'd better warn him that I don't want any of his cowboy shit this time. We can't afford to have Charlie know we're operating in his AO."

Vao chuckled. Lam Noc was famous for stealing enemy equipment right from under the noses of NVA units. Once he had stolen a motorbike and ridden it through the jungle with a dozen North Vietnamese hot on his trail. "I will tell him, *Trung Uy.*"

"Also," Santelli said, "the new *Dai Uy* will be inspecting the troops in the morning, so make sure all the men are standing tall. And I don't want to see anybody wearing trophy necklaces."

Some of the younger Nungs had started collecting ears from the enemy dead, which they dried out and wore around their necks. The Americans tried to discourage the practice.

"I do not like that, either," Vao agreed. "The dead, even dead Communist dogs, should rest undisturbed."

Santelli got to his feet. "If there's nothing else, I'll see you in the morning."

"Sleep well, *Trung Uy.*"

"You, too, Vao."

"I wish MACV-SOG had waited a week before giving us this mission," Reese said as he looked out over the approaches to the camp. "I should be taking that patrol out instead of Santelli."

He and Sergeant Pierce were walking the perimeter of the camp. So far the defenses looked good to Reese. The trenches were deep, the sandbagged weapons emplacements were well built and the barbed wire obstacles were tight. About the only thing Reese could find fault with was that there were too few claymores backing up the wire obstacles. Since the Tet Offensive, claymores had been extremely scarce throughout the country. He would have to wait before he could get more of the deadly mines. The trip-wired hand grenades in the barbed wire would have to suffice for now.

"Santelli will be okay, sir," Pierce said. "He's done real well so far, and this is his first big chance to get out there and really get his feet wet."

"That's what I'm afraid of," Reese said. "If he gets too wet, he might drown."

Pierce chuckled. Wet work was the slang for close-in killing, particularly a clandestine killing on a black operation. "He's going out with some of the best Nungs I've ever worked with. They'll keep him from getting into too much trouble."

"I sure as hell hope so. The other thing that bothers me is that he's taking too many men in for a recon."

SF recon teams were usually made up of only four to six men, few enough to move unseen and to hide in the jungle if they had to. Santelli's twenty-three-man patrol was more of a reconnaissance in force. They planned to break up into smaller teams once they reached their recon area, but until then they had to move as one body and would run a greater risk of being detected. If anything went wrong and they had to be extracted, it would take at least three choppers to pull them all out.

"That bothers me too, sir," Pierce said, "but that's the way SOG wants it, so the LT's just going to have to live with it."

"I know," Reese said. He took one last look out over the perimeter before turning back. "Let's go take a look at the 106 emplacements."

7

April 17, Camp A-410, Ban Phoc

After an early breakfast the next morning, Santelli and his team assembled on the open ground between the team house and the command bunker. He looked over his troops with confidence. It wasn't going to be an easy mission, that was a promise, but he couldn't think of a better group of men to try to do it with.

As he waited for his CO to appear, the lieutenant checked over each man to keep his mind occupied.

Most of the Nungs were dressed in tiger-striped jungle fatigues and boonie hats, their faces and hands camouflaged with green and black greasepaint. Most of them wore Army-issue OD towels draped around the backs of their necks as sweat rags. Lam Noc and the four men of his sterile team were dressed in faded olive NVA uniforms with NVA-style brush hats, rucksacks and field equipment.

Each man carried an NVA-style rucksack on his back filled with a double basic load of ammunition and grenades, extra water and rations. They would be humping almost eighty pounds a man, excluding their individual weapons, but they couldn't go with any less.

Four of the young Nungs were further burdened with the Prick-77 radios and extra batteries. The AN/PRC-

77 radio had a secure voice capability that would prevent enemy interception of their radio transmissions. The radios would be their sole link with the outside world, and they didn't need anyone listening in.

Except for the sterile team, which was armed with captured AK-47s, most of the Nungs were armed with M-16s. Santelli had, however, taken the precaution of adding two M-60s to the patrol, and four of the Nungs were packing Thumpers, the M-79 grenade launchers. The riflemen were carrying extra bandoliers of the 40 mm grenades for the Thumpers as well as extra link belts of M-60 ammunition.

The three Special Forces men carried a mixed bag of weapons. Sergeant Kowalski had his CAR-15, the shortened submachine gun version of the M-16 rifle, as well as an Army-issue .45-caliber pistol in a field belt holster. Sergeant Larry Webb, the demo man, had his M-16 rifle as well as his favorite 12-gauge Remington automatic shotgun and a Browning Hi-Power 9 mm pistol. Hotchkiss also carried a CAR-15 and a .45 pistol. All of the men sported knives and machetes.

We've got enough weaponry here to start a small war all on our own, Santelli thought. I hope to hell we don't need all of it. If we do, we're all going to be in deep shit.

Santelli looked over toward the command bunker and saw Captain Reese approaching with Sergeant Pierce at his side. He called the patrol to attention. "We're all ready to go, sir."

Reese glanced over the Nung troops standing in formation. "Have them stand easy. And I'd like to meet your Nung leader."

Santelli called Vao out. The old warrior double-timed up to Reese. *"Ni hao, Dai Uy,"* the Nung said, bowing slightly.

Reese returned the bow, but not so deeply. *"Ni hao, Vao."*

Vao smiled. "The captain speaks Chinese."

Reese returned the smile. "Not really. Just enough to get myself into trouble."

The Nung's smile broadened. "If you like, *Dai Uy,* I will get a young Nung woman for you and she can teach you our language properly."

Reese laughed. "Thank you, Vao, but I must respectfully decline. I don't need that much trouble."

Vao laughed. "The *Dai Uy* is wise not to let a woman into his house!"

"Introduce me to the rest of your troops," Reese said.

Vao spun around and shouted a command in Chinese, and the ranks of the strikers snapped to attention. Vao faced about again and saluted French-style with the palm of his hand forward.

"Dai Uy, the First Platoon of the A-410 Nung Mike Force is ready for your inspection."

Reese returned the salute and followed Vao as he stepped up to the first striker in the formation. The Nung he faced was typical of the men who had joined the Special Forces to fight Communists. He was well-built, of medium height and in his early twenties. Although he was supposed to be standing at attention, his open face wore a huge grin and he bore his heavy burden of weapons and equipment easily. He was proud to be defending his people from the Communists.

Reese quickly glanced over the striker's weapons and moved on to the next man. He knew Santelli had already inspected the team in detail. He was really giving the Nungs a chance to see him up close for the first time.

"The men look good, Vao," he said when he completed his walk-through inspection.

"Thank you, *Dai Uy*." Vao bowed slightly. "They fight good, too."

Reese smiled. "The Nung always fight well."

In the distance Reese heard the distinctive thrumming of approaching Huey helicopter rotors. "I hear your ride coming, Jack," he said, looking up. "Better get 'em down to the pad."

"Vao," Santelli said, "move 'em out."

The Nung shouted a command, and the men broke ranks and headed for the chopper pad. The three AH-1 Cobra gunships of the Light Fire team escort circled protectively like hawks while the first of the three slicks flared out and touched down on the small pad inside the wire.

Vao shouted orders and, hunched over to clear the spinning rotor blades, the first group of Nungs sprinted through the red dust kicked up by the rotor blast and scrambled on board. As soon as the first ship was loaded, it lifted off to join the other circling Cobras and the second one landed.

As Santelli climbed on board the last slick, one of the door gunners handed him a flight helmet. He slipped it on and plugged the cord into the intercom jack before he took his seat in the open side door. "We go back here," he called up to the pilot.

"Roger that!" the pilot yelled, twisting the throttle. "Hang on."

The pilot pulled pitch on the collective, the Huey's tail came up and they were away. The mission was on.

Reese watched the chopper disappear to the northeast before he turned back to the command bunker. Until Santelli crossed safely over into Cambodia he would monitor every move they made by radio. If they ran into trouble before crossing the border, he could still do something to help them. Once inside the Parrot's Beak, however, they would be on their own.

SANTELLI LET his jungle boots hang out the open door of the helicopter. As the cool air of the rotor blast buffeted his face and the noise of the blades rang in his ears, he felt his pulse beat faster and faster. There was something about riding in the open door of a Huey slick, locked and loaded for war, that was completely beyond his ability to express. Even after the countless times he'd done it, he still didn't know if it scared him more than it excited him.

From the air the countryside looked as peaceful and calm as always, but he knew appearances were deceiving. There he was, flying through the sky with a chopper full of men armed to the teeth, looking for someone to kill. Santelli was very conscious of the weight of the loaded rucksack on his back and the trigger of his Swedish K lying under the forefinger of his right hand. It was a powerful feeling.

He looked around at the Nung strikers sitting in the doorway beside him and saw that they, too, were feeling some of the same excitement he was. He could see it in their dark eyes and in the same tight grin on their faces that he knew was on his own. That slight smile hid the hammering of their hearts.

Whiskey, one of his interpreters, caught his eye and shot him a thumbs-up. Santelli's grin broadened as he answered by pumping his clenched fist up and down in the infantry "go faster" signal. Whiskey's laugh was carried away by the wind.

When the flight reached the insertion area, the slicks started making dummy insertions. While the Cobras circled protectively overhead, the helicopters would flare out over a likely landing zone for a moment before climbing back into the sky.

On the way in for the third insertion the pilot called Santelli on the intercom. "This is it, LT," he said, pointing at the small clearing in front of them. "The Lima Zulu is green."

Santelli signalled a thumbs-up, took off his helmet and got ready to exit the ship. No sooner had the skids touched down than he leaped and ran a few paces into the grass before going to ground. The Nungs from his chopper formed a ring around him as the other two slicks quickly off-loaded. In less than thirty seconds he heard the Huey pilots pull pitch and rise again.

They were down and no one had shot at them.

Santelli waited until the sound of the choppers had faded into the distance before getting to his feet. The Nungs quickly formed into a patrol formation and, with Sergeant Kowalski taking point, headed northeast for the Parrot's Beak and Cambodia. Santelli made his first radio report back to B-40 at Can Tho, telling them they were on their way.

The choppers had inserted them three klicks from the border, and even moving carefully the patrol covered the distance in a little over an hour. When they reached the border, there was nothing to indicate they were crossing an international boundary of great significance. Cambodia looked no different from South Vietnam. But Santelli knew better. They had just jumped out of the frying pan into the fire.

AS SOON AS REESE received Santelli's message, he turned to Sergeant Pierce. "Okay, Sarge, now we have to get back to my signing for the camp."

Even in the middle of the war, any new unit commander always had to wade through a pile of paperwork before he could assume command of his unit.

"What do you want to do first?" Pierce asked.

Reese thought for a moment. "Can I get you to call your chopper buddies and get me a ride down to Tan Son Nhut this afternoon? B-40 wants me to go to Amexco and sign over the unit's funds. I'd like to get that shit out of the road first, so I can get back here and keep a close eye on Santelli."

"No sweat, sir," Pierce said, glancing down at his watch. "I should be able to get someone to drop in here in the next hour or so."

"Good," Reese said. "I'll throw some gear into a bag and be ready in a flash."

Reese was back in a few minutes with a packed B-4 bag in his hands. He and Pierce started going over the unit's property books, another chore that couldn't be put off. Before long the chopper called that it was inbound and, grabbing his bag, Reese hurried out to the pad. "I'll be back tonight," he told Pierce as he left the bunker.

It was a short flight to Saigon, and as Reese's Huey approached Tan Son Nhut on the outskirts of Saigon, the pilot took his ship down for a low-level run over the hotel that housed many of the American nurses who worked in the hospitals in the Saigon area.

"Keep a sharp eye out!" he called back to Reese on the intercom. "Usually there's a couple of 'em sunbathing on the roof."

They buzzed the hotel, but there weren't any naked "round eyes" lounging on the roof. Still, it was a nice view of the city, anyway. A few minutes later the Huey entered the traffic pattern at Tan Son Nhut, the busiest airport in the world.

The pilot flared his ship out on the Hotel Three helipad and shut down the turbine. Reese asked him to wait before he climbed out of the Huey, squinting his eyes against the sudden glare. Settling the beret on his head, he started off across the base for the American Express bank near the big PX complex.

Once inside, he went up to the unit fund counter and caught the eye of the young Vietnamese woman behind the desk. She immediately rose and gracefully hurried to meet him. "Can I help you, Captain?"

"I need to sign over a unit fund. Special Forces Camp A-410 at Ban Phoc."

"So sorry, Captain," the young woman said, looking down at the countertop. "Jennings is unit fund officer and he not here this afternoon."

"Is there someone else here who can help me?"

"So sorry." The clerk kept her eyes downcast. "Jennings only one who can do this thing."

"When is he coming back?"

"Not until tomorrow, Captain."

Reese was ticked off, but he knew there was no use in taking it out on the woman. Her American boss was evidently an incompetent civilian. He could only stay in town overnight and try to get the damn thing squared away in the morning. If he had to hang around overnight, he wasn't about to get a room in the Tan Son Nhut BOQ. For an evening in Saigon, he was going to do it right.

Reese went back to the heliport, released the slick and arranged for him to pass the information on to Sergeant Pierce. Then he walked out the main gate of the air base and hailed one of the yellow-and-blue Renault cabs clustered on the side streets.

He had stopped riding around in cyclos, the motorcyle-engine-powered pedicabs, after one of his friends had had a grenade chucked into his lap while doing so. Although the man managed to get rid of the explosive before it had gone off, Reese figured life was risky enough in Nam without taking unnecessary chances.

"Continental Palace," he directed the cabdriver, naming his favorite old French Hotel.

"No sweat, *Dai Uy,*" the cabby said, accurately reading Reese's rank insignia on his beret. "You Green Beret, *Dai Uy?*"

"Yes," Reese answered with a smile. "I'm in the Special Forces."

The cabbie smiled back. "Numbah one."

Reese sat back in the little car and loosened the strap on his shoulder holster as the cab pulled out into traffic. Even a ride with a smiling Saigon cabdriver, however, wasn't without its perils.

8

Continental Palace Hotel, Saigon

It had been well over a year since Reese had last been in Saigon, and he was surprised to see how much the city had changed. Not only did it show scars from the Tet Offensive earlier in the year, but it was even more crowded now and dirtier than it had ever been. Back in the days of French colonial rule, Saigon had been a charming European-style city of one and a half million people. Now its population had swollen to nearly four million, many of them villagers from the countryside who had fled the Communists. In the process Saigon had lost much of its fabled charm.

In fact, by the spring of 1968 the capital of South Vietnam was one massive slum that showed the destruction wrought by the Allied forces driving the NVA and VC out of their hiding places during Tet. While the offensive had been a decisive defeat for the Communists, it had also dealt the refugees a severe blow. And the war had followed them to the cities where hundreds had died. Thousands more were now without any home at all.

Reese had often wondered about what had happened to all of the Japanese Kamikaze pilots who had survived World War II. During his cab ride into the city, he suspected that some of them were masquerading as taxi drivers in Saigon. Reese had driven in Parisian traffic and had even survived driving the autobahn between Frankfurt and Heidelberg, but he'd never seen anything as bad as this in his life.

With its French background, Saigon traffic had always been bad, but this was ridiculous. At one point he found himself on a two-lane highway carrying four lanes of traffic going in three different directions. It didn't seem to bother his daredevil cabbie in the least. Alternately using full throttle on the gas and blasting full volume on his tinny horn, the Vietnamese wove his way through the mess toward the heart of town.

"Continental Palace, *Dai Uy*," the cabbie announced as he slid the little Renault to a stop in front of the impressive building directly across the plaza from the National Cathedral. Reese reached into his wallet for Vietnamese piasters to pay the driver. "You no have MPC?" the man asked, looking annoyed. He evidently preferred the American military currency.

Reese shook his head and handed him the local currency. The driver loudly muttered something about *"Dai Uy* number ten thou" as he engaged the clutch and lurched back out into the steady stream of traffic, his horn blaring.

The Continental Palace had been built before World War I at the height of French colonial rule, a relic of a time long before the scourge of the Vietminh and the fall of Dien Bien Phu. The elegant hotel wouldn't have looked out of place along a tree-lined boulevard in the heart of Paris. Like any grand dame of those bygone days, however, the hotel was showing a little wear and tear. The place badly needed a paint job, and the carpets were shabby and threadbare. The last time Reese had been there, the solid oak dining room tables had been dressed in linen tablecloths and the waiters in immaculate white jackets.

Even in its current state the Continental Palace did its best to recall those kinder years. The only real concession management had made to the harsh realities of Saigon in the late 1960s was the addition of RPG screen around the veranda and the heavily armed security guards on duty in the makeshift sandbag bunkers by the main entrance.

Reese had no problem getting a room. After checking his weapon with the desk clerk, he was shown to a small suite overlooking the plaza. He showered, dressed and, much relaxed, descended the wide staircase to the dining room.

On another evening he might have gone over a few blocks to the Caravel Hotel's rooftop restaurant for a real American-style dinner of grilled steak and baked potato. Tonight he didn't feel like fighting his way through the hordes of reporters and junketing politicians for a table. Besides, he felt like seeing if the Tet Offensive had managed to ruin the cuisine at the Continental Palace as much as it had ruined the rest of the once beautiful city.

REESE PUT DOWN his knife and fork and signaled for his waiter. The meal had been superb. Even with the disruption caused by Tet, the French-trained chefs in the kitchen of the Continental Palace still knew how to create chateaubriand, and the sautéed mushrooms had been as good as any he had ever had in France. He was glad to find that despite the war certain things endured.

When the waiter arrived, Reese ordered coffee and a Napoleon brandy and wished he had a good cigar to top it all off. The best part of being in the army was that his European tour with the Tenth Group Special Forces at Bad Tolz, Germany, had done wonders for his appreciation of the finer things in life. Europe had taught him that there was more to dinner than meat and potatoes. Not that he didn't like a thick, juicy charcoal-grilled steak as only an American could cook it, but there was a lot to be said for French haute cuisine, or even for German fare.

As he waited for his brandy, he looked around the high-ceilinged dining room. Halfway across the room he noticed a dinner party of two young women and four field-grade officers, Saigon commandos by the look of them, staff REMFs from any of the dozen or more headquarters that dotted the city. His eyes paused on one of the women, a stunning dark blonde with long hair flowing down her back. She was speaking animatedly with the men about something. Reese strained his ears to catch their conversation, but they were too far away. He turned his eyes away before they noticed him watching them.

The waiter returned with his brandy and coffee, and Reese settled back to enjoy two of life's greatest pleasures. That was one of the things he missed most about his life in the Army—decent coffee. There was no shortage of coffee in the Army, but most of it was fit only to be used as rust remover.

"Excuse me," a female voice spoke from behind him.

Reese turned and recognized the blonde from the table he'd been watching. Caught completely off guard, he struggled to his feet. "Mike Reese," he said, sticking his hand out.

"Laura Winthrop," she answered, shaking his hand firmly. "May I impose on you?"

"Certainly," Reese answered, his eyes covertly running over her trim frame. Up close she was even more beautiful than she'd appeared from across the room. Her deep blue eyes, golden tan and long blond mane were stunning. "How can I help you?"

"Well," she said, smiling. "My friends and I are having an argument, and I want an expert to come to my defense."

"I'll be glad to come to your defense anytime," Reese said with an open grin. "But I'm not sure I'm too much of an expert on anything. Just what is it you're talking about?"

She cocked her head slightly. "The war, of course."

His smile faded. "I do know something about that," he admitted, suddenly cautious.

She glanced down at his green beret on the edge of the table, then back up at the CIB sewn above his left breast pocket with the jump wings above it. "I think you know a little more about it than those jerks do," she said, nodding her head toward the men at her table. "They're a bunch of REMF staff officers from MACV who've never spent a night in the field."

"What do you do here, Miss Winthrop?" He smiled, curious about her use of the infantry's slang abbreviation for noncombatants—Rear Echelon Motherfuckers.

"Laura, please," she said, smiling again. "I'm a correspondent for UP."

Reese's smile disappeared completely. If there was any group of people in Vietnam he hated more than the REMFs it was the members of the "press corps."

"Well..." He paused. As beautiful a woman as she was, she was an enemy. "I'm not too sure I can help you, Miss Winthrop."

Her own smile faded, and she appraised him with hard eyes. "I take it you don't much care for the press."

"It's nothing against you, Miss...Laura. It's just that..." Most of the reporters he'd met had been flaming assholes. The rest had been incompetent fools who fed on the tragedy of the war.

"You think we're all a bunch of assholes who work late into the night doing our best to make people like you look bad. Right?"

He grinned sheepishly. "Well, I wouldn't have put it exactly that way. But..."

"Some of us are that way. But most of us are just trying to do a job. And our job is to tell the people back home what's going on here."

Reese looked skeptical. "That may be, but there are a lot of us in uniform who feel that when you people do your job, as you say, it only makes our job even harder than it has to be.''

"I can see that,'' she said, her deep blue eyes locked on his. "But maybe that's because we're exposing things you want to keep hidden."

Reese didn't answer. Too many of the missions he'd undertaken on his last tour had been top secret. His war, the one being waged by the Green Berets, was the war the press seldom learned about. Even when they did, more often than not they got it wrong.

He suddenly realized that their conversation had become the center of attention in the dining room. Other conversations and the clinking of cutlery against fine china had hushed. "Look,'' he said in a lower voice, putting his hand on the back of the chair next to him, "I'm forgetting my manners. Would you care to sit down and have a drink with me while we talk about this? We're becoming the evening's entertainment."

She laughed lightly with a little swing of her hair. "Sure. Why not?''

"What are you drinking?'' he asked as he signaled for the waiter.

"Burgundy."

"Good choice in this place." He ordered the wine for her and another brandy and coffee for himself. "Now,'' he said, trying to lead the conversation toward less dangerous ground, "what's this argument you wanted my opinion on?''

Laura leaned forward slightly. "Whether or not we're winning the war now that the Tet Offensive showed that Westmoreland's overly optimistic reports about the 'light at the end of the tunnel' were pure bullshit. I say we haven't a hope of winning and, as far as I'm concerned, the fact that Westy's leaving and Johnson's bowed out of the presidency proves my point.''

Reese liked outspoken women. "Well," he said, "I've only been back in-country for a couple of days, and I managed to miss all the fun during Tet, but . . .''

"Fun?" she interrupted him sharply. "You think the Tet Offensive was *fun?*''

"Wait a minute," Reese said, his eyes narrowing. "I know Tet wasn't fun for any of the people who got caught up in it, GI or Vietnamese, but you have to understand that I'm a professional soldier. My job is to close with and destroy the enemy, and Tet gave us the chance to do just that. We kicked their asses so hard that it's going to take them months, if not years, to fully recover from it. From what I've been reading—''

"But you weren't here for Tet yourself." Her expression was intense.

"No, I wasn't," Reese said, controlling his growing anger. "I said I missed it, but I know what took place. I make it a point to keep up with what's happening in my profession.''

"But you weren't there when the Special Forces camps were wiped out—Lang Vei, Bu Dop?''

"No, I wasn't, and I lost friends there, but that doesn't change my mind about what happened. General Giap gambled and he lost big. More of the country is under government control now than it was before the attack, and I call that a victory for us.''

"At the cost of how many American lives?"

"Miss, in case you haven't noticed, there's a war going on and people get killed in wars—on both sides. For every American killed in Tet there were several hundred NVA and VC killed. Again that's a victory for us."

"So you think we're winning the war?"

"On the battlefield, yes," he said. "But you people are losing it for us in the newspapers and on TV back home."

Now it was her turn to speak sharply. "That's what all of you people say, but I'm not seeing anyone winning a war around here. All I'm seeing is a never-ending stream of enthusiastic bullshit coming out from MACV and a steady stream of body bags going back home."

"I won't disagree with you about MACV," Reese said, "but have you ever seen the war from the viewpoint of the Special Forces CIDG program?"

She shook her head. "No, I've never been to a Special Forces camp."

"Well, if you want to see the part of the war that's being won, come down and see me. I'll give you a guided tour and let you talk to the men who are winning this war."

"The famous Green Berets?" She almost smirked.

"No," he answered patiently. Like everyone else in Special Forces, he'd had more than his fill of the John Wayne image during the past two years. "Not the Green Berets, but the indigenous troops we have the honor to lead—the CIDG Yards, the Nungs, the ethnic Cambodes. Those are the men who are going to win the war for South Vietnam."

"You didn't mention the ARVINS," she said, referring to the South Vietnamese army troops. "You don't think they can win the war?"

"Oh, no, you don't," Reese said, his jaw set. "You're not going to get me to say anything like that. Some of the ARVIN units are damn good. Some aren't. The fact is that, man for man, the Special Forces CIDG programs are killing more enemy than anyone else in this entire country."

"Including the rest of the U.S. Army?"

Reese held his eyes steady on hers. "Including the rest of the American Army, yes."

"And why is it," she asked skeptically, "that I don't hear this at the MACV briefings?"

Reese smiled thinly and shrugged. "I don't know. Professional jealousy perhaps?"

She played with the stem of her wineglass thoughtfully, swirling the dark wine around the sides of the glass. "I'll tell you what. I just might take you up on that offer. I've just about had my fill of the MACV version of this war, so if you can show me something that's working in this crazy war, I'd sure as hell like to take a look at it."

She reached into her purse and took out a ballpoint pen and a small notepad. "Give me your unit designation, location and land line number."

He gave her the information. "Give me a call first, though," he told her with a big grin. "To make sure I'll be around. I wouldn't like you to sneak up on us and catch us losing the war."

She finished her wine, studied him over the rim of the glass and smiled. "No, we wouldn't want to do that now, would we?" Then she stood abruptly and extended her hand. "It's been nice talking to you, Mike. And I *am* going to take you up on your offer."

He got to his feet and took her hand. "Great, I'll look forward to it."

9

Parrot's Beak, Cambodia

While Reese was discussing the war with Laura Winthrop in the Continental Palace restaurant, First Lieutenant Jack Santelli was crouching in the deep night shadows beside a stand of bamboo, intently watching a long column of heavily laden North Vietnamese troops making their way down a trail leading to the southeast and Vietnam.

After crossing into Cambodia, Santelli had marched the Nungs all day, moving carefully and covering ground as fast as they could. This part of Cambodia along the Vietnam border was sparsely populated, so they had been able to make good time. The arrival of the NVA several years ago had driven most of the local peasants westward, creating a buffer zone almost empty of civilians. This and the sparse vegetation had made it easy for Santelli's patrol to move through the area quickly.

They had pushed on all day, not even stopping to eat. Those who were hungry had opened a plastic bag of freeze-dried rations, added a little water from their canteens and put the bag inside their fatigue jackets. In fifteen minutes their body heat warmed the rations and rehydrated them enough to eat. By late afternoon they had reached their patrol area deep inside the Parrot's Beak in a region of denser jungle, and Santelli had decided to call a halt.

He had pulled his men back into a night defensive position on a small ridge line a klick away from the trail to rest and eat. After an hour he split the patrol into small recon teams under the command of his SF NCOs and sent them out to start checking the area.

Santelli had taken the five-man "sterile" recon team himself and come across a well-traveled jungle path leading to the southeast just as night was falling. Now he crouched in the darkness and watched the enemy troops as they passed.

Every third NVA in the column carried a hooded lantern with a small candle inside to light their way. The glow of the lanterns was so faint that it couldn't be seen more than a few yards away. As close as he was, Santelli couldn't tell what the North Vietnamese were carrying. He only knew it had to be bad news.

This was the third such string of troops he had observed in little over an hour. Something big was going down; there was no question about that.

Santelli carefully backed away from his observation point and returned to the rest of his recon team securely hidden in the jungle. Lam Noc, the sterile team leader, and the skinny young Nung interpreter known as Whiskey were anxiously waiting for him. "What you see, *Trung Uy?*" Whiskey asked.

"*Beaucoup* MVA," Santelli answered. "They're moving supplies down the trail."

"What we do now, *Trung Uy?*" Lam Noc asked.

Santelli thought for a moment. "Lam Noc," he said softly, "I'd like you to go down there and play VC for me. Try to hook up with one of those units. Talk to them, try to find out what they're carrying and where they're going. But make sure you get back to our camp by first light, 0700 at the latest."

Lam Noc grinned in the dark. This was his favorite game, infiltrating enemy units and learning what they were doing. It was a dangerous game to play, but he was very good at it and liked the excitement. "No sweat, *Trung Uy,*" he said confidently, proud to have been chosen for the mission. "Can do."

"But don't steal anything this time," Santelli cautioned. "I just want you to talk to them."

"Okay, *Trung Uy.*" The young Nung smiled. "Their stuff is all shit, anyway."

Santelli bit off a laugh as Lam Noc grabbed his AK-47 and moved downhill toward the trail. As soon as the Nung was gone, Santelli took the rest of his team back up to the ridge line to hear the preliminary reports of the other teams.

Back at his patrol base Santelli talked quietly with the other team leaders as they returned before he made his radio report to the B-40 headquarters back at Can Tho. Santelli got out his map, hid under his poncho liner, shone his red-filtered penlight on it and carefully plotted the trail he'd found as well as the heavily trafficked trails the other teams had reported. All of them seemed to lead into an area of dense jungle at the very tip of the Parrot's Beak. He didn't like the way things were shaping up at all.

So far, though, all he could report was that the NVA were moving troops and supplies. They moved men and matériel in this area all the time, but there was far more activity than he would have expected from an enemy that was supposed to be licking its wounds. And the tip of the Parrot's Beak protruded into South Vietnam.

He called for the radio and, speaking softly, made his report. B-40 rogered his message and ordered him to move south in the morning to try to find where the enemy troops were assembling. They also told him to snatch a prisoner if he could.

Santelli passed the Prick-77 handset back to the Nung on radio watch. Prisoner snatches were always tricky. Not only was there the problem of taking the man alive without getting into a firefight, but then he would have to keep him with them until they could be extracted later. Since they were in Cambodia, he couldn't just call for a chopper to take the man out right away. The mission could be blown that way. If they caught someone, they would have to carry him with them.

Softly he called Kowalski over. "They want us to follow them in the morning and try to learn where they're going, and they want us to try to get a prisoner."

The intel sergeant was silent for a moment. "You know I like talking to prisoners, sir, but I don't think that's a real good idea this time."

"I know. But we have to do it if we can."

Kowalski shrugged. "Okay, LT. We'll give it a try."

"I'm going to catch a few zees," Santelli said. "Wake me if anyone calls."

"Right, sir."

Santelli wrapped his poncho liner around him and tried to find a soft place to sleep next to the radio operator. With the soft hiss of the radio squelch in his ears, he dropped right off to sleep. As an experienced combat soldier, Santelli had learned a long time ago how to sleep whenever he had half a chance.

ON THE BANK right above the trail, Lam Noc watched a party of two dozen NVA troops, a platoon, slowly snaking their way downhill, their covered lanterns flickering like glowworms. The last man in the file was older than the rest and a little heavyset. Lam Noc felt he might be a talker; in his experience fat men often were. When the man passed by him, the Nung silently dropped onto the trail and followed.

Twenty minutes later the platoon stopped along the side of the path for a rest break. Lam Noc stopped short of the group, around a bend in the trail. Shrugging out of his rucksack, he dug out a cold rice ball wrapped in a banana leaf. Getting back into his ruck, he slung his AK over his shoulder and sauntered up to the end of the enemy column, munching on the rice ball.

The heavy NVA he had spotted was on trail watch and started when he saw the Nung approach. He quickly swung his weapon up to his shoulder.

"Peace, Comrade," Lam Noc said, holding his hands out. Lam's parents had come down from the

North when the country was partitioned in 1954, so his accent and dialect were correct. Relieved, the NVA guard assumed he was a file closer, carrying messages between columns on the march. He lowered his assault rifle.

Lam Noc squatted on his heels beside the man. "You have no food, Comrade?" he asked when he saw the NVA eyeing his dinner.

"No, Comrade." The man was almost salivating. "Our cook, that motherless son of a dog, said he had no more for us today."

The Nung chuckled as he broke his rice ball in two and gave half of it to the guard. "Here, Comrade," he said, "you need to eat."

The guard gratefully took the food and stuffed the sticky pork-and-rice mixture into his mouth. He removed the NVA canteen from his belt and took a deep drink before handing it to Lam Noc. "Here," he offered, "try some of this. It'll rinse the taste of the trail from your mouth."

The Nung drank deeply. The canteen was full of raw rice wine. "Thank you," he said sincerely, then handed it back.

The guard looked closely at him. "I haven't seen you before, Comrade." Before Lam Noc could answer, however, the North Vietnamese went on. "But since Tet there are so many new fighters I haven't met. So many new comrades in the people's struggle. I guess it isn't surprising our cook often doesn't have enough food." He smiled briefly. "Maybe in the cities, though, there'll be enough rice for all of us."

Lam Noc almost jumped at that reference, but he made no remark. He had certainly picked the right man to talk to, and he was more than happy to listen to anything the NVA had to say.

"Yes," the guard continued, "I've heard the men of the South always have enough rice. I also hear they have imperialist whiskey and good French beer. The beer I can use." He smiled again. "But I don't know about the whiskey. I haven't tried that, have you?"

"No," Lam Noc answered, careful to keep the grin off his face. Like most Nungs, he loved whiskey, particularly Wild Turkey. "That'll be a new experience for me, too."

"I also hear—" the NVA chuckled as he absentmindedly scratched his crotch "—that all of their women are eager to make love to the brave fighters for the people's liberation. That, too, is something I'll have to try for myself when we get to Saigon next week."

Lam Noc had to keep himself from jumping up and running back to the lieutenant with what he had just learned. The NVA was planning another attack on Saigon next week!

"Say," the North Vietnamese said, looking at him curiously again. "What's your name, Comrade?"

"Fighter Vinh." Lam Noc answered calmly, but his heart was pounding. "Tran Co Vinh."

The Nung sighed. "I need to sleep now, Comrade," he said, settling back into the brush. "I need my strength for the women of the south." It would be dangerous for Lam Noc to get into a long discussion with the NVA about his family or his village. There was always the off chance that he came from the same area of the country. Lam Noc leaned back against his rucksack and closed his eyes.

A little later the Nung woke to the sound of equipment and weapons rattling as the NVA platoon got to their feet. The rest break was over.

"Go on ahead, Comrade," he told the guard as he undid his belt buckle and stepped off the trail. "I have to shit. I'll catch up with you later."

The NVA laughed and walked on.

As soon as the enemy column disappeared around the next bend in the trail, Lam Noc quickly pulled up his pants, buckled his belt, grabbed his weapon and faded back into the jungle.

"LT!" KOWALSKI WHISPERED URGENTLY.

Santelli was instantly awake. "What is it?" he asked, glancing at his watch. It was 0500 hours, the darkest part of night right before dawn.

"Lam Noc is back," Kowalski said. "He says he has to talk to you right away."

"Send him over."

The young Nung quickly related his news. Santelli frowned when he heard what the enemy soldier had said about going to Saigon. He was only supposed to break radio silence twice a day—at noon and midnight. Taking the SOI from around his neck, he swiftly encoded his message. Even with Prick-77 radios with secure voice transmission capability, this information was too important to risk possible enemy interception, and too important to wait till noon.

It took longer to send the message in three-letter code groups than it did in a voice transmission and even longer for the radio operator at B-40 to decode them and find someone to read the message. Dawn was breaking when B-40 got back to him.

Santelli called his American NCOs over to him. "Okay," he said, "here's the story. I reported the movement on the trails we found and passed on the information Lam Noc got about their hitting Saigon next week. But apparently it isn't enough for SOG. Our orders are to move south and try to find exactly where they're going."

Kowalski slowly shook his head. "We're going to have our shit hanging in the wind if we do that, LT. There's just too fucking much activity in this area for us to be stumbling around out here with a twenty-man patrol. If we were a five-man RT with strabo rigs and had an extract bird on standby, that would be one thing. But this shit just isn't going to cut it."

Santelli had to agree. The SOG RTs, recon teams, were small enough to hide in the woods and, if things went to hell on them, the strabo rigs they wore on their assault harnesses allowed a chopper to drop down over the treetops, hook onto them with a nylon rope and snatch them out in an instant.

"You're right," Santelli said, "but we're stuck with what we have. When we move out, we'll split up into our four teams and move to our new recon area by separate routes. We'll join up later in the afternoon at the rendezvous point to set up our new patrol base before splitting up into the teams again."

Webb had been listening intently. "Ah, sir," he said hesitantly, "that plan's okay for movement, but it still leaves us hanging if we run into trouble. We get into a firefight and it'll have to be each team for themselves. The others will be too far away to help."

"I know," Santelli said grimly. "But we run a better chance of not being detected if we split up." He opened his map. "Here's our primary rendezvous point." He grease-penciled a location on the map. "And here's a couple of alternates along the way."

The NCOs all marked their own maps.

"We'll put the radios on the patrol push and check in every two hours."

"Isn't that compromising our commo security, sir?" Kowalski asked.

Santelli nodded. "Sure it is. But that's the only way I can keep track of everyone. Are there any more questions? Okay," he said when there were none, "let's get the troops fed and break camp."

10

April 18, MACV-SOG Headquarters

Dick Clifford looked over the radio message that had been forwarded to him from B-40. Santelli's report fitted right in with the rest of the information he had been gathering. It all fitted perfectly, but he knew Colonel Marshall wasn't going to accept Santelli's conclusions that the North Vietnamese were massing their forces for another major attack on Saigon.

The colonel had completely bought the official line that Tet had crushed the NVA, and he wasn't going to like hearing what the patrol had to report. Marshall had reluctantly okayed the A-410 team's mission into the Parrot's Beak, but he had done it only to reinforce his own personal belief that there was nothing there to worry about.

Clifford finished his coffee and butted his cigarette before slapping Santelli's message into a classified folder and heading out the door for Marshall's office. Halting at the door, he knocked twice and waited for permission to enter.

At the regulation three paces in front of Marshall's oak desk, he halted and came to attention. "Sir, I have the initial reports from that team I sent into the Parrot's Beak."

"What do they have to say?" Marshall asked, leaning back and indicating that Clifford should take a seat. The colonel didn't like to read reports; he preferred his staff to give him the information orally.

"Well, sir, their initial report last night confirms what I suspected. They report observing several company-size NVA regular units moving down into the point of the Beak. The troops were loaded down with additional supplies and ammunition as well as their normal weapons and equipment. Our group broke radio silence this morning to send an additional report that one of the sterile CIDG troops talked to a man in one of the NVA units last night and learned that they plan to hit Saigon next week."

Marshall was silent for a moment. Then he snorted. "I don't buy that for a minute. What's the name and rank of the officer leading that recon patrol?"

"First Lieutenant Jack Santelli, sir."

"And this is his first mission into Cambodia, right?"

"Yes, sir."

"That's it, then," Marshall said smugly as he folded his hands in front of him. "He's just another junior-grade Special Forces officer playing super soldier and seeing a VC under every bush." Even though Vietnam was seen as a young man's war in the newspaper, the colonel still refused to take the judgments of junior officers seriously.

"But, sir—" Clifford started to protest.

"But nothing," Marshall interrupted. "I see this happening all the time with these people. From the way they've been treated in the press reports, it's no wonder they think they're winning this war all by themselves. Every time they go out in the field they find VC all over the place. But when we send in line units, the enemy mysteriously vanishes into thin air.''

Clifford knew this was all too often the case, but not because of faulty Special Forces field intelligence. It was the fault of inept tactics on the part of the line infantry units. How in the hell could you even hope to sneak up on a guerrilla force with artillery preps, recon choppers and transistor radios blaring?

Clifford knew better than to try to argue the point with the colonel. He also knew, however, that he had to do something before Marshall made his life even more miserable.

"Maybe I could go to the launch site, sir," Clifford offered, "and take control of this operation myself. That way I'll be getting their reports firsthand and can better direct their movements."

Marshall drummed his fingers on his desk for a moment. "Somebody had better do something to get this mess straightened up," he muttered. "I didn't send those people in there to give me this kind of shit. I want accurate, factual reports, not some Green Beret fantasy."

"Yes, sir," Clifford said, getting to his feet. "I can be on-site before nightfall."

"Do that."

Back in his office Clifford made a few phone calls and grabbed the packed B-4 bag he kept ready for those rare occasions when he went out on field operations. He really didn't want to go, but there was too much at stake this time for him to leave the mission completely in Santelli's hands.

MIKE REESE WAS BACK at the Amexco office at Tan Son Nhut as soon as the bank's doors opened in the morning. The errant Mr. Jennings, the unit fund bank officer who had been AWOL the day before, looked severely hung over, and Reese knew why he hadn't been at his desk the day before. From the look of his bloodshot eyes, he took his partying seriously.

It took only a few minutes for Reese to get the unit's funds signed over. When that chore was taken care of, a quick trip to the Army Aviation flight operations got him a chopper ride back to Ban Phoc within the hour.

"What have you heard from Santelli?" Reese asked when he found his team sergeant in the command bunker.

Pierce handed him several message forms. "We got their midnight report on time. And then they broke radio silence this morning to send an update. It looks like they landed right in the middle of a whole bunch of 'em, at least a couple of NVA regular regiments making their way south."

Reese quickly read over the messages. "What did SOG have to say about this?"

"They told them to move south, too, and try to locate their assembly area."

"You're shitting me!" The essence of a good recon was to find the enemy and then get the hell out of the area before he found you. Santelli didn't have enough men to fight if they got into big trouble. And, worse than that, if they did step in it, it would be difficult to pull them out of Cambodia in time.

"No, sir," Pierce said. "They want Santelli to keep on their trail."

Using the wall map, Reese plotted the locations the lieutenant had reported. "It looks to me like Jack's hit on a major operation. If they're moving men and supplies down into the point of the Beak, they're planning to kick the living shit out of someone before very long."

"That's what I think, too, sir," Pierce agreed. "The question is, who are they going to hit?"

Reese reread the morning message. "I'd go along with this," he said, tapping the page. "I think they could get a lot of mileage out of another big attack on Saigon."

"What do you mean, sir?"

"Well, just look at where we are right now," Reese explained. "Westy's been kicked upstairs and Abrams is still trying to figure out what in hell the politicians want him to do next. The Paris peace talks are starting up again, and Johnson threw in the towel the week before last. The press is already completely against us, and if the enemy can make it look as if we can't even defend Saigon, it'll make us look that much worse at home. It'll give them a real advantage at the negotiating table."

Just as he finished, the radio broke in with a message from an incoming chopper that it would be landing in five minutes. "Are we expecting any visitors today?" Reese asked.

Pierce looked puzzled. "Not that I can think of, sir."

Reese grabbed his beret and shoulder holster. "We'd better go see who the hell it is, I don't need guests in the middle of an operation like this."

"Roger that, sir," Pierce agreed fervently.

The sergeant popped a smoke grenade and dropped it at the end of the PSP to show the pilot of the lone Huey which way the wind was blowing. As the slick flared out and touched down, Reese saw that it didn't have Army markings. Instead, it was painted olive drab and had a small U.S. flag on the tail fin.

"Ah, shit," he muttered. "The fucking Company."

Reese's earlier experiences with the CIA had been all bad. MACV-SOG had a number of CIA men working with the black operations section, so this visit had to be connected somehow with Santelli's mission.

Reese recognized the pale, skinny man who stepped out of the Huey as the guy who had briefed him on the mission at B-40. "Nice to see you again," Clifford said to Reese, his hand held out. "I'm the controller for that recon team you have in the Parrot's Beak."

"Is there something wrong?" the Green Beret asked as they shook hands.

Clifford instinctively glanced around the helipad. "Is there someplace we can talk?"

"Come on into the bunker," Reese said, turning smartly on his heel.

Sergeant Pierce offered Clifford coffee or beer. The CIA man declined both and got right down to business. "We think we've got a problem with the reports we've been getting from Lieutenant Santelli."

"And just what might that be?" Reese asked curtly. Even if his people had been loaned to SOG, he wasn't going to take any shit from these guys, particularly this CIA man.

Relatively insensitive as he was in his work, even Clifford could see that Reese wasn't impressed with the Company. He started over. "What I mean is that my boss, Colonel Marshall, the SOG operations chief, wants to make sure we're getting accurate information."

When Reese didn't reply, Clifford continued. "And since your men haven't worked for SOG before, he sent me up here to keep an eye on the mission."

Reese looked Clifford up and down slowly as if he were debating whether or not to throw him out on his ass. "Are you telling me that you think my man is lying? That he's sending back false information?" He spoke slowly and softly.

Clifford involuntarily stepped back a pace. "No!" he answered. "I don't think that myself, but the colonel..."

"What about this colonel of yours?" Reese asked. "He thinks that Santelli's seeing things and he sent you out here to take command of the mission? Is that it?"

Clifford was used to taking a certain amount of shit from SOG's Special Forces men, but usually not quite this much. Not when he was supposed to be running the particular operation.

"Look," the CIA man said, "we don't seem to be communicating very well. Why don't you call B-40 and talk with Captain Bob Williams in the S-3 shop? He knows who I am and he can explain what I'm doing here.''

"I'll do that," Reese said, turning his back on the CIA man. Clifford was left standing there like an idiot. Since he hadn't been invited to take a seat, Clifford leaned back against the wall and wondered why it was always so fucking difficult to work with the Special Forces.

Reese turned back to the radio, his face grim. "B-40 tells me that until further notice you'll be running this operation from my camp."

Clifford caught Reese's emphasis of the possessive pronoun and wisely decided not to make an issue of it. He felt the same way about his own little office.

"And," Reese continued, "I'm supposed to make my facilities available to you. So what do you need to operate here?"

"Not much," Clifford said carefully. "A place to bunk and access to your radios and maps."

"You can sleep in the team house and mess with the team," Reese said. "As for the rest of it, coordinate with my team sergeant, Sergeant Pierce here. He'll see you get everything you need."

"Thanks," Clifford said.

Reese locked eyes with him. "Don't mention it," he said as he brushed past and climbed the stairs out of the bunker.

"Well, sir," Pierce said, stepping up, "let's get you squared away."

"Thanks, Sergeant."

"Glad to help, sir."

JACK SANTELLI and his sterile team of six Nungs were finding it tough going as they headed south into the point of the Parrot's Beak. The terrain was rougher, the jungle foliage much thicker and NVA units were crawling all over the place. The reports he was getting from his other three teams were the same: no one was making good time.

At noon he called a halt and, after studying his map, he decided to change the evening rendezvous point to the second alternate location. The teams would have to hurry to arrive at the original location, and if they hurried, they would get sloppy. One false move and they'd have NVA on them like stink on shit.

He called his change in plans into B-40 with his normally scheduled report. The radio operator at Can Tho told him that the SOG mission controller had moved to Ban Phoc and that he was to send all further reports directly to him, using the A-410 frequency and call sign. He rogered the message and radioed the change in plans to his NCOs with the other teams.

"Okay," he told Lam Noc as soon as he was done, "let's get going."

11

Parrot's Beak

Sergeant Gil Kowalski bent to pick up an empty tin can he had spotted beside the trail they were crossing. It was a favorite North Vietnamese army ration item, a tin of herring packed in Red China, and it had been opened so recently that it still had a thin coating of soybean oil inside. The ants inside the can hadn't had time yet to eat it clean.

Down the trail he saw several more herring cans. At least a platoon-size unit had stopped here for lunch, probably not more than an hour ago. He checked the dirt and noted that the boot prints all headed southeast, the same direction he was going. He motioned the Nungs quickly across the trail and ducked back into the protection of the jungle himself.

Checking his map, he decided to swing west to get farther away from the trail they had crossed. This was the second sign of major enemy activity he had come across in as many hours. With so many NVA around, they had to be especially careful to avoid having the living shit shot out of them.

He took a quick compass reading and moved out again, taking up the point position himself. Even with the new rendezvous point, they had to get a move on if they were going to join up with the lieutenant on time. Of course, if they moved too fast, they wouldn't make it at all.

An hour later Kowalski topped a small ridge line and halted the team for a short break. They had made good time but were still a little behind schedule. The team was tiring quickly from the pace and needed to rest for ten minutes or so. Tired troopers didn't pay close attention to what they were doing, and he couldn't afford to have any screwups today.

While the Nungs rummaged in their rucks for something to eat, he ducked back along the way they'd come to watch their backtrail while he ate his own lunch. The jungle in this part of Cambodia wasn't triple canopy as it was in the Central Highlands of Vietnam. From where he was on the ridge line, Kowalski could see much of the route they'd taken through the breaks in the treetops.

He was opening a C-ration can of ham and lima beans when he spotted a flash of movement about a quarter of a mile away. Dropping flat, he parted the leaves in front of him and watched, his dinner temporarily forgotten. There it was again—a moving flash of North Vietnamese khaki glimpsed through the vivid jungle greenery.

Stuffing the partially opened can into his pant pocket, he grabbed his CAR-15, hurried back to the rest of his five-man team and signaled them to move out. The men crammed the rest of their lunch into their mouths, then formed themselves into a defensive formation to watch their rear and moved out on the run while Kowalski got on the radio to Santelli.

"One Zero, this One One. Over," Kowalski whispered urgently into the radio handset as he ran.

"This is One Zero, go." Santelli answered.

"This is One One," Kowalski whispered. "I've got NVA tracking me about a half a klick behind, and they're coming on fast. I don't know if I can shake them. Over."

"This is One Zero, roger. Send your location. Over."

"We're at 638294," Kowalski said, reading the grid coordinates off his map. "Moving to the southwest. Over."

"Roger, you're about three klicks to my west. Can you break trail and join up with me? Over."

"This is One One. That's a negative. I'm afraid I'll lead them right into you if I try that. I have to stop them here. Over."

"One Zero, roger." Santelli's voice was hard. Kowalski was sacrificing himself for the mission. "What do you want to do? Over."

"I'm going to send four of my Nungs on ahead to the rendezvous point," Kowalski said. "I'll take the radio and keep Kent with me and see if we can lead these guys away from you. That way if anyone hears the firefight, you won't be in the vicinity. Over."

"One Zero, roger," Santelli answered. "Keep me informed, Ski. Good luck. Out."

Kowalski called a halt. After showing the Nungs the planned evening rendezvous point, he took the Prick-77 radio from the radio telephone operator. It would be tougher for the Nungs to make it to the rendezvous without the radio, but he had to have it with him so he could keep Santelli informed.

They moved out again, heading as fast as they could to the west. As they ran, every five hundred yards or so one of the Nungs would drop off and disappear into the jungle, making sure his boots left no tracks to show where he had gone.

Finally Kowalski was left alone with Kent, his Nung interpreter. Of all the men on his team, Kent was the best colleague for this little job. Not only was the young man fearless in battle; if something happened to Kowalski, Kent could use the radio to report back to Santelli. This was one of those times when everyone, even the valuable interpreter, was expendable for the sake of the mission.

Kowalski motioned Kent to drop back to take up the drag position covering their rear. The Nung flashed him a grin of understanding as Kowalski passed him to take up the point. The Green Beret smiled back. If things did go to hell today, at least Kent was a good man to die with.

Running at an easy, mile-eating pace, the two men penetrated deeper into the jungle, gradually drawing the North Vietnamese farther away from the rest of the patrol.

SANTELLI HANDED the radio handset back to his RTO and took out his map again. The shit had just hit the fan, as the old saying went. Things had been just a little too easy so far. Now the situation was getting back to normal—all fucked up.

As much as he hated leaving Kowalski out there to go it on his own, he knew he really didn't have any other choice. Even with all four teams together, he still didn't have enough people to get into a major pissing contest. There were simply too many damn NVA running around in this part of the woods. Ski was right: if he could pull a successful ambush on that NVA tracking team and get away clean, they could continue with the mission. If not, they would have to break it off and run for the border. As he knew all too well, his recon would be blown once they made a major contact.

He quickly plotted Kowalski's last position and the remaining distance to the new rendezvous point. When he got there and joined up with the other teams, he would reassess the situation. Right now all he could do was keep moving and hope Kowalski and Kent could take the enemy out without getting hurt. If anyone on his team could pull this off, however, it was the Polish redneck.

Santelli folded his map, stuffed it back into the side pocket of his tiger-striped pants and signaled his team to move out again. They still had a couple of klicks to cover.

KOWALSKI DROPPED to the ground, his chest heaving as he fought to catch his breath. He scrambled his way back into the heavy bush along the side of the faint trail and brought his CAR-15 up, sighting back along the way he had come. He had led the enemy team as far from the others as he could. Now it was time to take them out. He had been running for over half an hour and was too exhausted to go any farther.

The green and black camouflage paint on his face and the green and black stripes of his uniform still enabled him to vanish against the jungle background. Sweat streaked his cheeks and forehead. He pulled three loaded magazines from the bandolier around his neck and laid them close to hand on the ground in front of him. Taking a fragmentation grenade from his ammo pouch, he held the spoon securely against the palm of his left hand and pulled the safety pin.

He heard the faint sounds of someone running down the path and knew it was Kent. The Green Beret raised himself enough to wave the Nung off to the other side of the trail. The North Vietnamese would be following right on the interpreter's heels. If Kowalski and Kent were going to get out of this alive, they had to take them all out in this one ambush.

Kowalski's thumb flicked the selector switch of his CAR-15 down to rock and roll, full automatic fire, and his forefinger unconsciously tightened around the trigger. He forced himself to slow his breathing. The M-26 frag weighed heavily in his left hand. He had been running for so long that he was light-headed and could feel the blood singing in his ears. It had been a long time since he'd run through the jungle with a radio strapped to his back, and he'd forgotten just how heavy the fuckers could be.

He couldn't see Kent across the trail. He looked back down the trail and spied the North Vietnamese point man crouching, looking at their boot prints in the red dirt and trampled brush. The soldier was packing what looked like a brand-new AK-47. Kowalski smiled thinly to himself.

The guys who were tracking them were good, he had to admit that. But from the khaki uniforms they wore and their new equipment, he figured they were NVA regulars, fresh troops just down from the North. This was what the sergeant was counting on to make his ambush work. Troops who were new to jungle fighting tended to bunch up in the woods to keep their comrades in sight. He was betting on this tendency so that their entire team would be in the killing zone together when he opened up on them.

The North Vietnamese got to his feet and slowly scanned the jungle in front of him before turning around and waving his comrades forward. Kowalski knew that as soon as the point man reached their ambush position, he would see where their footprints ended and would instantly know they had moved off the trail. By that time, he hoped, the rest of the enemy would be well within range.

He let the point man approach closer and closer until he could clearly see the star embossed on his brass belt buckle. He could even smell the man's sweat, but still he held his fire. Kent would wait for Kowalski to shoot first.

Back down the trail the rest of the five North Vietnamese trackers slowly came into view. Like the point man, they were alert, but as Kowalski had hoped they were bunched up beautifully. One of them carried a radio on his back, the second man from the drag. He would have to die first.

The point man was less than ten yards away from him now, approaching the place where he and Kent had turned off the faint trail.

Kowalski took a deep breath. It was show time!

With a snap of his arm he lobbed the grenade over his head and onto the trail behind the point man. Almost simultaneously he ripped off a long burst from his CAR-15 at the man carrying the radio.

The sudden shock of adrenaline rushing through Kowalski's veins made everything seem to move in slow motion, and his body went into overdrive. Out of the corner of one eye he saw the point man bearing down on him with his AK, bringing it up to fire. It would be Kent's job to deal with that threat.

The grenade was still turning through the air when the NVA radioman took Kowalski's burst of 5.56 mm full in the chest. He spun around and went down on his face just as the grenade exploded. The sergeant heard Kent's M-16 open up on the point man at the same time. Meanwhile he was busy burning through the remainder of the ammunition in his CAR.

When the bolt of his CAR locked to the rear on an empty magazine, he ducked. In one smooth movement he punched the magazine release, dropped the empty one out and slammed a fresh one in its place. Hitting the bolt release to chamber the first round, he came up onto one knee and emptied the weapon into the killing zone again.

One of the NVA had dived off the trail and was returning fire. Accurate fire. Kowalski heard the rounds tearing through the bush around him. He flattened and reloaded his SMG again. Rolling to one side, he came up once more, the CAR blazing.

He was right on target this time. The AK fire abruptly stopped and a sudden silence descended.

Kowalski slowly got to his feet and looked down the trail. There was no movement. Motioning Kent to stay where he was, he cautiously stepped out into the open, panting slightly, his CAR-15 at the ready.

Four of the NVA were dead, their bodies sprawled over the trail. The fifth was still alive, gasping for breath, his hands clamped over a gaping grenade wound in his belly. Ignoring the wounded man's eyes, Kowalski calmly stepped up to him and whipped the K-bar fighting knife from the sheath taped to his assault harness. Smoothly he jammed it up under the man's jaw, plunging the blade into his brain stem. The North Vietnamese shuddered violently, kicked his feet in the dirt and was still.

Kowalski tugged the knife free, wiped the blade on the dead man's clothes and resheathed it. Motioning the Nung to cover him, he ran back down the trail for a hundred yards and ducked off into the bush on the side again. He waited for several minutes to see if the tracking team had had a backup following them. The jungle was quiet except for the rustle of the soft breeze through the leaves.

The Green Beret sergeant finally went back to the ambush site and quickly searched the bodies. He picked up the fallen AK-47s, their magazine carriers, grenades and the shot-up radio and threw them all as far back into the bush as he could. Kent followed him, hoisting the bodies by the arms and dragging them off the trail.

Now that they had shaken off their pursuers, they had to change direction and try to get back to the rest of the patrol before nightfall. As desperately tired as they both were, this was no time to slack off now. He motioned Kent to move out again, and as they dog-trotted through the breaks in the underbrush, Kowalski reported the successful ambush to Santelli.

Camp A-410, Ban Phoc

Reese's jaw tightened as he listened in on Kowalski's radio message to Santelli. When Dick Clifford arrived to control the mission from Ban Phoc, Reese had switched his backup radio over to the patrol's internal frequency so that he could monitor the traffic between the teams as well as hear what Santelli was sending at the scheduled report times.

"That's blown it," he said, turning to face the CIA man when Kowalski had signed off. "We've got to get those people out of there ASAP."

"I'm not sure we can do that," Clifford replied carefully. "The colonel..."

"Fuck your colonel," Reese snapped. "My people are in danger out there. I want that mission closed down so I can extract them before dark."

Clifford shook his head. "I don't have the authority to order mission closure."

"You're the controller and you can't terminate the mission?"

"No. I can't."

"Who the fuck can, then?"

"Colonel Marshall," Clifford explained. "But his orders are that he wants the mission to run to completion."

"Even if it means losing the entire unit?"

Clifford successfully kept himself from shrugging in response to Reese's question. As far as he was concerned, losing men was what this war was all about. As an Intelligence officer, he didn't have a commander's attachment to the people who fought and died on the missions he controlled. Rarely was anyone that he knew personally killed.

"Colonel Marshall wants a thorough recon of this area," he repeated patiently. "And he didn't give me authority to pull them out ahead of schedule." Clifford didn't bother adding that he had his ass on the line and desperately needed the recon to vindicate his own prediction.

Reese clenched his fists at his sides. This was just one more example of why he always hated working with the CIA. They were always a little too willing to spend the lives of good men when they really didn't have to.

"Okay," he said reluctantly, "then how about letting me put a platoon on standby in case they run into more trouble and need reinforcement?"

Clifford slowly shook his head. "I don't have authority to mount a rescue mission, either. I'd have to run that by the colonel first."

Reese coolly appraised the CIA man as if he were measuring him for a body bag. "It looks to me as if you don't even have the authority to wipe your own ass without the colonel's permission."

Leaving Clifford with his mouth hanging open, Reese turned and left the bunker. Outside, the afternoon sun baked the red earth of the small camp. Most of the off-duty Nungs were taking afternoon naps, and the place looked deserted. The only sign of life was the work party filling sandbags to rebuild the 106 mm recoilless rifle pit at the north end of the camp. Reese saw that his team sergeant was supervising the work party and headed over.

Wiping the sweat from his eyes, Pierce stepped out of the sunken pit to meet him. "How's it going with Super Spook, sir?"

"I'm about to tear that fucker a new asshole," Reese growled. "Kowalski had a shoot-out with an NVA tracking team. They got away, but they've blown their cover, and Clifford doesn't think it's serious. He says he can't pull them out yet."

Pierce frowned. "Has the LT called for an extraction?"

"Not yet," Reese admitted, "but I still don't like their being in the middle of so much activity. If they step in it and need extraction in a hurry, it's going to take us far too long to get anyone in there to pull them out. When I asked Clifford about mounting one of the platoons just in case, he said he didn't have authorization to reinforce them."

Pierce buttoned up his fatigue jacket and brushed the dust off his pants. "I'll tell you what, sir. Let me talk to that contact I mentioned earlier. I may be able to put something together."

Reese locked eyes with the sergeant. "You do that, Sarge. I'll alert Second Platoon."

"That's Baker's bunch," Pierce said. "You'll find him going over the ammo inventory. Tell him to drop that and get cracking."

MASTER SERGEANT Ray Pierce hurried to the holdout bunker in the middle of the camp by the mess hall. Even though the camp defense plans called for the final defense to be conducted at the command bunker if they were ever overrun, Pierce had been in too many shitstorms not to have made other provisions in case something went wrong with the original plan. If things were so bad that the NVA were inside the wire, there was a good chance that someone wouldn't be able to make it to the command bunker in time. Hence his bolt hole, the holdout bunker.

This was a well-ventilated underground chamber, like a VC tunnel, big enough to hold four men and enough supplies to withstand a week's siege. He had also scrounged a spare radio to keep in there. This was also the radio he used to conduct his "unofficial" business. It had a buried ground-plane antenna that allowed him to reach all the way to Saigon. Using a bootleg call sign, he could talk to almost anyone in the entire IV Corps area of operations.

Pierce lifted the concealed trapdoor and climbed down. It was cool underground, although the air was stifling. He made another mental note to try to find a hand-cranked blower to circulate the air. Something like one of those things they sold back in the States for use in civilian fallout shelters.

Switching on the Angry-9 radio, he contacted his warrant officer buddy in Tay Ninh at the operations shack of the Sixty-Ninth Helicopter Assault Company, the Black Knights. It should be no problem to lay on a three-slick lift and a Light Fire team to be available at a moment's notice. The warrant officer took his request and told him to call back in an hour to confirm. Pierce switched off the radio to save the battery and went back up to report to the captain.

So far the veteran sergeant was impressed with what he had seen of his new commander. He appeared to be a man after his own heart, a real soldier instead of another ticket puncher. However, Reese seemed to get wound up a little too tightly when things weren't going exactly his way. He would have to learn to settle down and realize that some things were best left to the regular Army NCO corps to get done. Things like getting helicopters to make an end run around obstinate CIA men.

Pierce had been in the Army all of his adult life. In fact, he had still been two weeks shy of his seventeenth birthday when his father signed the papers that sent him off to become a professional soldier in 1947.

His father had just returned to the small ranch in Montana he'd left in 1942 to go into the Army. The elder Pierce, an Irish cowboy, had left to fight the Germans immediately after Pearl Harbor, leaving his Santee Sioux wife and twelve-year-old son behind. A year after he left his wife had died and he hadn't had the heart to return. The young Pierce had been taken in by his mother's relatives and had spent the rest of the war years raising cattle on their small ranch.

The day his father had shown up in Montana had been a shock for the boy. His uncles had told him he had been killed in the closing days of the war in Europe. The day after his father arrived he'd taken the boy aside and told him he wasn't going to stay in Montana, that he was moving on to a job in Alaska and couldn't take the boy with him. Concerned about his son's future, however, the elder Pierce had convinced him he should consider making the Army his career. Accordingly the eager young man had gone to Billings with him, where he'd taken the oath of allegiance to the United States and boarded a bus for the basic training camp at Fort Polk, Louisiana, the same day.

Three years later when the well-armed North Korean army jumped the border to invade South Korea, Pierce was a PFC rifleman in an infantry battalion of the Twenty-Fifth Infantry Division stationed with the occupation forces in Japan. His poorly prepared division was immediately rushed across the Sea of Japan and thrown into the meat grinder that was to become known as the Korean Conflict, a so-called police action that to all intents and purposes had looked a lot like a real war.

By the end of his first week in combat, Pierce was promoted to squad leader, and by the end of the first month, he was acting platoon sergeant as an E-5. All the other platoon NCOs had been killed or wounded.

After the Pusan perimeter, he volunteered for the First Ranger Battalion and spent the rest of the war with that elite unit.

He finished the war with a Combat Infantryman's Badge, a gold combat jump star on his parachute badge, a Silver Star, a Bronze Star and two Purple Hearts on his Ike jacket. He also lost his temporary master sergeant's stripes in the Army-wide reduction in force that followed the signing of the cease-fire at Panmunjom.

Pierce got out of the Army at the end of his first enlistment and returned to the ranch in Montana. But, after his second knockdown, drag-out fight in the local ranchers' bar when some cowboy made a comment about halfbreeds, he went back to the only place where he knew he'd always be welcome—the U.S. Army.

The peacetime Army had been good to him, but it wasn't until he joined the fledgling Special Forces in 1963 that he really found a home. The brainchild of President John F. Kennedy, the early Special Forces was a collection of experienced combat veterans from all over the Army. No one cared where you came from. All they cared about was that you were deadly serious about the profession of arms and were willing to train hard to become a member of the most elite fighting force in the world.

Pierce had found peacetime service a little too tame for his taste, and the Special Forces' worldwide mission of counterinsurgency looked like the best bet for him to see more combat. His bet had paid off. He was on his third and last tour in Vietnam since 1965 and had seen enough combat for any man in one lifetime, even a dedicated professional soldier.

Now he had only nine months left before he could retire. He wasn't slacking off, though. There were still important things he needed to do, like getting his new captain squared away. And seeing what he could do to help keep a certain young LT out of trouble.

"WELL, I'LL BE a son of a bitch!" Santelli whispered softly to himself as he peered through his binoculars. "We hit the fucking jackpot!"

The officer and his Nung team were still a little over two hours short of the planned rendezvous point when they stopped for a rest break halfway up the side of a ridge overlooking a narrow valley. Santelli took his field glasses out for a long-range look around the area. Focusing in on the other side of the valley, he spotted the biggest enemy supply dump he had ever seen.

The huge camp, which was hidden under the trees, had been so carefully constructed that it would never be spotted from the air. The NVA had cleared most of the underbrush from the closely packed trees and had selectively cut down some of the trees themselves to open up the ground beneath. Enough of these had been left standing so that their branches formed a solid canopy overhead, effectively hiding the storage area from even the closest aerial observation.

Only at certain angles could one see beyond the screen of brush left along the tree line and discern what was under the trees. From where Santelli was he could see small bamboo huts, probably troop barracks, interspersed among large stacks of supplies. A larger structure stood far back in the center of the camp, probably the headquarters. Camouflage nets were draped over everything. As he watched, dozens of North Vietnamese troops went about their business, apparently issuing the supplies rather than stockpiling them. Several of the nets were pulled back, and men took long wooden crates from the piles and headed back deeper under the trees with them. Troops were being outfitted for something big, but what?

He put the field glasses down and charted the dump's location on his map. From his rucksack he pulled out a small camera fitted with a special lens for long-range shots. Rapidly he snapped several photographs of the area, overlapping each picture to compose a photo mosaic of the entire area when developed.

Santelli still had several hours before his next scheduled communication with Ban Phoc, so he decided to spend some of that time watching the enemy. Maybe he could figure out what they were up to. At least the temperature had cooled down, thanks to a thin layer of clouds covering the late-afternoon sun. Hiding in the bush almost felt bearable now. The cool air made him feel drowsy, and even the swarms of gnats that followed him everywhere were sluggish.

He was just about to doze off when Whiskey nudged him. *"Trung Uy!"* the Nung hissed softly, pointing over to the far left. "Look, they come!"

Moving into the tree line from the far end of the valley was a long line of NVA infantry in dark olive-green uniforms. Santelli snapped his field glasses up to his eyes. They all had full packs and combat equipment and were wearing North Vietnamese pith helmets. These weren't the local force VC or NVA who had been hiding out in the hills since Tet; these were NVA regulars, fresh troops just down from the North.

Santelli watched as at least two companies of infantry moved into the hidden supply dump. The supply people quickly issued them ammunition and other equipment from the stacks. In a little over half an hour the troops were on the move again, heading southeast, away from Cambodia and toward South Vietnam.

"Whiskey," he said, "I want to follow these guys for a couple of klicks and see which way they're going."

The Nung nodded and went to alert the rest of the team. By the time Santelli called his report into Ban Phoc, he should have the goods that SOG wanted. Not only would he have the supply site to report, but also the route this enemy battalion was taking.

That should be more than enough for them. Maybe he could talk the controller into letting them have an early extraction. He had discovered what they'd come to find within the five days allotted to their mission. Now that Kowalski had made contact, he didn't want to stick around any longer than he absolutely had to. There were just too many goddamn hostiles running around in the Parrot's Beak.

13

Parrot's Beak, Cambodia

Santelli was on point as his team moved down the ridge line leading into the small valley where he was to meet the rest of his patrol. The heavy jungle in this part of the Parrot's Beak offered few good pickup zones, and the far end of this valley was the closest suitable site to bring the slicks in. As soon as they joined up with the other teams and secured the PZ, he would make his report on the NVA supply dump and arrange to get them the hell out of there ASAP.

The lieutenant was just starting down the side of the ridge when the Nung RTO handed him the radio handset. Kowalski was calling. "Strider One One, this is One Zero. Over," Santelli answered.

"This is One One," Kowalski radioed. "I've joined up with the rest of my team and we're closing in on the rendezvous point, but I'm afraid we picked up another enemy tracking team. Over."

"One Zero, roger. Where are you right now? Over."

"This is One One. We're at 692385, moving east. Over."

"One Zero, wait one."

Santelli quickly pulled out his map. They were still two klicks away from the PZ and at least two more hours away from being extracted. With NVA that close on Kowalski's tail, they'd end up trying to extract under fire—and that was a no-go.

Pushing the transmission switch, he spoke softly. "Strider One One, this is One Zero. Over."

"One One, go."

"One Zero, I'm right ahead of you at 693411. There's a trail running along the center of the ridge line. Double-time up here to my location and bring your shadows with you. I'll have a welcoming committee waiting for 'em."

"Roger," Kowalski answered. "We're on the way and they're right behind us. Over."

"One Zero, roger. We'll be ready. Out."

Taking the six Nungs back up the trail some two hundred yards, Santelli began to set up their reception. The faint path they were following widened out slightly as it followed the ridge. The dense foliage provided good cover and concealment. If he couldn't resolve this situation right here, he would have to forget about an early extraction and see if he could find some place to hole up for the night.

Taking two claymores from the Nungs' rucksacks, Santelli set them up with their backs facing large tree trunks. Then he had one of the Nungs step out onto the middle of the kill zone. Lying behind the claymores, Santelli used the built-in sight on top of the mine to aim both of them at the grinning Nung's blackened belt buckle. When the mines detonated, the seven hundred steel balls from each would blast a swath fifty yards wide down the trail. If any of the NVA were left alive after that greeting, the recon team would finish them off with their small arms.

With the claymores sighted in and the detonators attached, he camouflaged them with brush and trailed the firing wires along the ground and behind the neighboring tree. When he detonated the mines, his men would spring out and rake the killing zone with automatic fire. If everything went as planned, the business would be over in less than thirty seconds.

The Nungs spread out on his right side, well back in the underbrush. They waited, straining to hear any sound of approach, alert to the slightest noise.

Ten minutes later Kowalski and his team came into view, and Santelli stepped out to meet him. The older American's faded tiger-striped uniform was dark with sweat, and he was panting as he reported to his patrol leader. "There's at least a dozen of 'em," he gasped, crouching beside the trail. "'Bout half a klick behind us and coming on fast."

Santelli pointed out the planned pickup zone on his map. "Move on up to the PZ and wait for us there. If I can't stop them, take the rest of the people and get the hell out of here. Find a place to hide and try for another extraction later."

"We can stay here to help, LT," the sergeant insisted.

"No." Santelli shook his head firmly. "We can take care of it. I want you back there to take over in case you have to run again."

Kowalski got to his feet stiffly and motioned Kent and the Nungs to follow him. "Good luck, LT."

Santelli clasped his outstretched hand. "Catch you later."

As soon as Kowalski and the Nungs were out of sight, Santelli settled back down behind his tree. He pulled the bolt handle on his Swedish K out of the safety notch at the rear of the breech and eased it forward into the firing position. Then he laid an extra magazine from his ammo pouch and the submachine gun within easy reach, took one of the claymore clacker firing devices in each hand and waited. He noticed the familiar pre-ambush sensations: pounding heart, shallow breathing, sweating palms and forehead, and he licked his dry lips.

Santelli had originally wanted to get into the SOG business to see a lot of action, but recently he had begun to have second thoughts about it. He had overlooked the fact that the primary reason the SOG units saw so much contact was because they operated in the enemy's backyard. Naturally that meant they were cut off from the usual air and ground support that the Mike Forces enjoyed in South Vietnam. Being alone out there with no one to call on for help when something went wrong added an entirely new dimension to the war, one he could do without.

The Special Forces officer had barely concealed himself when an NVA point man in an olive-colored uniform slowly walked into view. The man was young, his uniform and equipment brand-new, matching the AK-47 assault rifle in his hands. Good. He was a fresh kid, not a hardened, experienced jungle fighter.

The point man walked into the killing zone and stopped for a moment, peering quite a way down the trail. When he saw it was clear, he turned around and waved his comrades forward.

From his position Santelli grinned. The NVA obviously didn't like being stuck out on point. His eyes darted from side to side without really seeing anything. Rookies like him never wanted to be at the forefront alone in the jungle; they needed the comfort of knowing their buddies were close behind.

The North Vietnamese waited until his comrades were only a couple of yards behind him before he moved out again. Santelli let him pass his hiding place. He was more interested in the main body and would catch up to the point man later.

The rest of the enemy patrol were obviously rookies, too, ten men crowding nicely together in a tight little bunch. Santelli waited patiently until they were in the middle of the killing zone, right where the Nung had stood when he'd sighted in the claymores. It was time to rock and roll.

He slammed down on the clacker firing handles and the two mines detonated as one. Fourteen hundred .25-caliber steel balls swept the jungle trail at waist height. Seven of the ten North Vietnamese were blown off their feet by the blast. The other three were cut down instantly when the Nungs opened up on them with full automatic fire.

Santelli dropped the clackers, snatched up his submachine gun and spun to his left. The point man had turned halfway around, a look of horror frozen on his face and his AK still held at port arms. Santelli didn't give him time to react. He dumped half a magazine into him, and the North Vietnamese pitched forward onto his face.

Spinning around the other way, Santelli unloaded his remaining rounds into the tangled pile of bodies on the trail until the K's bolt locked back on an empty magazine.

The sudden silence reverberated through the jungle. Nothing moved for a few moments. Santelli dropped the empty magazine from his K and noisily slapped a new one into place. He pulled the bolt back into firing position and cautiously got to his feet. The sharp smell of cordite and fresh blood hung in the air as he stepped out, his finger on the K's trigger. He stopped in the middle of the trail and took a deep breath, surveying his handiwork.

The Nungs followed Santelli out to check the bodies. All eleven of the NVA were dead, one with a radio on his back. This didn't concern the lieutenant, who doubted that the man had even had time to key the mike before he was gunned down.

The Nungs checked the bodies for documents, then dragged the corpses back into the thick brush. Their weapons quickly followed them. Santelli tried to scuff dirt over the dark stains on the trail, but there was just too much blood to hide. Anyone passing that way would know in an instant that there had been a firefight.

"Trung Uy." Lam Noc, the Nung leader, came up beside him. "You go. I take these Nungs and we stay behind to kill more NVA if they come."

Santelli shook his head. "No. We're all getting out of here. I'm not leaving anyone behind."

"You take film back to Can Tho," the Nung reasoned with him. "Show them what we find. This *beaucoup* important, *Trung Uy.* We stay and kill more enemy so you can get away."

"As soon as we reach the PZ," Santelli said, "I'm calling for an extract and I'm going to get all of our asses out of this place." He locked eyes with the Nung leader. "And I mean *all* of us."

The Nung shrugged. "Okay, *Trung Uy.*"

"Come on," Santelli growled. "Let's get the fuck outta here."

Santelli and the six Nungs turned and started down the trail, loping at the steady mile-eating pace of airborne troops. At that speed they would be at their rendezvous point in a little over an hour.

REESE AND PIERCE were both in the radio room in the command bunker when Santelli's call came in. Clifford quickly recorded the location of the supply dump, the enemy KIAs from the ambush and the coordinates of Santelli's proposed PZ.

"Roger, One Zero," Clifford answered. "Hang tight till I can get back to you. Over."

"This is Strider One Zero, wilco. Out."

Clifford immediately encoded the information for transmission back to MACV-SOG headquarters at Tan

Son Nhut and sent the three-letter code groups. MACV-SOG was back on the horn within half an hour. The CIA man decoded the response and turned to Reese. "It's a no-go on the early extract," he said matter-of-factly. "Colonel Marshall wants to put a B-52 Arc Light strike in on that supply dump tomorrow morning. We'll need a BDA after the strike and, since Santelli's already in position, he can do it."

As far as Reese was concerned, a bomb damage assessment after an Arc Light strike was only a nice-to-have item. It didn't begin to compare with the importance of saving the lives of his troops.

"If they can last through the night," he said, stating the obvious. "That was their second contact in less than six hours and the enemy must have figured out that someone's working in their backyard. Even if Santelli's reports are only halfway accurate, they're in the middle of at least a regiment if not a couple of them. Their asses are really hanging in the wind if they can't find a good place to hide."

"I know," Clifford admitted. "They're in a tight spot, but I've got to have that BDA for the colonel. We're under a lot of political pressure about using the B-52s in Cambodia, and he wants to know what kind of results he's getting from those missions."

"I'd like to have a little chat with your colonel about wasting good troops someday," Reese said sharply.

Clifford had had about all the shit he felt like taking from the Green Beret today. He already had his ass on the line with Marshall about this mission, and he needed all the cooperation he could get.

This wasn't the first time the CIA man had had problems with Special Forces people about how to conduct a mission. Usually, though, he could talk them into doing things his way if he invoked the colonel's name enough times. For some reason that tactic wasn't working with Reese.

"Captain," Clifford said, putting his clipboard down, "can we step outside and talk for a minute?"

Reese smiled as he unbuckled his shoulder holster and put his weapon on the table. "Sure, why not?"

Camp A-410, Ban Phoc

The sun was just setting over the Delta when Reese climbed up the command bunker steps and emerged into the cooler night air. Already the night creatures were beginning to stir on the plains around the camp.

There was a natural rhythm to the war that Reese had come to expect. This was the time of day when he should be relaxing before readying himself for the night's activities. Even the enemy had stopped moving so that they could prepare dinner. He looked over at the mess hall and saw the strikers who had been on early guard duty lined up for their dinner. Santelli and his people wouldn't dare risk lighting a fire to warm their cold rations tonight. And they sure as hell wouldn't be relaxing, not if they wanted to stay alive until morning.

"Reese," Clifford said, coming up behind him. "I think we've gotten off on the wrong foot here."

"I'd say that's a pretty accurate assessment," Reese agreed coldly, locking eyes with him. "But then you've got your job and I've got mine."

"Maybe we can start over and see if we can work together," Clifford said patiently.

"Not if you're going to risk the lives of my men unnecessarily," Reese replied. "Those people did their job and they did it well. They deserve to be pulled out and I—"

"Look, goddamn it," Clifford interrupted, "I'm under the gun on this thing, too. This colonel I work for is constantly on my ass about the reports I get from the field. He's a suspicious old fuck and doesn't trust you people out here."

"Well, maybe he can drag his ass out here and take a look for himself then."

Clifford wanted to laugh at that suggestion, but he suppressed the urge. He didn't want to piss off Reese any more than he already had. "That's why he sent me up here. I'm supposed to do his looking for him. I'm controlling the mission, but the fact remains I've still got to follow his lead."

"I appreciate that," Reese said, "but the fact also remains that as far as I'm concerned, you and your colonel are a bigger threat to us than the goddamn NVA. My men have done their part of his job. They've found the evidence of the buildup you were looking for, and it's time to pull them out of there before they get wasted."

Even though the Green Beret had only been on the job at Ban Phoc for a couple of days, he obviously considered Santelli's patrol his own people. Reese was too emotionally involved to take an objective view of the situation.

"Look," he said, "you must know there's a limit to what I can do without the colonel's approval, but I'll try to work something out. I really don't want those people killed any more than you do."

"I doubt that," Reese said bluntly, "but I'll have to take your word for it right now. What do you think you can do for my men?"

"After Santelli does the BDA, I'll do my best to get them out. I promise."

"What if Marshall wants them to count water buffaloes or some shit like that?"

"I said I'll try to get them out," Clifford repeated.

Reese took a deep breath. He still didn't trust the CIA agent. "Why don't you let me put together a rescue mission? I can suit up two platoons of Nungs and have them standing by in case they get into trouble."

Clifford shook his head. "I'm sorry. I can't do that. Marshall would have my ass if I let you put more troops in there. Extracting them is one thing, and reinforcing them is something else entirely. There's no way he'll agree to that."

"Why?"

"For one thing, we have to clear all these Cambodian operations with MACV Headquarters, and they're as sensitive as hell about Cambodia right now. Particularly with the press screaming their heads off about violating the neutrality and the rest of that bullshit."

"Fuck the press," Reese retorted.

Now Clifford got really mad. Between the press corps getting hints about black ops from drunken GIs and the South Vietnamese blabbing to their VC buddies, he didn't know which caused him the most trouble. SOG had a way of dealing with South Vietnamese traitors, but there was very little they could do about American reporters.

"You can get away with saying shit like that," he said hotly, "because you're way the hell out here fighting your own personal little war. I've got to guard against those goddamn people every day."

"War's hell, isn't it?"

Clifford inhaled deeply. He couldn't let Reese get under his skin. "I've got my orders. I'll do what I can for your men, but I've got to have that BDA done tomorrow."

Reese looked at him for a long moment. "You do what you have to and I'll do the same."

Clifford didn't bother to reply. He turned and went back to the bunker.

IN THE MEANTIME, Reese went looking for Sergeant Pierce. Like Clifford, Reese had a job to do as well and he was going to do it.

He knew he was putting his career on the line if he crossed swords with Colonel Marshall. At the very least Reese knew this was probably going to cost him his job. If Santelli and his people weren't pulled out, they wouldn't have lives, let alone careers. It wasn't easy for him to disobey orders purposely, but sometimes a commander had to make tough decisions. Reese would gladly risk losing his command if he could get Santelli and his men back safely.

He found his operations sergeant in the team house. "Sarge," he said as he walked into the NCO's room.

"I want to put together that rescue mission in the morning."

Pierce looked up from the tattered western novel he was reading. "Super Spook said no go on the extract?"

"Not only that," Reese said. "He's calling in an Arc Light on that supply dump in the morning and he wants Santelli to do a BDA on it."

"Shit!" The sergeant sat up immediately and swung his legs over the edge of the bunk.

"Exactly what I said."

"How many people you want to take?"

"I was thinking about each of us taking a fifteen-man Nung team in. That would be small enough that we could move fast, with still enough people to fight if we had to. That would leave the Cambode platoon and the heavy weapons people behind to defend the camp."

"That sounds about right, sir," Pierce said, lacing up his jungle boots and reaching for his fatigue jacket. "I'll call the Sixty-ninth about the lift ships and tell Vao to get the Nungs going."

"Do that," Reese said. "I'll either be in the bunker or my hooch. Get back to me when you've got it set up."

"Yes, sir."

PIERCE LEARNED that the Nung leader had been called over to the Nung shrine. Pierce walked to the northern point of the star-shaped camp and found a small crowd of half a dozen Nungs gathered in front of the small building. The shrine was unimpressive, just a small box made out of two-by-fours and covered with sheets of roofing tin. Bright red banners trimmed with light blue and inscribed with black Chinese characters hung on poles flanking an incense burner in front of the building.

Inside was an altar where the Nungs gave offerings and paid homage to the Great-Grandfather General, the spirit of the Chinese general who had brought them to Vietnam a thousand years ago. They prayed to their god for success in battle as well as for good luck in their personal lives. They believed that when they died in battle, they would go to join the heavenly army of their Great-Grandfather General.

The Nung priest, an old man well past the age for active-duty soldiering, tended the shrine. He made the daily offerings and served as the Great-Grandfather General's voice in the camp. Most important, he interpreted omens and foretold the future by casting ancient knucklebones on the ground and reading the patterns they made on the red earth.

It was a ritual from prehistoric times, dating back to an era when men had killed one another with sharpened stones. Pierce wasn't automatically skeptical of the Nung rituals; they reminded him too much of the rituals of his mother's people, the Santee Sioux.

When he had been a young boy, a few of the older men had still danced the ghost dance as it had been done in the days before the Sioux had wiped out Custer and his men at Little Big Horn. The old men would put on their brightly decorated ghost shirts and dance the ancient steps and talk with the skulls to gain wisdom from the spirit world. Although Pierce had been too young to take part in these ancient ceremonies himself, he had never forgotten them or how they had made him feel.

Pierce felt the same way every time he saw the priest talk to his knucklebones. He paid close attention to what the bones foretold, and some of his best combat intel had come from what the old priest had seen in the cracked, brown ancient bones worn shiny with use. He didn't know how the old priest knew what he knew, but as far as he was concerned, it didn't matter. The bones told the truth.

The team sergeant found Vao and several of the other Nung leaders standing immediately outside the small hut. Inside, the priest was trying to light the incense sticks in the pots on the altar. Each time he put a match to one, however, it went out.

Suddenly the old man cried out shrilly in the ancient Nung dialect and pointed a shaking finger at the offerings on the altar. The glazed ceramic bowl of rice wine had cracked and the colorless liquid was trickling down to collect on the packed earthen floor. The priest peered intently at the pattern the wine made as it soaked into the dirt. He let out a moan and started babbling in Chinese. The men watching recoiled and started to mutter among themselves.

"What's going on, *co ba?*" Pierce asked Vao, using the Nung term for brother.

"A bad omen, *co ba,*" the old warrior answered, his face somber. "Real bad."

The old priest took a red cloth from a shelf, unfolded it and bound it around his head, completely covering his eyes. Carefully moving the rest of the offerings aside, he sat on top of the altar with a small red-and-black-lacquered box cradled protectively in his hands. It contained his divining knucklebones.

He carefully opened the box and chanted as he reached his right hand in, grabbed the bones and tossed them onto the ground before him. He peered at them through the cloth covering his eyes, seeming to see the pattern they made on the ground. Then he moaned again and spoke rapidly in the Nung dialect.

At first Vao tried to keep up a running translation for Pierce, but the priest spoke too fast and he soon gave up. When the old man finally fell silent, his head bowed, Vao turned to Pierce, his own face set. *"Co ba,"* he said solemnly, "things look bad, very bad. The Great-Grandfather General says that very bad things come to us very soon. He says we must be prepared to suffer from our enemies."

"What kind of danger does he see?" Pierce asked, a chill tickling the back of his neck.

Vao shrugged. "The priest must make more sacrifices before he knows."

The priest continued casting the bones, but the god didn't speak again. Finally one of the younger men led the weary old man away to rest in the small hut beside the shrine. The gathering broke up and Pierce followed Vao back to the hooch he shared with the other Nung leaders. Pierce couldn't help but wonder if maybe there were unseen forces working in the war that Westerners couldn't see.

He pulled out one of the chairs from around the makeshift wooden table and sat down. "We have a mission in the morning. The captain and I are going to take thirty men into the Parrot's Beak and look for Santelli and his men. They're cut off and we have to get them out of there."

Vao stiffened and seemed to listen to something that Pierce couldn't hear.

"What is it?" Pierce asked.

Vao refocused his dark eyes, and a broad smile broke out on his dark, wrinkled face. "I heard a tiger call my name, co ba."

Pierce shivered. He had heard nothing, but then he wasn't as old as Vao. The Santee Sioux believed that the spirits of the animals spoke to the tribal elders and the old warriors. If old Vao claimed he had heard a tiger speak to him, then Pierce believed him.

Vao called out, and a young Nung appeared with two bottles of beer in his hands. "We will drink beer while you tell me of this mission, *co ba.*"

Vao sipped the Vietnamese beer and listened impassively to Pierce's outline of Reese's plan. When Pierce was finished, Vao smiled. "I will go with you on this mission," he said.

Pierce hadn't planned to take the old jungle fighter, and he paused before responding. He had wanted to take younger men, men who could keep up a brutal pace through the jungle. It was on the tip of his tongue to tell the old man that he was staying back this time.

But Pierce knew it would be futile for him to say that. If Vao had said he would go, there was nothing Pierce could do to stop him. If he tried, the other Nungs would stack their arms and stay in the camp.

"Okay," he said. "You can go."

Vao smiled as he raised the bottle again to his lips.

15

Parrot's Beak, Cambodia

Santelli handed the radio handset back to the Nung RTO and looked out over the darkening jungle. Night fell fast in the jungle once the sun went down. Already the night creatures were stirring and the bugs were out in force.

They had found a good place to hole up not too far from the PZ. Now achieving that goal wasn't as important as it had been. The MACV-SOG controller had just handed them what amounted to a death sentence. It was suicide to attempt a bomb damage assessment in this area now. For a brief moment the lieutenant considered disregarding his orders and making a run for the border. If they pressed on and moved all night, they could be out of danger by midday tomorrow. He considered it and then put the thought aside. He was too good a soldier to blatantly disobey a mission order, no matter how insane it might be.

He knew SOG headquarters really didn't understand the seriousness of his situation. And there was always the off chance that there might be a pressing reason why they wanted him to remain to do the BDA, bad situation or not. A reason that somehow affected the "big picture," as they called it back at the Puzzle

Palace. Even so, after that second ambush, the enemy had to know there was a recon unit working in their area, and they were going to be beating the bush looking for them.

Digging into his side pant pocket for his map, he unfolded it and studied it. SOG wanted their damn BDA, but there was no reason he had to risk more than one of his teams to get it for them. He swiftly plotted a course back to the supply dump location. Maybe he and the Nung sterile team could get in there unseen while he left the rest of the patrol where they were. It was risky doing it that way if they ran into trouble. But what the hell?

He called Kowalski and Webb over. "I've just been on the horn to our mission controller," he told them. "The good news is that he's calling an Arc Light strike in on that supply dump tomorrow. The bad news is that we won't be extracted yet. They want us to do a BDA after the strike."

"That sucks heavily, LT," Kowalski said bluntly. After the day's two ambushes, the Alabama-born intelligence sergeant had completely lost any tact he might normally have had. "We're going to get our asses shot off if we go fucking around in there again."

Santelli nodded. "I know. That's why I'm going to take the sterile team in myself and do it while you people hang tight here and wait for me to come back."

"That sucks, too," Kowalski growled. "Why don't you let us all go in together? That way if we step in it, we'll have a decent chance of fighting our way out."

"No. I don't want to risk any more people on this thing than I absolutely have to."

Kowalski had been in the woods with the lieutenant enough times to know that when the LT made his mind up there was no point in trying to argue with him. He was a good lieutenant, but he could be a bit stubborn. "Okay," he said, shrugging. "You do the BDA, then what?"

Santelli paused to consider. "Then we try to get the fuck out of here one way or the other. If they won't give us an extraction, we'll walk out."

Laying the map on the ground, the two hunkered down to study it. Santelli outlined the timetable for the BDA and made his assignments for the rest of the patrol. "Ski," he said when he was finished, "put out some LPs tonight and make sure they keep their eyes open."

"Don't worry," Kowalski promised. "I'll see to it."

When the briefing was over and the sergeants went to set up the night positions, Santelli dug into his rucksack. Opening a can of beans and franks with the P-38 can opener he wore on the dog tag chain around his neck, he wolfed them down. Usually he ate light when he was in the field, but the firefight today had given him an appetite. He even added a can of crackers and cheese to the menu and followed it with a can of peaches.

Packing the empty cans back into his rucksack, he found a relatively soft spot on the ground close to the RTO, wrapped his poncho liner tightly around him, rested his head on his pack and tried to sleep.

For once he couldn't put the mission out of his thoughts. They had been lucky so far, real lucky. As far as he knew, the two ambushes today had been completely successful, with no survivors and no radio messages sent to alert the enemy. Their luck wouldn't last forever. The two NVA patrols would be missed. The enemy would go looking for the missing men and, sooner or later, they would find the bodies, by smell if by nothing else.

As long as the NVA thought they were alone in their part of Cambodia, Santelli's teams could operate in relative security. Once the NVA started actively looking for them, they were bound to find them sooner or later. And that was the problem. The question was, could he get the BDA done before the bastards found them? Fuck it, he told himself. He'd worry about it in the morning.

Santelli rolled halfway over and away from a rock poking him in the back. Again he tried to wipe his mind clear. He would need all the rest he could get if he was going to make it back to the enemy supply dump unseen.

AFTER GRABBING a quick meal in the mess hall, Reese toured the perimeter to check the guards. As long as Clifford was in the bunker, he wanted to spend as little time there as possible, himself. He didn't want to make feelings between them any worse than he absolutely had to.

When he had inspected the entire perimeter, he checked in with the duty radio operator before going

back to his cubbyhole in the team house. As he prepared for bed, he had to look at the date window on the
face of his watch to see what day it was. Having been
in-country for a little less than a week, he was nonetheless having a hard time trying to keep track of everything that had happened. And it didn't look as if
things were going to slow down for the next couple of
days at least.

He hadn't planned to get in quite so deep this fast.
At least Sergeant Pierce had the air assets laid on for
the rescue attempt if it was needed. He knew he had
really lucked out in getting a team NCO who had his
shit together as well as Pierce did. But then the SF
wasn't a place for sergeants who couldn't function well
both in and outside the system.

For all the attention the Special Forces received in
the press, they still had to operate on the fringe of the
Army system most of the time. There was a great deal
of professional jealousy in the regular Army aimed at
the Special Forces, particularly among the general officers. This was the primary reason that even though
the CO of Fifth Group had almost four thousand
Americans and some forty thousand indigenous troops
under his command, he was only a colonel. Fifth
Group had over three times the strength of the vaunted
First Air Cav Division, and if those forty-four thousand men had been Army REMFs of some variety or
other, they would have been commanded by at least a
two-star general. The conventional generals weren't
about to give that kind of authority to a commander of
unconventional special warfare troops.

The generals who ran the Army in South Vietnam were all graduates of World War II and Korea, both big wars fought with massed troops. The idea of small Special Forces units operating almost independently of the regular Army scared the hell out of them. The fact that these small units were the most successful combat organizations in-country didn't matter. Their existence threatened the status quo, and the regular Army chain of command did everything it could to downplay the SF's successful operations. If it was ever discovered that conventional generals weren't needed in Vietnam, they would all be out of a job.

One of the main reasons the Special Forces units were as successful as they were was that they were as unconventional in dealing with Army red tape as they were in kicking Charlie's ass. The SF NCO corps were the key to making the SF work the way it did. Reese could lead the troops in to get Santelli out of the Parrot's Beak, but he knew he couldn't do it without Pierce.

THE NEXT MORNING Santelli woke just as dawn broke over the jungle. The air was damp and chill, so he kept his poncho liner wrapped tightly around him as he sat up and looked out over the terrain below their position. The morning mist obscured the jungle, muting the vivid daytime greens into greenish-grays. As soon as the sun rose a little higher, the mist would burn off and he would take the team out.

Around him the Nungs were waking up and seeing to breakfast. Santelli mixed powdered coffee, sugar and water in his canteen cup and started drinking it cold. It was too dangerous to try to heat anything for breakfast. The smell of hot coffee would carry for half a klick on the morning mist and announce their presence to anyone in the neighborhood. Until they got safely back into South Vietnam they'd eat cold rations.

He sipped the cold brew, grimaced, then sipped again. He had to have his caffeine in the morning, cold or not. He broke out a can of fruit cocktail to accompany the coffee. They'd be traveling light this morning, packing only their weapons, canteens, ammunition and one of the radios. It was risky to leave everything else behind in case they got cut off, but Santelli wanted to move fast, and he was willing to take the risk.

This was the day he was going to get to do a real SOG-type covert mission. The upcoming job was about as clandestine an operation as he could ask for, and he felt his excitement build as he stripped his rucksack for the equipment he would take with him.

His brush hat looked too American, so he stuffed it back into his ruck. Then, taking the sweat rag from around his neck, he tied it around his head. From a distance it would make him look more like a VC.

His camera went into one of his side pant pockets and a couple of cans of C-rations into the other. The field glasses would hang around his neck and his notebook found a place in his breast pocket. Everything else he would need was already on his field belt and assault harness.

He checked his grenades and, after thinking about it, added two more frags to his load. Breaking open the boxes of 9 mm ammunition, he reloaded the magazines he had emptied yesterday. He would have liked to have had a couple more, but eight would have to do. Besides, if he got into a situation where eight 30-round magazines wouldn't do the trick, two more really wouldn't help that much.

Kowalski walked up as the lieutenant was filling the last of his magazines. "You about ready to move out, LT?"

"Yeah," Santelli said, glancing at his watch as he got to his feet. "I'd better get this show on the road. The B-52s are due in at 1100 hours, and I don't want to have to rush it on the way in."

"I wish you'd let me go with you, sir," the sergeant said. "I don't like staying behind on this one."

Santelli grinned. He and Kowalski had had some interesting times in the woods over the past several months, and the veteran intel sergeant was a good man to have at one's side when the shit hit the fan. "I know, Sarge. I know. But I need you to stay here. If we step on it, I want you to take the rest of the people out."

"If you get cut off, I'm coming in after you," Kowalski said, pressing his point.

Santelli shook his head. "No, Sarge," he said emphatically. "If we can't make it back, you get the hell out of here with those film cans."

"I've been thinking about that, sir." Kowalski scuffed his feet in the dirt. "Why don't you let me send the film back now with Whiskey and a couple of the

Nungs? They can get through, and that'll leave the rest of us here to bail you out if anything happens."

"I appreciate the thought, Ski," Santelli said sincerely. "But you know as well as I do that if we're spotted going in or coming out, we're going to get our asses blown away, pure and simple. There's no way to avoid it. I don't want to risk losing the film with a small team. You just stick to the plan, okay?"

"Yes, sir," Kowalski said. "But I still don't like it."

"I don't like it either, Sarge. Believe me, I don't."

Lam Noc, the leader of the sterile team, walked up carrying one of the Prick-77 radios. "We about ready, *Trung Uy?* Here's the radio."

Santelli looked beyond him and saw the other four Nungs waiting for him. In their dark olive NVA-style uniforms and khaki chest-pack AK-magazine carriers, they looked exactly like the NVA troopers they had killed the day before. Only their distinctively Chinese faces could give them away. That and the fact that they all looked well fed. But there were even a few Nungs in the North Vietnamese army, so they should pass if they were spotted.

"Good." Santelli smiled as he slipped his arms into the radio pack harness and settled it on his back. "Let's get going while it's still cool."

Sergeant Kowalski watched as the six men quickly faded into the jungle. Damn it! He hated to be left behind.

16

April 19, U Tapao Air Base, Thailand

At U Tapao in southern Thailand three B-52 crews prepared for an Arc Light strike in the Parrot's Beak. While the flight crews received their classified target briefing in an air-conditioned building, out on the flight line sweating ordnance men loaded the last of the twenty-four Mark 82 750-pound high-explosive bombs onto the external underwing racks of the bombers. An additional eighty-four bombs had already been loaded into their internal bomb bays. On takeoff the B-52s' eight thundering J-57 engines would strain to their limits to lift the 220-ton weight of the loaded aircraft off the ground.

Originally designed as an intercontinental, city-busting nuclear weapons delivery system for Strategic Air Command, the venerable old B-52 Stratofortress had been called into action in the jungle war of Southeast Asia. Commonly known as Buff, short for Big Ugly Flying Fucker, the B-52s had been converted to "Iron Bombers" for this purpose. The CBC, or Conventional Bomb Carrier, versions of the B-52D with the "big belly" modifications could carry more than a hundred 750-pound high-explosive bombs, over thirty-nine tons. By comparison, the famous B-17 bombers of World War II fame had carried a bomb load of only slightly over four tons.

The Buff was one of the most feared weapons in the entire American arsenal. The jet bomber delivered its payload with pinpoint accuracy from thirty-five thousand feet, so high that the bomber couldn't be seen or heard by enemy troops on the ground.

A North Vietnamese unit would be cooling their heels in the jungle, thinking they were safe. They would have no way of knowing they had been spotted by a Special Forces recon team or that the sound of their movement had been transmitted by a seismic device planted in the jungle. They could be casually eating or resting from their march when their world would suddenly end. A rain of high-explosive bombs from a plane they could neither hear nor see would land right on top of them and instantly wipe them off the face of the earth.

While most of the B-52 Arc Light strikes were made against remote targets like the one they were preparing to hit today, the B-52s had been put to use as tactical bombers in a close air support role at the siege of Khe Sanh earlier in 1968, a first for a heavy jet bomber. Guided to their targets by a radar station located within the Marine base, the Buffs had been able to deliver their bomb loads with even greater accuracy. The attacks had been so precise, in fact, that after a carefully controlled test the Buffs had started dropping their bomb loads as close as five hundred yards in front of the Marine positions—close-in tactical air support from thirty-five thousand feet.

A campaign of around-the-clock bombing had been instituted at Khe Sanh. Every ninety minutes a flight of three heavily laden B-52s had taken off from one of their bases in either Guam, Okinawa or Thailand for the twelve-hour round-trip flight to Khe Sanh. Every hour and a half the Buffs had unloaded their high-explosive cargoes on the NVA gun positions and trenches in the hills surrounding the base. The blitz had been devastating and unrelenting and it had killed thousands of enemy troops without the loss of a single American life.

Since the siege in Khe Sanh, the Buffs had been given more missions supporting ground units in contact, but they still ran Arc Light strikes on preplanned targets, as well, targets like the NVA supply dump that Santelli had spotted.

After the mission briefing, the crew members of the three bombers were driven out to their planes on the tarmac.

The B-52 looked mean and purposeful. Its landing gear was short, and it crouched with its belly almost touching the runway, like a tiger ready to spring. Its tail swept up and back over forty feet above the ground, like a shark's fin. Its fuel-laden wings bent gracefully downward like a hawk's cupped wings as it glided in for a landing, the olive drab high-explosive bombs tucked under its wings like eggs. Four J-57 jet engines hung in twin pods under each wing. Looking almost too small to propel the big bomber, the engines pushed the plane along at over six hundred miles an hour.

The green-and-tan camouflaged Buffs with the flat black bellies usually flew without the personal markings often seen painted on fighter planes. But one of the bombers in the three-plane flight this morning wore a small, smiling mouth on its nose. "Grin" was painted right above the smile. The other half, "and Bare It," was painted near the tail turret, next to a cartoon figure of a man bending over with his pants around his ankles.

The six-man crew of Grin and Bare It climbed aboard and began going over the lengthy preflight checklist. They were the fifth crew she'd had since she'd been stationed in the war zone. Some of the men weren't much older than the plane itself.

In the extreme rear of the bomber the Air Force tech sergeant gunner methodically checked his four .50-caliber machine guns in the tail turret, their ammunition supply and the gun aiming radar. Then he settled back to read his copy of *Playboy.* Unlike the grunts in Nam who had to wait for their copies to reach them by ship, the Air Force had a supply of the latest issue flown in once a month.

As soon as they were in the air, however, the sergeant would put down the magazine and nap. There was very little chance of their encountering enemy MiG fighters on their mission. He was just along for the ride on the off chance the North Vietnamese air force or the Cambodians decided to participate in the game.

In the nose of the plane, Captain Jim Huntington finished reading off the prestart checklist to his co-pilot, First Lieutenant Ray Sloan.

"Let's get the old bitch cranked up," the pilot said as he stowed the checklist back in its pocket.

"You're not grinning, Jimbo."

"Fuck you."

This was the fourth mission the crew had flown in as many days, and they were all bone weary. They had been due for a two-day stand-down starting today, but the high-priority mission had put them back in action. The one saving grace was that they would be flying from Thailand, a much shorter flight than one of those ass-busting twelve-hour humps from Guam, like the ones they had flown during the Khe Sanh siege.

Huntington was praying for an engine malfunction, which he well knew wasn't too likely. He had the best damn crew chief in the entire Buff fleet. If he'd had a marginal engine, Mac would have changed it during the night. He sighed. There was no way out of it; they were going to have to fly this damn mission today.

"Okay, light 'em up."

The copilot hit the starter for the number four engine. With a whine of the starter motor and a cough of black smoke, it burst into life. When the tachometer showed fifteen percent, the pilot moved its throttle to flight idle. The number four generator quickly started the other seven engines, and Huntington ran the turbines up to forty-five percent rpm. He radioed the flight leader that he was ready. When the leader rogered, Huntington switched the steering ratio from takeoff/land to taxi. The call came, the pilot eased off the brakes and the huge bomber slowly rumbled to the end of the runway to its position immediately behind the flight leader.

"Flaps full," Huntington called out as he switched the steering ratio back to takeoff.

"Flaps going down," Sloan called back. "Ten percent, thirty percent, fifty percent, flaps full."

Huntington advanced his throttles, keeping his eyes on the rpm, fuel flow and exhaust gas temperature gauges. The big bomber quivered under the strain of holding back under the thrust of eight screaming J-57 engines. Everything was in the green. The flight leader took off ahead of them, the wake of his jet exhaust rocking Grin and Bare It.

"We're go," Huntington announced as he pushed the throttles up to the one hundred percent position. The airframe shook as the engines howled and black smoke belched out the exhausts. With one more brief glance at the gauges, the pilot came off the foot brakes. The B-52 started forward down the concrete runway, steadily gathering speed. With several hundred yards of pavement left, the loaded bomber reached rotation speed and lifted gracefully into the sky.

For the next few minutes the crew was busy pulling up the gear and flaps and setting the engines as they rose. The three planes flew in a triangular formation, with Grin and Bare It off the portside wing of their flight leader. They soon reached their cruising altitude of thirty-five thousand feet and settled in for the first leg of their flight to the Parrot's Beak.

In the tail gunner's compartment of Grin and Bare It, the tech sergeant adjusted his oxygen mask and settled down for his high-altitude nap. Until the bomb run it was sack time for him.

SANTELLI LAY in the bush on the ridge line overlooking the NVA supply dump. The five Nungs lay around him in a defensive formation. They had been able to make it back to the ridge line with no problem. They'd only had to stop twice and hide while an enemy patrol crossed their path.

He knew that making his way back out wasn't going to be as easy. Once the Arc Light hit, the place would be crawling with NVA. They'd recognize the connection between their overdue patrols and the bombing and would know that a recon team had been operating in their backyard. Blasting the shit out of their hidden supply dump was only going to piss them off even more and send them out for blood.

That was why Santelli had chosen to make his bomb damage assessment from the ridge line instead of going in closer to actually count bodies. A second set of photos taken after the bombing would have to suffice. Orders or not, there was no damn way he was going in any closer.

He studied the second hand on his watch. Arc Light strikes were always on time, and he wanted to cover his ears before the bombs hit. He automatically glanced at the clear sky, even though he knew he wouldn't be able to see the planes at their thirty-five-thousand-foot bombing altitude.

When there was just a minute to go, he signaled the Nungs and clapped his hands tightly over his ears.

It was show time!

A LITTLE OVER an hour after takeoff the three B-52s turned for the run on the target. Onboard Grin and Bare It the radar navigator quickly ran through his pre-IP checklist. When the radios were locked on the beacon transmitting from inside South Vietnam, he fed the navigational information into the bombing computers and reached for his bomb run checklist.

"IP in ninety seconds," Huntington called back.

"Roger."

The radar navigator flicked the switch on the master bomb control panel to auto. Now the computers controlled the bomb drop. He would center the electronic cross hairs of the radar scope on the blip and the computer would take into account everything from airspeed, ground speed and altitude to wind drift, and fly the plane directly into position to hit the target dead center. When the ballistics were right, the computer would open the bomb bay doors, drop the load and close the doors again.

"IP," the pilot called back, releasing the controls.

The radar navigator peered through his radar scope at the blip, his thumb resting on the D-2 bomb release switch.

"FCI centered," the pilot called back.

"Roger. Bomb doors coming open. Sixty seconds to drop."

The red light came on and the radar navigator's thumb stabbed the D-2 switch. "Bombs away."

One by one the olive drab 750-pound bombs left the wing racks and bomb bay, headed for the Cambodian jungle below. In a few seconds almost forty tons of high explosive would ruin someone's day down there.

"Doors closing," the radar navigator called out.

"Roger." Huntington took control of his plane again and followed the leader into a slow banking turn to take them back to their base in southern Thailand. Another mission, another thirty-nine tons of HE. Flying a Buff was a great life, but he needed to take a leak, badly.

EVEN FROM THEIR observation position half a mile away, the concussion of the Arc Light strike buffeted Santelli and his Nungs. The ground rolled and shook under them as if they had been caught in an earthquake. The air was thick with red dust and the acrid smell of detonating high explosives.

Santelli had seen the first of the enormous bombs hit the center of the supply dump. The gout of black smoke shot through with angry red flame made him think of a giant hand flattening the trees. He had also seen the small figures of the North Vietnamese vainly trying to run for cover after the first explosion. There was no place to hide from an Arc Light strike. Then, as he tried to keep his eyes open, the smoke and dust forced him to shut them tightly.

The rain of bombs unrelentingly blasted a quarter square mile of jungle, churning it into a tangled, blasted, smoking ruin. After what seemed like an eternity, the rumbling ceased and the jungle was deathly still. Then he heard the faint cries of the survivors.

Snapping his field glasses up to his eyes, Santelli peered through the screen of smoke and dust to see what remained of the camp. He could see nothing. As soon as the dust settled a little, he brought the glasses up again.

The hidden supply dump was now open to the sky. Jagged stumps of trees dotted the ground between steaming bomb craters. Tangled, shredded foliage and branches littered the ground. He knew that shredded, bloody pieces of North Vietnamese troops also littered the ground. It looked like Hell created in this very small piece of the Cambodian jungle.

He snapped a series of photographs of the blasted camp with his camera. As he had done before, he overlapped the shots to ensure that he recorded the damage completely. Then he took the radio handset from his assault harness. "Rocky Lariat, this is Strider One Zero. Over."

It was a moment before Clifford's voice answered. "Strider One Zero, this is Rocky Lariat. Send your traffic. Over."

"This is One Zero. The Arc Light was right on the mark. Target completely destroyed. Bravo Delta Alpha is completed and I'm returning to my Romeo Oscar November. Over."

"This is Lariat. Roger, copy. What body count did you get? Over."

Santelli frowned. How the hell should he know how many enemy had been killed? He sure as hell wasn't about to go down there and count body parts. "One Zero, estimate a reinforced company Kilo India Alpha. Over."

"This is Lariat. Roger, good work. Report back in when you've joined up with the rest of strider element. Over."

"Strider One Zero, wilco. Out."

Hooking the radio handset back on his harness, he turned to the Nungs. "Let's get the hell out of here!"

17

Parrot's Beak, Cambodia

Santelli crouched in the clump of bushes and watched the squad of North Vietnamese heading straight for his group. The black and green stripes of his uniform and the two-tone green splotches of his face paint made him almost invisible against the foliage. Despite the camouflage his luck had just run out. He had fucked up in a major way.

Because of the tangled thickness of the jungle they were traveling through, he hadn't spotted the NVA patrol moving their way until it was far too late to evade them. Now all they could do was try to fight their way out. If they tried to cut and run for it, there was too great a chance the enemy would hear or see them. They were outnumbered by at least two to one. Their only hope was to achieve complete, overwhelming surprise in the confrontation.

The problem was that they had left the claymores behind, so he couldn't use them to even up the odds a little. They were going to have to fight their way out with just their small arms and grenades.

The five Nungs were spread out around him in a classic L-shaped ambush, their fingers poised on their triggers and their grenades close at hand. In the middle of the long arm of the L, Lam Noc flicked the selector switch on his AK-47 down to semiautomatic fire and silently focused the sights on the last man in the enemy patrol. He was the best shot in the team, so he would try to take out the men farther back in the rear of the formation while the others took care of the point man. His first shot would signal the rest of the team to open up.

Lam Noc set his sights high on the point man's chest and then waited until the NVA was well within the killing zone before he inhaled deeply and tightened his finger around the trigger. Then he squeezed and the assault rifle spit.

At the rear of the enemy patrol the North Vietnamese soldier threw his arms wide and flipped over onto his back, blood spurting from the hole in his heart. The Nung calmly shifted his point of aim and fired again.

The jungle erupted with gunfire as the others opened up simultaneously. Three of the enemy went down in the first burst, but the other enemy troops dived for cover and returned heavy fire immediately.

From the short end of the L, Santelli fired his borrowed grenade launcher almost point-blank into the bush in front of him, hoping the rounds would travel far enough to arm themselves. Thanks to the low-hanging forest canopy, he couldn't lob his deadly little 40 mm grenades up into the air as he usually did because they would hit the tree branches and explode.

The first round detonated with a crack and a little puff of black smoke. Snapping the breech of the grenade launcher open with a practiced flick of his wrist, he stuffed another one of the fat cartridges in, snapped it shut and fired again. This time, however, the grenade didn't explode. Santelli didn't even try a third time. Dropping the M-79, he reached behind his back and swung his Swedish K submachine gun around.

He triggered off a quick burst just as an NVA stuck his head up to throw a Chicom stick grenade. The 9 mm rounds tore into the Vietnamese's upper body at the same instant that the grenade left his hand.

"Grenade!" Santelli shouted, throwing himself to the ground.

It seemed to take forever for the Chicom stick bomb to land. He could see it tumbling end over end in the air, looking like a soup can stuck on the end of a short piece of broomstick. He could almost see the faint trail of smoke, its black powder fuse train left in the air as it sputtered toward him, and he covered his head with his arms.

With a dull crump the bomb exploded off to his side. Almost simultaneously a heavy piece of shrapnel slammed into his back, momentarily stunning him. But there was no time to worry about the pain now. He rolled off to the side and came up firing, his SMG blazing.

After firing off his first three well-aimed shots, Lam Noc flicked his AK's selector switch back up to automatic. He emptied the remaining rounds in a single long burst and dropped back behind cover to reload. Dumping the empty magazine, he slapped a loaded 30-round magazine in its place and slammed back on the charging handle to chamber a round.

An AK bullet slapped into the tree by his head, spraying wood splinters into his face. He snatched a grenade from his ammo pouch, pulled the pin and tossed it out in front of him. The instant it exploded he jumped up and drilled a full magazine load of 7.62 mm into the killing zone before dropping back down again.

Santelli took cover when the bolt of his K locked to the rear on the empty magazine. More AK fire followed him. He rolled over to the right as the rounds tore into the ground where he'd been lying a second before. Dropping the empty magazine, he slammed a fresh one into the bottom of the K. Maybe they had bitten off a little more than they could chew this time.

The hollow thud of a Chicom grenade and the shower of dirt and debris from it spurred him into renewed action. Snatching a hand grenade from his pouch, he pulled the pin, held it in his left hand, then stuck the muzzle of his submachine gun around the edge of the tree. He triggered off half of the magazine in one long burst and pitched the grenade as far as he could, ripping off the rest of the ammunition simultaneously.

The explosion was followed by a high-pitched scream. That was a little more like it, Santelli thought grimly.

He reloaded before crawling off to the side to take up a new position behind a fallen log. Peering around the end of the log, he spied a man's leg through the dense foliage. The leg was clad in the olive-green of an NVA uniform. He aimed carefully and put a short burst of 9 mm into it.

The NVA screamed as the rounds smashed the bone in his thigh. The man rolled over, twisting around to duck under cover. Santelli sent another three-round burst after him, but he had disappeared.

By now the firing had subsided to scattered shots. Santelli kept low as he dodged through the bush toward the sound of Lam Noc's firing. Parting leaves in front of him as he ran, he stepped on a fallen tree branch that broke with a loud snap, and almost ran into an NVA with his back to him. He was evidently trying to sneak around to Lam Noc's rear. At the sound of the breaking branch, the enemy trooper spun around immediately. Then it was a race to see who could reach the trigger first.

Santelli won.

His long 9 mm burst tore into the middle of the man. Some of the rounds hit the AK itself, knocking it out of the NVA's hands, the rest plowing into the man's body. The enemy soldier gave a short grunt and went down on his knees, his belly shot open. Santelli stepped crisply up to him, delivered another shot to his head and quickly moved past the body.

By the time he reached Lam Noc's position, the Nung was getting back on his feet. Three NVA bodies lay sprawled in front of him. The jungle was silent.

After a few seconds of deathly quiet, Santelli cautiously stepped out into the open, his weapon at the ready and his finger on the trigger. He looked up and down the trail. There was no movement anywhere. Their ambush had been successful once again. Even with the odds against him, he'd been able to pull it off one more time.

Silently he waved the men forward. The Nungs went from one dead North Vietnamese to the next, first ensuring that they were dead and then searching the bodies for documents.

Santelli searched out the enemy radioman and was pleased to see that his radio had been shot up. He vaguely remembered seeing the man go down in the initial burst of fire. Unfortunately, however, the North Vietnamese RTO had been holding the radio handset in his hand, which meant he might have been transmitting when he'd been cut down. If he'd been talking with his headquarters, the NVA at the other end would have been able to hear the gunfire and would know why he'd suddenly stopped transmitting.

There was nothing to be done about it now, except get the hell out of the area as fast as they could.

"Trung Uy," Lam Noc called softly. Santelli turned and saw the Nung kneeling beside a tree, his rifle trained on an NVA. "This one still alive."

Santelli walked over. The soldier, an older North Vietnamese, was lying on his back with bullet wounds in both legs. His hair was cut short, he looked well fed and, like the rest of them, his uniform was fairly new. He was a hard hat, an NVA regular, not a Vietcong.

The man stared at Santelli, the whites of his eyes gleaming. He clasped his hands in front of himself, trembling, glancing from Santelli to Lam Noc.

"Do him," Santelli said curtly. Regardless of what MACV-SOG had said about snatching a prisoner, there was no way he was going to try to take a wounded man out with them.

Lam Noc smiled as he pulled his K-bar from the sheath tied to his boot top. The wounded man struggled to sit up as the Nung's hand flashed, burying the blade in the hollow of his neck. The NVA was dead in seconds. Lam Noc wiped the knife on the man's jacket and resheathed it in his boot top. Then he dragged the body deeper into the bush.

Santelli took the radio handset from his harness, held it up to his ear and pressed the talk switch. There was no hiss; the Prick-77 was dead. The shrapnel from the Chicom stick grenade that had slammed into his back must have hit it.

Shrugging out of the radio harness, he found a jagged hole where the fragment of Red Chinese steel had penetrated the case. He shuddered as he let the dead radio slip to the ground. If he hadn't been wearing the unit, the frag would have torn into his lungs. His problem now was that he couldn't contact Kowalski to report that he was okay.

He disconnected the handset from the damaged radio and stuffed it into his pocket. Then he opened the battery box in the bottom and, pulling the battery out, bent the connectors until both poles touched. The battery gave a small pop as it shorted out. Now all the NVA could salvage from the radio was junk parts and a useless battery.

Motioning the Nungs to follow him, he glanced at his map and compass and began to move out. All he wanted to do was put as much distance between them and the ambush site as he could.

FROM HIS NDP LOCATION on the ridge line several klicks away, Kowalski heard the rattle of small-arms fire echoing through the jungle. Sometimes it was hard to pinpoint a sound among the trees and thick vegetation, but the firing seemed to be coming from the direction of the supply dump. Santelli was in contact!

While the Nungs jumped for their fighting positions, Kowalski snatched up his radio handset and switched to the Ban Phoc frequency. "Rocky Lariat, Rocky Lariat. This is Dusty Strider One One. Over."

"Rocky Lariat," came Clifford's voice seconds later. "Go."

"This is One One," Kowalski answered. "Be advised that Strider One Zero element is in contact. Over."

"This is Lariat. Copy One Zero in contact. Do you have commo with him? Over."

"That's a negative at this time, but I hear firing from his location. Over."

"This is Lariat," Clifford said. "Roger, good copy. Maintain your position until you hear from One Zero and then get back to me ASAP. Over."

"One One, roger. Out."

Kowalski set the handset down and gazed out over the luxuriant jungle. He could still hear faint echoes of the firing in the distance. His lieutenant was in contact, and the only thing he could do for him was to sit tight?

"Kent!" he yelled. "Saddle up! We're going after the LT."

Pleased, Kent called out his men in Chinese as Kowalski turned to Larry Webb. "If you don't hear from me in an hour, you're in charge."

"That SOG guy's going to shit himself."

"Fuck 'em," Kowalski growled as he slung another bandolier of ammunition over his shoulder. "My orders to you are that if I don't come back, you're to take everyone who's left and get the hell out of here."

Webb frowned. "I don't know about that, Ski. I don't want to leave you behind."

"You let me worry about that," Kowalski said sternly. "Just do what I say. If you don't hear from me in an hour, get the fuck out of here as fast as you can. If I'm still alive, I'll catch up with you."

"Good luck."

"Yeah, sure," Kowalski said doubtfully.

18

Parrot's Beak, Cambodia

Kowalski and his Nung team had scrambled into their gear and were ready to move out when he heard the distant firefight abruptly end. Switching the Prick-77 radio over to the patrol's internal frequency, he keyed the mike. "Strider one Zero, Strider One Zero, this is Strider One One. Over."

Only the hiss of the carrier wave sounded in his ears.

He tried again without success. Switching back to the Ban Phoc frequency, he called Clifford again.

"This is Rocky Lariat. Go ahead," the CIA man answered immediately.

"This is Strider One One. The firefight has ended, but I still can't make contact with One Zero. Over."

"Lariat, roger, copy," Clifford replied. "Just stay put and wait for further orders. Over."

"One One, wilco. Out."

One of the Nungs on the perimeter interrupted his dark thoughts to report movement in the jungle below. The sergeant dropped the handset and crawled over to look for himself. Parting the leaves in front of him, he looked down and caught a brief flash of North Vietnamese uniform through the valley's foliage. The Nung was right; an enemy patrol was moving below them. He saw a couple of flankers out to the sides who looked as if they might be coming up the side of the ridge line.

Kowalski gave a silent alert before ducking back into his firing position. Laying out a couple of loaded magazines on the ground beside him, he watched the enemy's slow progress. It was their turn in the barrel now. If Santelli was still alive, he was going to have to look after himself for a while. If the NVA discovered them, they'd be too busy running for their own lives to worry about him. And even if the enemy didn't find them, there was nothing the sergeant could do to help until they were clear of the area.

BACK IN PIERCE'S holdout bunker at Ban Phoc, a grim-faced Reese turned to his operations sergeant. They had monitored Kowalski's message about Santelli and heard Clifford's reply. "Better give your buddies a call, Sarge. I think it's time we got into this."

"You sure you really want to do this, Captain?" Pierce asked as he reached for the radio handset.

Reese ran his hand across the back of his neck. "Actually, Sarge, I'd rather not. But I can't just sit here and listen to Santelli and his people go down."

"That SOG colonel is going to shit himself."

Reese grinned. "Maybe it'll do the old bastard some good. Get his brain working again." Pierce switched the radio frequency as Reese got to his feet heavily. "As soon as you've got them on the way," the captain said, "get the Nungs formed up. I'm going to get into my war suit. I'll be back to you in just a minute."

Reese was halfway to the team house when Pierce called after him. "Sir!" Reese turned around. Pierce was scrambling out of the bunker. "We've got us a problem."

"What now?"

"I can't get the choppers. My contact says their CO's got the unit on a maintenance stand-down today. I think that's bullshit, though. They're probably all hung over."

"Oh, shit!" Reese's mind raced. "Can you get us enough ground transportation to do it? A deuce-and-a-half with a jeep escort?"

The operations sergeant frowned. "I could try, sir. But by the time I got them up here and they drove us to the border, it would set us back at least half a day, if not more."

"Who's in charge of that Aviation company?"

"A Major Rett Butler."

Reese squinted at Pierce. "You're shitting me? He calls himself that?"

The sergeant grinned. "That's not his real name, but he's from Georgia, and he thinks he's some kind of modern Southern cavalier."

Reese shook his head. "Jesus! No wonder you're having trouble with this guy! Delusions of grandeur from a fucking Georgia cracker chopper jockey!"

Pierce smiled. "Butler may be a little off-the-wall, sir, but he runs a pretty good outfit. We've used them a lot for things like this."

"Do you think it would do any good for me to talk to him?"

"Depends on how hung over he is."

Reese grinned. "Drunken rednecks I can handle. How fast do you think you can get me a ride to Tay Ninh?"

Pierce reached for the radio mike. "I'll have something on the pad in thirty minutes, sir."

"While I'm gone," Reese added, "get the people ready, but keep them out of sight. I don't want Clifford to see them if he goes to take a leak. Somehow I'm going to get us a ride to Cambodia."

THE SLICK FLARED OUT and neatly set itself down on the end of the runway at the Tay Ninh Army Airfield. The base camp to the west of Tay Ninh City was huge. Along with the airfield maintenance facilities, a brigade of infantry, artillery and armored units and several support units shared the camp. The place had the look of a dusty Army post in southern California. Rumor had it that the camp even boasted a soft ice-cream shop over by the R and R center.

Reese wasn't thinking of ice cream as he jumped down from the Huey and strode across the tarmac toward the battered tropical hut at the other side of the airfield. On the flight line in front of the hut half a dozen UH-1C Huey Hog gunships sat parked side by side. They all wore red-and-white sharks' mouths painted on the side of their gun turrets with colorful names painted under the canopies on their noses.

Off to one side were parked another half-dozen slicks and a couple of the smaller OH-1 Loach scout ships. The Hueys all had crossed lances and the legend Black

Knights painted on their noses. The Loaches sported unit insignias on their rotor mast towers. Except for a couple of men stripped to the waist as they slowly polished the canopy of one of the gunships, Reese didn't see much maintenance work going on.

The sign above the door of the hut read Operations, Sixty-ninth Assault Helicopter Company, The Black Knights. The unit crest, a white crusader's shield with a black bar sinister and crossed gold lances over the motto *Noli Conjugere Nobiscum,* was prominently displayed under the sign. Someone had written The Sixty-niners in black grease pencil beside the unit chest.

Somebody had a sense of humor around here, Reese thought as he opened the door. The black bar sinister through the shield on the crest proclaimed that the company was a bunch of bastards who shouldn't be fucked with. The added message indicated they were cocksuckers, as well. He'd find out what was what soon enough.

Inside, was a large room, obviously the pilots' ready room. A ring of folding metal chairs was set against the walls, which were covered with war trophies. A big pool table dominated the center of the floor. Two men in faded Nomex flight suits were leaning over it, completely engrossed in a game of eight ball.

"Can you tell me where I can find your CO?" Reese asked one of them, a warrant officer pilot, judging from the insignia on his flight suit collar.

The pilot looked up from his shot. "Try his office," he said, pausing before he added the regulation "sir."

Reese stared him straight in the eye. "And just where can I find his office?"

The pilot took his time, lining up his shot, and making it before looking up again. "In the back," he said, motioning with his head.

Without a word Reese turned and walked to the back of the room. He needed the help of these guys, but he would remember that particular pilot's bad manners. He knocked on the door.

"Come!"

Reese opened the door and stepped into the room. An infantry major wearing an unzipped flight suit sporting pilot's wings and a big Black Knights patch on the breast sat behind a cluttered GI-issue steel desk. A thin cigar was clamped in the side of his mouth. "What do you want?" he growled, looking up from the piles of paperwork scattered over the desktop.

"My name's Mike Reese, sir. And one of your bastards told me I'd find you here."

The major leaned back in his chair and grinned around the cigar. "And which particular bastard was that?"

"The thin black-haired warrant officer bastard with a bad attitude and a bent cue stick."

"Yep, that's Marcelli. He's a bastard all right." The major chuckled and stood up to offer his hand. "I'm Rett Butler, the biggest, baddest bastard in charge around here."

Reese shook his hand. "I'm the new A-410 camp commander down in Ban Phoc."

"Have a seat, Captain. What can I do for you today?"

"Well, sir," Reese said, taking a seat in a folding metal chair by the desk, "I'm looking for some last-minute chopper support for a priority mission I've got to run in about an hour."

Butler grinned. "You've come to the right place, Captain. We may be a bunch of bastards around here, but we can sure as hell fly and we can shoot straight, as well. Where do you want us to take you?"

"How about the Parrot's Beak?"

The major's grin faded abruptly. "We may be bastards, buddy, like the sign says, but we're not out of our fucking minds. Nobody flies into the Parrot's Beak, man! What in hell's wrong with you?"

"Well, sir, I've got a platoon cut off in Cambodia and the CIA mission controller won't give me—"

"I don't have anything to do with the goddamn Company," Butler said abruptly, sitting down and yanking his chair forward to the desk. "So you better shag your ass outta here, son, while you still can."

Reese stared at Butler for a long moment before standing. "The word I had was that you people really have your shit together, but that doesn't seem to be the case, does it? You'd better change that sign outside, Major. You guys don't have the balls to be bastards. As far as I'm concerned, you're nothing but a bunch of pussies."

Butler was on his feet like a shot. "You just wait a fucking minute, mister. I don't have to take this kind of shit from some fucking Green Beanie."

Reese stood his ground, his arms crossed. "And furthermore," he said with a slight smile, "I don't think you look a damn bit like Clark Gable, either."

"You motherfucker!" Butler roared as he started out from behind his desk. Reese waited. If he had to kick a major's ass to get the choppers he needed, he was more than ready to do so.

Before Butler could reach him, however, the door smashed open as the two warrant officer pilots stormed into the room, cue sticks in their hands.

"Get the hell outta here!" Butler yelled at them.

The two glared at Reese for a second before reluctantly turning around and closing the door behind them.

Butler took a deep breath. "That crack about Clark Gable was a low blow," he growled. He reached for his cigar from the overflowing ashtray.

Reese merely smiled.

Butler took a deep drag on the cigar. "Okay, let's start from the beginning again. Just what in hell is your problem?"

Reese stepped over to the big map on the wall. "I've got some people cut off inside the Parrot's Beak and I've got to get a rescue mission on the way ASAP."

"I'm not crossing that goddamn border and that's that!" Butler snapped at him.

"Fine," Reese said quietly, knowing he'd won the battle. "I can live with that. Just drop us off on this side and be ready to come and get us if we get into trouble on the way back out."

There was a momentary pause. "How many ships are you talking about and how much blade time?" the major finally asked.

"I've got two groups of fifteen troops, so I'll need a four-ship lift and a Light Fire team escort. It's forty-five minutes to Ban Phoc, fifteen to load on and another thirty to forty-five to the border. Call it seven choppers for three hours? Twenty-one hours total."

"I don't know why in hell I'm doing this," Butler muttered to himself as he walked over to take a closer look at the map. "I've gotta be outta my fucking mind to even think about it."

"Rhett Butler would have done it."

"Asshole."

"And," Reese added, "I need this ASAP. My operation sergeant had this laid on with your ops people, but when he called in for it he was told you were on some kind of maintenance stand-down."

Butler had the decency to look a little sheepish. "We had a party last night," he mumbled. "Some of the nurses from the Eighth Evac came over."

"Are your people sober enough to fly?"

Butler grinned. "Shit, Captain, we fly best when we're half hung over."

"The last thing I need is a fast ride back to Ban Phoc so I can get my people ready."

Butler walked over and opened the door. "Marcelli!"

"Yeah, boss?"

"Get this Green Beanie back to Bum Fuck ASAP."

"You got it."

Butler glanced down at his watch. "We'll be there fifteen minutes after you touch down."

"Thanks."

Butler switched the cigar to the other side of his mouth. "Don't thank me, Reese. Just thank God I didn't kick your ass."

"Maybe next time."

"Asshole."

19

Tay Ninh Army Air Field

Reese ran out to where the Loach scout ship sat on the tarmac with her turbine whining and her rotors spinning. He opened the right-hand door and slid into the seat, reaching for the shoulder harness buckles. The warrant officer scout pilot didn't even give him time to strap himself in before he hauled up on the collective, sending the small Loach rocketing into the air.

Stomping on the rudder pedal, the pilot pivoted the Loach around and lined the bird up to the southwest. Then, nudging forward on the cyclic and twisting the throttle all the way up against the stop, he sent the ship screaming across the base camp barely a hundred feet off the ground.

Seen from above at speeds of 150 miles an hour, the sparsely vegetated plains and abandoned rice paddies along the Cambodian border flashed by. At Ban Phoc Reese jumped out as soon as the little Loach's skids touched down.

The team sergeant met him outside the bunker. "I've got the Nungs standing by, sir."

"Good," Reese said. "I've got the slicks coming in right behind me. There's been a slight change in plans.

We're not going to fly all the way into Cambodia. They're going to drop us off on the border."

Pierce frowned. "That's going to make this even more difficult, sir."

"I know," Reese replied as they hurried toward the team house. "But that was the best I could do. And I damn near had to assault a major even to get them to do that."

"Rett Butler?"

"The very same Southern gentleman."

Reese grinned. "I've got to get suited up. And, after I get changed, I'm going to go have a little chat with our resident spook."

"Good luck, sir."

Reese grinned again. "I don't think I'll have too much trouble with him. I'm sure he'll be more than willing to listen to reason on this."

Pierce laughed. "Right!"

Dick Clifford looked up from the radio as Reese descended into the command bunker. The Special Forces officer was dressed in a tiger-striped uniform completely bare of insignia and was wearing his full combat gear. "Going somewhere?" the CIA man asked in some surprise.

"Matter of fact, I am," Reese said with a slow smile. "A little jaunt into the Parrot's Beak."

"You can't do that," Clifford warned, raising one eyebrow. "I don't have clearance from Marshall for a rescue mission yet."

Reese just smiled more broadly as he took an SOI from the nail above the radio table and slipped the small paper pamphlet around his neck.

"Damn it, man!" Clifford exploded. "You can't do this until I get clearance!"

"Who's going to stop me?" Reese demanded, staring back at Clifford. "You?"

"Marshall's going to have a shit fit!"

"That's your problem."

"Look," Clifford said, getting to his feet, "I can't let you do this. It's going to be my ass, too, if you move your troops out of here without authority."

Reese called up through the door of the bunker. Two young Nung strikers stepped into the bunker with their M-16s at the ready.

"Hey, wait a minute!" Clifford cried, backing away.

Reese ignored him. "If this man touches the radio, shoot him in the legs and then call the doctor."

"Yes, *Dai Uy.*" The Nung grinned broadly. "We will shoot both legs."

Reese turned back to Clifford. "Since you're not a field soldier," he said with a tight smile, "I think I should warn you about the destructive power of the 5.56 mm M-16 round. If they do shoot you, you'll be lucky to save the leg. At the very least you'll never walk normally again."

Clifford's pale face was pasty white now. "I'm going to see your ass in jail for this," he said, his voice quavering.

"Maybe," Reese agreed, "but I won't have to see all of my people in body bags." He turned to go. "I'll call in right after we do our insert and tell them to let you go. Then you can call your colonel and tell him anything you want to. By that time it won't matter."

"You won't get away with this!" Clifford yelled after him. "I swear to Christ I'm going to—"

Reese stopped halfway up the steps and turned around. "Why don't you hold that thought till I get back?" he suggested. "Right now I'm kind of busy."

ON THE EMPTY GROUND between the bunker and the mess hall Pierce had mustered thirty Nung strikers. The radioman, Torres, and Silk Wilson, one of the team's medics, were also suited up for the mission. The radioman had insisted on going along, and the medic's services would probably be needed before the mission was over.

As Reese walked up, he was surprised to see old Vao, the Nung commander, standing in the formation with the younger men. "Is Vao coming with us?"

Pierce grinned. "I'd have to tie the old fuck up to make him stay here. He always wants to go out with us on the hot missions."

Reese hesitated. "That's fine with me just as long as he can keep up with the rest of us."

"You don't have to worry about that, Captain," Pierce said comfortably. "He's a tough old bastard. I've seen him hump the legs off some of these young kids."

"Which bunch am I taking?" Reese asked.

Pierce pointed at the first row of fifteen men. "You're going with Vao. He knows the Parrot's Beak and he'll keep you out of trouble. I've also given you an extra interpreter and Torres."

"Okay," he said, and glanced down at his watch. "Let's get 'em down to the pad. Those slicks will be coming in any minute now."

The three Huey gunships of Butler's Light Fire team appeared a few minutes later, tailed by the four slicks of the lift element. The guns circled protectively overhead as the first Huey flared out above the small landing pad in a flurry of red dust. As soon as it touched down, the Nungs ran to it and scrambled aboard. The moment the first ship was filled, it lifted off and another one slid into place.

Reese climbed into the back of the last Huey and sat in one of the canvas jump seats against the rear bulkhead. He shot the pilot a thumbs-up as he buckled his seat belt. The pilot hauled up on the collective, pulling pitch to the rotor blades, and the Huey rose. After joining up with the other three lift ships, the fleet banked away to the northeast and the Cambodian border.

Well away from the camp the four slicks split into two groups. Reese planned to drop his and Pierce's teams off at different LZs so they could move in on different axes to Santelli's location. That way, if one of the teams ran into trouble, the other could still continue to try to link up with Santelli's patrol.

Reese didn't want Butler's chopper pilots to get into any more trouble than they already were. He had carefully picked landing zones a klick back from the border. That way, when the shit hit the fan over this little exercise, they could always plead ignorance and say they didn't know where Reese was planning to take his people. It was a thin excuse, but it should be sufficient to keep them from going to jail with him.

He settled back and watched as the countryside slid past below him. This time, however, he was taking what he thought would be his last look at this strange and dangerous but sometimes wonderful country.

It was ironic that after he had fought so hard to get himself assigned back to a Special Forces unit in Nam he was setting himself up for a court-martial before he had been back in-country for even a week. And he was risking it for men he didn't really know.

Mike Reese would have laughed had anyone said he was doing something heroic by risking so much for Santelli and his men. As far as he was concerned, what he was doing was simply demonstrating good military leadership. They were his people, they were in trouble and he was going to give them a hand. Even had they not been his men, he probably would have done the same thing.

He tried to relax and take his mind off Santelli and the rescue mission, but it didn't work. He kept going back to the thought that in all likelihood this would be his last mission as a Special Forces officer. If he somehow managed to keep his captain's bars, his next job would probably be running the garbage dump at Khe Sanh.

AFTER MAKING two dummy insertions, the warrant officer pilot flying the lead Huey turned around to

Reese. "LZ coming up in zero one," he shouted over the noise of the rotor blades.

The Special Forces officer unbuckled his seat belt and got ready to leave the slick as soon as her skids touched the ground. The pilot flared out over a small grassy clearing and came in for a hot landing. Before the pilot had even killed all of his forward momentum, Reese was out the door with the Nungs close on his heels.

The pilot glanced over his shoulder before shooting Reese a thumbs-up as he pulled pitch. The captain waved back as the slick pulled itself up into the air and banked away to make another dummy insertion before returning to base. If everything went the way he had planned, Reese would be seeing that same Huey in a little over a day's time.

20

Camp A-410, Ban Phoc

Dick Clifford was still sitting in his chair when he heard the radio come alive with a burst of rapid-fire Chinese. The smiling Nung came over, answered the call and, after a brief conversation, slung his M-16 over his shoulder.

"Captain say you can go now," he told Clifford happily. "He also say he no listen to radio anymore, so you no can call him."

The CIA man got to his feet slowly and stumbled back to the radio console. Jesus Christ! What the hell did Reese think he was doing?

Clifford had been hoping against hope that he could talk Reese out of this once he could get back to the radio, but even that faint chance of salvaging something out of this mess was gone now. Now all he could do was get on the horn back to Tan Son Nhut and tell Marshall what had happened.

Clifford came from a rigidly conventional background, one that valued conformity to social norms and authority over individualism. Even though Reese had blithely put the CIA man's ass into the same sling, Clifford couldn't help but admire the Special Forces officer.

The CIA was considered to be the most freethinking of the governmental services, yet it, too, placed a high value on following orders and not thinking for oneself. In fact, Clifford thought of himself as a man who "played the game" while a part of him desperately wanted to break free of the mold. For that reason he secretly envied Reese's stubborn insistence on doing things the way he wanted to. And doing what he felt was right, regardless of the consequences.

The suspicion flashed through his mind that Reese just might be the only guy in the whole goddamn country who knew exactly what he wanted to do and exactly why he wanted to do it. In a war that was notorious for its confused, muddled thinking, especially at the highest levels, Reese was a breath of fresh air. It was really too bad he was going to wind up with his young ass parked in Long Bien Jail for the rest of his tour.

Clifford keyed the radio mike and cleared his throat. Then he paused, released the switch and put it back down. Did he really want to blow the whistle on Reese?

On second thought, did he really want to take the fall with him and wind up stationed in Bumfuck, Ethiopia, for the rest of his own brief career? He admired Reese in a perverse way, but the primary rule of the game in Nam was something known as CYA—Cover Your Ass.

He took a breath and firmly pushed the transmission switch.

SIGHTING HIS COMPASS on a distant terrain feature in Cambodia, Pierce set a killing pace, the mile-eating slow run of the Airborne-trained troops. One of the reasons he set such a pace was that the thinly covered terrain along the border didn't offer enough cover and concealment for a unit as large as his. Any enemy lurking in the neighborhood would spot them in a minute. He wanted to get his people deeper into the Parrot's Beak and the Cambodian jungle as soon as he could.

As he ran, Pierce automatically kept a close watch on his surroundings. As soon as they entered the dense jungle some five klicks in from the border, they stumbled onto a North Vietnamese infantry company that had halted in the thick jungle right in their path. By the time Pierce spotted the enemy unit, he had almost stepped on one of their campfires.

He was afraid to pull back and bypass their camp. With the limited visibility he couldn't see how far the NVA were strung out or where their positions were. There was too great a chance of stumbling into them again or of being heard as they tried to break contact. Pierce's small force would be hopelessly outnumbered in a fight. The team could only go to ground right where they were and try to wait them out.

The Nungs lay in the wet foliage for several hours and watched as the North Vietnamese leisurely cooked their lunch, collected their gear and slowly ambled off to the south. The NVA gave Pierce's people an unexpected rest break of sorts—if one could call lying absolutely still in such close proximity to the enemy for several hours a rest—but it also cost them valuable time. They would have to make it up if they were going to arrive at the assembly point on time to join up with the captain. Pierce now pushed his people even faster.

The Nungs were moving at a dogtrot along a tree line that edged a small clearing when Pierce, close to the point man, noticed that the jungle made a slight jog to the right in front of them some 250 yards ahead. Nice place for an ambush, he thought. Then, just as he motioned one of his Nungs forward, the distant tree line exploded with automatic weapons fire.

The first burst took out both the point man and the slack, both of whom were hit with full bursts from about seventy-five yards away.

"Move it! Now!" Pierce shouted as he dived for cover in the trees to their left. The rest of the strikers sprinted after him, returning fire while they ran as the enemy fire shredded the vegetation around their fleeing figures. Even as they penetrated deeper into the jungle, they continued to run as hard as they could, crashing through the bush. It was every man for himself until they could get away.

Minutes later Pierce found a good concealed spot and halted. The panting Nungs quickly pulled into a tight defensive perimeter around him and tried to catch their breath.

Pierce turned to the interpreter at his side. "Lin," he gasped, "see how many made it."

"Yes, *Dai Si,* the Nung answered, using the Vietnamese term for master sergeant.

In the meantime Pierce whipped out his map and compass. Then Lin quickly came back.

"It's number ten, *Dai Si*. Three men dead and two more hurt. One man can walk okay. The other is hurt bad, hit in back. Sergeant Wilson say he hit in lung, but we no leave him. We take him with us, no?"

"Yeah," Pierce reassured the Nung, "we'll take him with us, Lin. Tell Sergeant Wilson to come up here."

"Yes, *Dai Si*."

"Shit!" Pierce muttered softly to himself. "What a fucking mess."

Wilson flopped down in the bush beside him. "You get the casualty report?" he gasped, wiping the sweat from his eyes.

"Yeah, I got it."

"Other than that, though, we're okay."

Pierce knew Wilson was right. It could have been a hell of a lot worse. Had the enemy waited just a few more minutes to pop their ambush, they could have gotten even more of them. Even with two fuck-ups today his luck was still holding. Now all he had to do was to shake these guys off and continue on to the assembly area to meet up with the captain on time. He turned his thoughts back to his map and compass.

Through the jungle behind them Pierce could hear faint voices growing louder as the enemy followed their broken trail. Unlike so many of their contacts in South Vietnam where they had the advantage of knowing the territory better than the enemy, they were playing on the NVA's home turf this time. It looked as if the enemy wasn't going to cut and run; they were going to try to hunt them down.

Pierce knew it wasn't going to be easy getting away from a North Vietnamese regular infantry unit working in familiar territory. Just for starters the enemy had probably checked the bodies of his dead and discovered they were Mike Force strikers. The North Vietnamese had a burning hatred for the Special Forces Mike Force Nungs, and it was very unlikely they would just let them go.

Pierce turned to the medic. "Silk, we've got to break this shit off and make a run back for the border. I don't think those guys are going to let us go, and they've got radios. Even if we can get away from this bunch, they'll just call ahead and let their buddies know we're coming."

"What about the captain?"

Pierce shrugged. "I know, but we can't take the chance of their following us to the assembly area. I'm afraid he's going to have to try to get through to Santelli on his own. I don't think we can help him now."

"I hate to break it off," Wilson said, "but you're right. Let's hat up and get out of here while we still can."

Pierce stood. "Okay, I'll take point, and you take a couple of guys and cover the drag. We'll head southeast, back to the fence. Tell Lin to put the wounded strikers in the middle, but they've got to keep up with us. I'll try to get through to Reese and let him know what's going on, and then I'll see about getting us an extraction once we're back across the border."

"Then what are we going to do?"

Pierce looked grim. "Evacuate the wounded, move a few klicks north and try again."

Wilson looked at him and slowly shook his head. "Jesus, man, you're out of your fucking mind!"

Pierce grinned. "You could say that."

Wilson grimaced. "Shit!"

REESE HANDED the radio handset back to Torres. Some rescue operation this was turning out to be. They weren't even halfway to their objective yet and already half the rescue force needed rescuing. This was supposed to have been a clandestine operation, but the way it was turning out he might as well have brought the entire First Air Cav with him and announce his presence to the entire world.

There was nothing he could do to help Pierce now. Reese had to keep driving on to try to reach what was left of Santelli's force. He wondered momentarily if Clifford had been right, after all. Instead of having only a small part of his unit in deep shit, now he had everyone in trouble.

He called for the radio again, and Torres handed him the handset. Keying the mike, he called Kowalski, "Strider One One, this is Dusty Strider Six. Over."

"Six, this is Strider One One. Over."

"This is Six. Send your status. Over."

"This is One One. One Zero has joined back up with us and we're holed up on a ridge line at 674242. We've got NVA swarming all around us, but so far they haven't spotted us yet. Over."

Reese grinned broadly. At least something was going right today. "This is Six. Let me talk to One Zero. Over."

"This is Strider One Zero. Go," came Santelli's welcome voice.

"This is Six," Reese said. "We're southwest of your location and moving as fast as we can. Five has run into trouble, and I don't think we'll be able to reach you till after dark. Do you think you can hold on till then? Over."

"This is One Zero. That's affirmative, Six. As long as the enemy doesn't get the bright idea they need to take a look at this particular ridge line we're sitting on, we'll be okay. Over."

"This is Six," Reese radioed. "Keep your heads down and hang on. We'll be there as fast as we can. Over."

"Take all the time you want, Six," Santelli answered. "We're not going anywhere."

THE PURSUING North Vietnamese weren't making life easy for Pierce. They were doing okay, so far, but trackers were hot on their trail and showed no signs of slacking. The footrace would continue even after the team recrossed the border unless he could get some help real fast.

Burdened with the wounded striker, they couldn't possibly outrun the North Vietnamese for very long. All the enemy had to do was keep rotating fresh men up to their point position and they could run his people right into the ground.

That was an old Apache trick, and it worked as well in the jungles of Southeast Asia as it did in the deserts of Arizona.

Right now the Nungs were taking turns carrying the stretcher. But they couldn't keep that up much longer. Also, once the North Vietnamese figured out their general direction, they would call other NVA units in to cut them off.

Were it a little later he might have been able to keep going till nightfall and evade his pursuers in the dark. At this time of day, though, there was just too much sunshine left. And as soon as they slowed down, the NVA would be all over them in a flash.

As much as he hated to, Pierce knew he had to try to find a PZ somewhere right across the border and call for an emergency extraction. He pulled a sweat-stained map from under his tiger-striped shirt as he ran. From what he could tell there was a possible PZ right across the border about half an hour away, at the rate they were going. He yelled for the Nung with the radio.

Panting into the radio as he ran, Pierce got through to his buddies back at the Sixty-ninth Helicopter Company in Tay Ninh. True to his word, Rett Butler had two slicks and a Light Fire team from his Lancer Flight immediately available. All Pierce had to do now was to stay ahead of the North Vietnamese and get to the Papa Zulu on time.

It sounded simple enough, but it was going to be tight, real tight.

21

Parrot's Beak, Cambodia

Pierce called Wilson for a quick conference and told him the extraction was on its way. A big grin spread across the medic's face. "You keep on going," he panted, "I'm going to take one of the Nungs and drop back. If I can ambush their point, they'll deploy and it'll give us a chance to break free."

Unlike the medics in regular Army units, Special Forces medics were soldiers first and medics second. Besides carrying an aid bag along with the rest of his combat gear, Silk Wilson got his buckle in the dust when it was necessary.

Growing up in the black ghettos of Chicago had given Wilson a taste for street combat and a deep sense of loyalty to his own people. His gang experiences had led him to the Army, and the Army had shown him how to heal as well as how to kill. And Special Forces had given him a place where he could be judged on the basis of his worth as a man.

The color of his beret counted for much more than the color of his skin in the SF, and he was loyal to his new gang. He was far closer to most of the white men in his A-team than he had ever been to the other black kids in his street gang at home. He felt particularly close to Pierce. When he had first joined the team, the Indian sergeant had taken him in hand and eased him through the transition from street smart to jungle smart and made a real soldier out of him.

The only way this extraction was going to work was if someone kept the enemy off their backs and that someone had to be him. Pierce had to lead the rest of the Nungs to safety.

The medic had a good idea, but Pierce didn't think it was going to work today. "You're just going to get yourself killed," he told him. "The NVA's coming on too hard. They'll just shoot you up and bypass you."

"I can stop 'em, man," Wilson insisted. "And I can run faster than you can, too, old man," he added with a big grin. "You get the rest of these guys out of here, and I'll catch up with you later!"

"Take care."

Wilson grinned as he spun around. "You got that shit right, Sarge." Grabbing one of the strikers, he loped back down the trail.

Pierce and the men with him ran much more slowly now. Carrying the litter with the wounded man was wearing them down quickly. It was bad enough that they had been forced to leave the Nung dead where they'd fallen in the ambush. But he had never left a wounded man, American or Indigenous, behind yet, and he wasn't about to start that shit now.

To their rear Pierce heard the sharp rattle of automatic weapons fire and the dull crump of grenades. Wilson had sprung his ambush on the enemy point.

Pierce picked up the pace. "Move it!" he yelled.

As he ran, Pierce prayed that Silk would somehow be able to break free and make it back. The medic was a hell of a good man, and it would be a shame to lose him on a mission as fucked up as this one was.

Now it was only another ten or fifteen minutes to their PZ.

IN THE AIR Rett Butler was inbound to Pierce's pickup zone in his Huey gunship with a Light Fire team at his back. The three gunships were loaded down with everything the company armorers could hang on them. Following behind as fast as they could go were the two slicks of the lift element.

Butler keyed his throat mike. "Dusty Strider Five, Dusty Strider Five, this is Lancer Lead on your push. Over."

"Lancer Lead, this is Strider Five," Pierce panted into the radio. "Go ahead."

"This is Lead," Butler radioed. "I am inbound to your Papa Zulu, Echo Tango Alpha six mikes. What's your situation down there? Over."

"This is Five. I'm at least ten mikes November Whiskey from the Papa Zulu and I'm up to my ass in alligators. Can you scratch for me? Over."

"This is Lancer Lead. Roger, Five, can do. We'll be there *muy pronto*. Be prepared to pop smoke. Over."

"Five, roger. Out."

The pilot switched back to the gunship frequency. "Lancer Flight, this is Lead. Time to go to work, boys. Two, you turn the wick up and follow me. Three, you stay with the lift ships. Over."

A chorus of "rogers" followed as one of the Huey gunships broke away to follow their leader. In the left-hand seat of Butler's Black Knights chopper, Warrant Officer "Surfer Joe" Hawkins, gunner extraordinaire, tightened the fingers of his Nomex gloves. On his weapons control panel he flipped on the arming switches to the 7.62 mm minigun pod, the automatic 40 mm Thumper in the ship's chin turret and the 2.75-inch rockets in the pods on the pylons. He swung the gunsight into position in front of his face and wrapped his fingers around the firing controls. He was ready to rock and roll.

PIERCE AND HIS interpreter had dropped back to take up the drag while the Nungs ran on ahead with the wounded. Behind him he heard more firing, both AK and M-16. He should never have let Silk try to stop them with only one man at his side. At least one of them was still alive. He hoped it was the medic. Taking a deep breath, he yelled at his Nungs to run faster. "Move it, goddamn it!"

Through the breaks in the treetops the sergeant saw black specks in the sky closing fast—the gunships. He keyed the handset to the radio as he ran.

"Lancer, this is Five. I have you in sight to my November Echo and I'm popping smoke. The target is right behind me—a company of November Victor Alpha. Smoke out. Over."

He pulled a smoke grenade from his assault harness, pulled the pin and dropped it onto the side of the trail as he ran. Behind him thick purple smoke billowed up through the tops of the trees.

Butler spotted the column rising through the jungle and glanced down at his map. Pierce was still right inside the Cambodian border. Damn that Reese for getting him into this! The shit was going to hit the fan if anyone found out about this unauthorized mission. But this was no time to go back on his promise.

"Strider Five, this is Lancer Lead," Butler radioed back. "I've got Goofy Grape. Over."

"This is Five, roger purple. Go get 'em. They're right on our ass. But keep an eye out for a round eye in cammies—one of my men is back there, too."

"Roger, Five, good copy. Move past the smoke and continue to the Papa Zulu. We'll cover for you."

Butler switched back to his internal frequency. "Lancer Guns, this is Lead. Hit behind the smoke and watch out for the good guys. They're wearing cammies today."

It almost looked as if the lead gunship was going to fly right into the ground as it passed not thirty feet over Pierce's head. He could feel the rotor blast and the concussion of the explosions as the gunner fired everything he had into the jungle behind him—rockets, 40 mm grenades and the 7.62 mm minigun. It felt as if the world were ending behind him.

The strikers beside him were running as fast as they could now, drawing on their absolute last reserves of energy. Pierce put his head down and ran flat out himself. It was all up to the gunships now. If they could keep the enemy off their asses while they ran the last few hundred yards to the clearing, they'd make it.

He glanced behind him and saw a figure in a tiger-striped uniform stagger out of the smoke from the rocket explosions. It was Wilson.

Pierce stopped in midstride and turned around. The medic was coming but not fast enough. As he watched, Wilson stumbled and fell onto the side of the trail. There was no sign of the Nung who had been with him.

"Lin!" Pierce yelled at the Nung interpreter who had stopped when he had. "Keep going!" The Special Forces sergeant started running back.

Lancer Lead had cleared his first firing run and was banking for another pass when he saw the first of the Nungs break out of the tree line into the open ground. "Lancer Four," he called to the first of the two slicks, "this is Lead. They're coming. Get those birds on the ground now!"

The slicks turned into their final approach and, with their door gunners hammering at likely enemy hiding places, flared out and settled to earth a few yards from the running Nungs. The four strikers carrying the litter with their wounded comrade nearly threw their burden in and clambered aboard the first bird themselves. It lifted off instantly. The other men ran back to the second slick.

While the other men scrambled right on board, Lin ran up to the pilot's window. "No go! No go!" he yelled. "*Dai Si* and *Bac Si* come soon!"

The slick driver shook his head and yelled back, "Get on. I can't wait!"

"No, wait! Please!"

Rolling in for his next firing run, Butler saw the Nung interpreter waving his arms as he yelled through the window at the slick pilot. "Lancer Four, this is Lead. What's going on down there?"

"This is Four. This guy says his advisers are coming, but I don't see them."

"Are you taking fire?"

"That's a negative."

"Hang in there until you do."

"Roger, copy."

Butler leveled out his gunship, and the gunner started to play with his firing controls again. He walked the chin turret from side to side as they swooped in low over the edge of the trees, peppering the jungle with 40 mm grenades. Lead looked down through the foliage and spotted two figures in tiger-striped cammies. One of the men seemed to be trying to carry the other.

"Four, this is Lead. We've got two more men in there, and we're not leaving without them. Let's give Charlie a taste of hell."

As Lead pulled out of his run, the other two gunships came charging in side by side right behind him, their rotors almost touching. Their noses blazed with fire, and 2.75-inch high-explosive rockets lanced out from the pods on their pylons.

The forest was coming apart below them. The rockets, miniguns and Thumper rounds stormed through the jungle, shredding the foliage and dropping trees as if they were matchsticks. Several more fires from the explosions billowed even more smoke into the already darkened sky. It was getting difficult now for the pilots to see their targets.

The ships of Lancer Flight were doing all that men in flying machines could possibly do to protect the two men still on the ground. Now it was up to Pierce and Wilson to make it to the PZ.

Pierce was panting and could hardly breathe. The thick, blinding smoke was choking him. Coughing and stumbling with Wilson's full weight on him, he staggered toward the PZ, the medic on his back in a fireman's carry. Wilson was hit in the leg, but Pierce knew if he could get him out, the wound wouldn't be serious.

He was oblivious to the destruction going on around him, the rockets slamming into the trees, the crump of the Thumper rounds detonating and the chattering of the miniguns as the three gunships worked the woods right behind him. Over the burning jungle Butler's Black Knights flew figure eights in the sky, directing the fire from the other two gunships.

Pierce was also unaware of the wound he'd taken himself, a small piece of rocket shrapnel in the shoulder, as well as the weight of the man on his back. He was totally oblivious to everything except the need to keep going, to keep putting one foot in front of the other until he cleared the trees.

His strength was rapidly leaving him. His energy reserves were all but drained. He was moving solely now on stubborn willpower. As long as he was alive, he would keep on running.

Out of the smoke in front of him two figures mate-
rialized, running toward him. Pierce tried desperately
to raise his weapon to fire on them, but his aching arms
wouldn't obey his brain's commands.

"Don't shoot!" one of the figures shouted. "Goddamn it, don't shoot!"

They were the two door gunners from the slick still
waiting on the ground. One gunner hauled Wilson
from his back and, cradling the wounded medic in his
arms like a child, sprinted for the bird. With Wilson's
weight suddenly gone, Pierce stumbled and fell. Hands
grabbed him by the assault harness and jerked him
harshly back onto his feet.

"Run, goddamn it, run!" the other gunner screamed
in his ear.

With the gunner pulling him along Pierce started
running again, and they broke out of the trees. The
slick was already in a ground-effect hover, her skids a
foot off the ground as she neared the tree line, the rotors at full rpm.

The gunner shoved Pierce into the passenger compartment and scrambled in behind him. The second
they were both safely inside, the pilot hauled up
sharply, the turbine screaming, rotor blades clawing the
smoke-filled air.

Pierce slumped against the frame of the open side
door, fighting to catch his breath and clear his lungs.
Wilson lay on the floor plates, coughing and hacking,
while one of the Nungs tied a field bandage around the
bullet wound in his thigh. It wasn't bleeding much and
didn't appear to be life-threatening. Wilson would be

okay once they got him back to camp. Only now could Pierce begin to feel the pain in his shoulder, and relief. Even with the Nung casualties, they had gotten off light.

One of the door gunners handed the sergeant a flight helmet and, pointing to the gunship flying beside them, motioned him to put it on. As soon as he plugged the end of the cord into the intercom jack, he heard Butler's voice over the headphones. "Five, this is Lancer Lead. Do you read?"

Pierce keyed the mike. "Lead, this is Five. Go ahead."

"This is Lead. Do you want me to carry your wounded to the Dust-off pad?"

Pierce thought for a moment. If he kept his wounded out of the hospital, no one would be able to ask them any questions, such as where they had been when they were hit. The problem was that the Nung on the litter was hit in the lungs. He would probably die if he didn't receive proper medical attention. Repairing a lung shot was more than the A-team's medics could handle. Fuck it! Enough men had been killed already.

"This is Strider Five. The other slick has one man who needs medical attention. The rest of us are okay."

"This is Lead, roger. I'll drop the rest of you off at Ban Phoc before I take him to Eighth Evac. Over."

"Five, thanks a lot."

"This is Lead. No sweat. Just tell your captain he owes me."

22

Parrot's Beak, Cambodia

A very grim Mike Reese had monitored the frantic radio traffic between Pierce and the rescue choppers. It was a bitch about the Nung casualties, but at least Pierce and Wilson were safely out. It was obvious that the team sergeant wouldn't be able to replace his losses and get back to Cambodia in time to be of any help with the mission. Now it was completely up to Reese, Sergeant Torres and the fifteen Nungs to pull this thing off.

He halted his small unit for a short rest break and called Torres back from the point position for a quick conference. "You heard about Pierce?" Reese asked the radioman.

Torres squatted beside his captain. "Yes, sir. I monitored." He shook his head. "If the Indian could step on his dick that way, then we'd all really better watch our asses."

"You've got that shit right," Reese agreed. "And since we won't be joining up with him now, I want to try to reach Santelli before dark. If we can get through to him, we can get the hell out of here tonight instead of waiting till morning. I don't want to spend any more time in this place than we have to."

Reese unfolded his map. "We're here right now and Santelli's over here. We were to join up with Pierce here." He pointed to a spot off to the right of a direct line from where they were in relation to Santelli's ridge. "But now that he's out of the picture I want to move in on Santelli by the most direct route."

Torres studied the map. "It's going to be a little tougher going that way, Captain," he said after a moment. "The terrain's rougher and it looks like the jungle's thicker."

"I know," Reese said, "but even so it'll save us some time. I want you to take point again and I'll rotate it with you."

"When do you want to get started?"

Reese took a long drink from his canteen and got to his feet. "As soon as I give Santelli an update on our plans. I want to cover ground as fast as we can, but I want you to be careful up there, *real* careful."

"You got that shit right, Captain," Torres said, looking up the trail. "There's a bunch of 'em running around in here all right. I can feel 'em."

"I hear you talking."

BACK IN THE command bunker at Ban Phoc Clifford sat by the radio and stared at the familiar sandbag wall in front of him. He had just signed off with Colonel Marshall again. He had informed the colonel that Santelli had finally returned to the rest of his unit and had reported that the Arc Light strike had literally been a smashing success.

Marshall had been glad to hear that the B-52 raid had been on target, but when the CIA man reported that Santelli thought he was surrounded by NVA and cut off from his escape route, the colonel hadn't been at all concerned. When Clifford had requested a cross-border helicopter extraction to rescue them, the colonel had turned it down flatly. He wanted Clifford to calm Santelli down, have him wait until dark and then get the hell out of there with those films. Most of all, the colonel wanted the BDA evidence back at SOG headquarters ASAP.

More and more Clifford was beginning to understand Reese's side of this thing. How in hell could you work with a man who thought the way Marshall did? All the colonel cared about was covering his ass on the use of the Arc Light strike in Cambodia. He didn't give a shit about the men who had called in the strike and who had risked their lives to make the BDA he'd insisted on. If the bomb damage assessment photos showed the strike had taken out a major enemy installation, Marshall would be a hero. On the other hand, if they showed nothing, the colonel would blame the fuck-up on Santelli and Clifford.

It was a win-win situation for Marshall. Unless Reese got through to Santelli in time and was able to get him out of there, it was a real no-win situation for the lieutenant.

This wasn't the first time Clifford had controlled a cross-border mission that had stepped in deep shit. He'd had people killed before, but he had never controlled a mission as fucked up as this one. He also knew that a large part of it was his fault, not theirs. He had wanted this recon made so that he could use the information to back up his own prediction of a new enemy attack and force the colonel to act on it.

Maybe he had made a mistake sending Reese's men in there. While they were very good at what they did, they didn't have the specialized cross-border recon training the other RTs had been given at Project Delta. Maybe he should have tried for yet another SR-71 Blackbird overflight for even more photos. The problem with that was that Marshall didn't trust recon photos any more than he did the findings of the recon teams in the field. The colonel firmly believed the North Vietnamese were beaten because MACV had said they were. He wasn't about to accept anything that conflicted with that belief.

Clifford shook his head. It was that kind of head-up-the-ass thinking that was losing the goddamn war. He was drinking yet another cup of the A-team's high-octane coffee, putting off making another call to Santelli for an update on his situation, when he heard the sound of helicopters approaching the camp.

Clifford scrambled up the steps from the bunker and saw two slicks coming in on final approach to the helipad. Several Nungs had gathered at the pad. Sergeant Hayes, the A-team's senior medic, was standing by with two Nung stretcher teams. Obviously something had gone completely wrong.

Pierce was the first man off the bird, and the veteran sergeant looked exhausted. Sweat had dried crusty white on his tiger-striped uniform, and a small patch of half-dried blood covered his right shoulder. Behind him the Nung medics were helping more wounded men off the chopper.

"Sergeant, what happened?" Clifford asked.

Pierce eyed him coldly before he answered. "We got our asses shot off, that's what. Four Cidge KIA and a couple more wounded, including Wilson."

"Where's Captain Reese?"

"He wasn't with us," Pierce replied. "His plan was to put our two groups into different LZs and then move in on separate routes."

"Why did he do that?" Clifford had controlled recon missions but had little knowledge of the actual tactics used by the teams on the ground.

"To try to keep something like this from happening." Pierce gestured at the wounded being taken off the slick. "We got spotted on the way in and we're out of it now, but he can still keep on going."

"But if they found your team, they'll be on an increased alert and they'll find him, too."

"He knows that," Pierce said grimly, "but he doesn't have any choice if he wants to get the lieutenant and those people back in one piece." Pierce spit on the ground in front of him and challenged the CIA man with his eyes. "That colonel of yours hasn't left him any other option."

"Look," Clifford said, taking off his sunglasses so that Pierce could see his eyes, "I know I've caused you and Reese a lot of trouble with this whole thing and I'm really sorry, but that's how my orders read. Maybe I could have argued a little harder with the colonel about this mission, but I never thought it would turn into such a complete monkey fuck.''

Pierce almost believed him. ''That's the thing about war, mister,'' he said bitterly. ''You've always got to figure a fuck-up factor into every operation. I can see where you might not be familiar with the fuck-up factor—I think you civilians call it Murphy's Law—but your colonel's been around long enough to know better.''

''Is there anything I can do to help?'' Clifford's thin face showed only concern.

Pierce stared at him long and hard. It might be a real help if the CIA man was really on their side for a change. He decided he'd give the guy one more chance. If he got in the road again, he could always throw his young ass in a CONEX container for safe keeping until it was over.

''About the best thing you can do right now,'' the sergeant said, ''is stay off the radio to that colonel of yours. I need to work out some plans with the captain and the LT, and I don't need your colonel giving me a raft of shit about what we're trying to do. I've got most of my team over there, and I want to get them back in one piece if I can.''

''You've got it, Sergeant,'' Clifford said. ''Tell me what you want me to do.''

''The first thing you can do,'' Pierce said, ''is fill me in on what you've told the colonel so far. We can take it from there.''

Clifford looked at the people still clustered around the landing pad. ''Let's go into the bunker.''

Pierce smiled for the first time. "You afraid these guys might find out we have a mission across the border?"

Clifford shrugged. "Sorry. Old habits."

Once the two men were seated inside the bunker, Pierce poured himself a cup of coffee while Clifford filled him in.

"You haven't told him we mounted our own rescue operation?" Pierce asked, surprise in his voice.

Clifford grimaced. "No," he said slowly, "I was holding off on that for a while."

"Why?"

"Trying to save my own ass," he admitted. "I was hoping you guys would get through okay and I wouldn't have to tell him anything about it."

Pierce thought for a moment. "He turned down your request to extract Santelli, you said?"

Clifford nodded.

Pierce looked pleased and took a swig of coffee. "Okay, I want you to get on the horn and tell him about Reese's operation right now."

"You're shitting me! Why?"

"Insurance," Pierce explained. "You have to understand how a colonel's mind works. Right now Santelli's mission is a secret. Even if it goes completely crazy and everyone gets killed, no one will ever know a thing about it because it's a SOG mission. But the captain went in there on his own, and that means someone who's not cleared for SOG operations flew him in there. If they talk and it gets out, it'll cause Marshall no end of trouble with the politicians and the press. The only way he'll be able to put a lid on this thing is if he authorizes the mission after the fact. That way he can cover his ass with the SOG security regulations and keep anyone from talking.''

Clifford smiled. "It's devious, but just crazy enough that it might work."

"The best part," Pierce continued, "is that once he authorizes the captain's mission that will allow you to call on SOG resources if he gets into any more trouble."

Clifford thought for a moment. "Marshall's going to shit a brick." He slowly shook his head. "And he's going to hang me by the balls for this."

Pierce leaned forward. "All you have to do to cover your ass with him is to blame it all on the captain. Tell the colonel that Reese got pissed when he wouldn't authorize an extract and just took off on his own. Tell him you tried to stop the captain, but he had two of his Nungs hold a gun on you until he took off."

Clifford looked up. "That's what really happened, you know."

Pierce grinned. "The captain does seem to know how to make things go his way."

Clifford shrugged. "I'll do it. I can't get in any more trouble than I already am."

"Good man," Pierce said, wincing slightly as he got to his feet. "While you're taking care of that, I've got a few things to take care of around here."

"What are you going to do?"

"After I get this shoulder fixed," the sergeant said, "I'm going to put together another rescue operation."

"Oh, shit."

REESE FROWNED as the shadows lengthened in the jungle of the Parrot's Beak and took out his map again. Damn it, anyway! They hadn't covered as much ground as they should have. Torres had been right about the rough terrain. And, if that hadn't been bad enough, they'd had to stop cold for almost an hour while Torres had taken two of the men and made a recon of a major trail they'd come across, one bearing signs of recent heavy foot traffic.

A stony-faced Torres had retrieved an empty tin of canned herring packed in Red China and an empty pack of North Vietnamese cigarettes. An NVA regular unit had stopped for a meal in the area in the past couple of hours. The enemy usually weren't so sloppy about leaving signs behind, but they'd obviously thought they were safe in their Cambodian sanctuary.

Since the NVA's tracks ran in the same direction they were going, Reese had been forced to detour off course for a couple of klicks, and that had cost them valuable time. They were still a little over an hour away from making the linkup with Santelli's force, and it was growing dark fast, too fast.

Reese hated to call a halt, but it was too dangerous to move so many people through the jungle at night. It was noisy and, more important, there was just too great a chance of stumbling into the enemy in the dark. The best thing they could do was find a place to lie low until the next day. They would move out again at first light. Now they needed somewhere high enough to keep them out of the way and from which they could watch all the approaches.

He caught up to Torres. "I think we'd better stop," he told the young sergeant. "What do you think?"

"I think so, too, sir," Torres replied. "We won't be any help to the LT if we get our asses caught in a sling tonight."

Reese would have liked the sergeant to try to talk him into pushing on, but he knew he was right. With just fifteen men they didn't have enough firepower to get into a nighttime firefight.

"Okay, Sergeant, as soon as you can find us a good night lager position, we'll park it and wait till morning."

"Yes, sir."

23

Parrot's Beak, Cambodia

Night descended suddenly in the tropics, and just as darkness fell over the jungle Reese's small unit reached the crest of a sparsely covered ridge. "What do you think, sir?" Torres quietly asked Reese.

The Special Forces officer looked around and down into the already pitch-black jungle below. "This'll do nicely, Sarge. We've got good observation of the approaches and there's enough cover for us up here."

"That's what I thought."

"We'll use a patrol star formation tonight," Reese ordered. "Get 'em set in and have 'em eat."

"Right, sir."

As each of the Nungs reached the top of the ridge, Torres had them pull into a tight defensive perimeter instead of digging in like infantry grunts would have done. Since there were so few of them, digging defensive positions would have been useless and would have given away their overnight position to the next NVA unit that stumbled onto the empty holes. Their only real chance was to lie low, remain completely silent and pray that any North Vietnamese roaming around would miss them in the dark.

The men lay on their bellies in a large circle, facing out with their boots touching those of the men on either side. They would lie immobile all night, awake or asleep. If they had to urinate, they would just roll over onto one side, urinate from where they lay and roll back into position. No one would move or speak until first light.

If anyone heard anything or thought he saw movement, he would tap the boot of the man next to him and communicate with hand signals. That second man would pass the message down the line to the next man in the circle. And so on.

They put their claymores out in the trees around them, without trip-wiring the explosives. The mines were rigged for command detonation only, not early warning, and would only be used as a last resort if they were discovered and forced to make a run for it. Their weapons were ready in their hands, and they'd placed their grenades within easy reach.

As the Nungs moved into their positions, Reese summoned the RTO to bring the radio. His first call was to Santelli to let him know where they were.

Reese keyed the handset. "Strider One Zero, Strider One Zero," he spoke quietly, "this is Strider Six. Over."

"One Zero, go."

"This is Six. We've halted for the night, but we'll get going again at first light. I think we can reach you in a little over an hour. Over."

"This is One Zero. That may not work," Santelli's voice was strained but controlled. "Our situation has changed in the past couple of hours, and I'm not sure we can hold out that long. I'm pretty sure we've been spotted. They've been moving units in below us and we're completely surrounded now. I've even seen them putting in some mortars, and I think they're waiting until morning to hit us so that they don't miss any of us in the dark. Over."

"Six, roger. Wait one and I'll see about putting something together to go tonight. Over."

"One Zero, roger. Like I said, Six, we ain't going anywhere. Out."

Reese urgently called for Torres and Vao and told them the news.

"Shit," Torres muttered.

"We're going in to get them out tonight," Reese said.

"That's going to be a gold-plated bitch, sir."

"I know, but the way I see it we don't really have any other choice." Reese turned to Vao. "I'm going to need your best night fighters. Men who can move quietly and who aren't afraid to use a knife."

Vao smiled faintly. "I have many such men, *Dai Uy*. How many do you need?"

"I'll take three and Torres will take three. We'll be going in light, and I want the others to stay back here to give us a patrol base. When we come back, we may have NVA on our tail and I'll need the men here to fight a rearguard action for us if we need it."

The old Nung nodded. That was the kind of operation he understood.

"Okay," Reese continued, "here's how it's going to work. Torres, you're going to take your people around to one side of the enemy and start a diversion. I'll be on the other side of the circle, waiting to open a hole as soon as you distract them."

"How are you going to do that?" Torres asked.

"Well, since we don't have any silenced weapons with us, I guess we'll have to use knives."

"Wait one, captain," Torres said, getting to his feet. "I've got a present for you."

The radioman ran back to his rucksack and dug around in it for a moment. He came back with a small matt-black case in his hands, opened it and handed it to Reese. Inside lay a silenced Ruger Mark 1.

"What the hell are you doing with this?" Reese asked.

"Well, sir," Torres grinned, "me and the LT started packing them with us on our missions. Mostly we use them to shoot small game when we run out of rations in the long humps."

"I'll be damned!" Reese smiled as he took the pistol from the case and weighed it delightedly in his hand. "This is going to make things a lot easier. How's it sighted in?"

"Dead on at fifty feet."

Reese thought for a few moments as he stared at the small weapon. "Now that we have this, let's change the timetable a little. I'll open the hole in their lines before you start your diversion. I can join up with Santelli's people, lead them to the hole and we'll be ready to escape when you open up on them. We'll be exposed for less time if we do it that way.''

"That makes sense," Torres agreed.

"Okay," Reese continued, "I want you and your people to carry as much firepower as you can pack. I want the NVA to think they're facing at least a dozen guys. Blast the hell out of 'em, but be ready to pull back as soon as I call and tell you we're clear."

"Then what?"

"I don't think they'll follow you at night, so as soon as you're clear, haul ass back here. As soon as I get back with Santelli's people, we'll pull out and start back. What do you think?"

"It's tricky, captain," Torres replied. "But we may be able to pull it off."

"I know it's risky," Reese said, "but we've got to make it work if we're going to get any of them out of there alive." He folded his map. "Get the men ready and then try to get some sleep. After I call Santelli, I'm going to try to get through to Pierce and let him know what we're doing."

Torres looked surprised. "But that will let the spook know what we're doing, too."

Reese grinned in the darkness. "What's he going to do about it? Send us to Vietnam?"

SANTELLI HANDED the radio handset back to his RTO and called softly for Kowalski and Webb. The captain's plan was crazy, just crazy enough that it might work. If this was a sample of how his new commander's mind worked, Santelli was really going to enjoy working with him. Provided he had a future.

"What's the word, LT," Kowalski asked.

"Well," the lieutenant said, grinning in the dark, "the captain's coming to get us tonight."

"You're shitting me, sir!"

"I wouldn't do that to you, Ski. You're my favorite sergeant."

"How's he going to do it, sir?" Webb asked.

Santelli briefed them on Reese's plan.

Kowalski frowned. "It might work, but it's going to be tight, real fucking tight."

Santelli peered down into the surrounding bush at the NVA units he knew were hiding in the darkness, waiting to kill them in the morning. "You got a better idea, Ski?"

Kowalski shook his head. "Can't say that I do, LT."

"Okay, then, let's do it," Santelli said. "I want our people to leave everything behind except for their weapons, canteens, ammunition and what rations they can carry in their pockets." He turned to his demo man. "Webb, you gather all the rest of the gear into a pile and leave a little something for Charlie to find."

Webb grinned. "Can do, LT, can do."

While Santelli and Kowalski talked to the interpreters, Webb went to work. As one of the A-team's two demo men, he loved pitting his skills against the enemy's booby trap experts. The NVA would be extremely suspicious of so much equipment left behind and would take great care to look for booby traps before they tried to salvage any of it. Accordingly, he decided to booby-trap everything twice. The first charge would be somewhat obvious, but the second charge would be more difficult to find.

As soon as the Nungs retrieved the gear they would take with them, Webb removed all the remaining claymores from the rucksacks and started stacking the packs in a pile in the center of their little hill. Under each rucksack on the bottom of the pile he placed a hand grenade so that the weight of the pack would hold the spoon in place after the pin had been pulled. It was a typical booby trap, and the enemy would surely find the grenades. Once they did, all it would take to render the grenades safe was to put a nail or piece of commo wire back into the safety pin hole. No big deal.

The NVA would be sure to make all the grenades safe before they moved anything. And when they thought they were so damn smart for having found the Yankees' amateurish attempts to booby-trap them, they'd start moving the packs. If this worked, Webb should get a good body count. It was too bad he wouldn't be able to stick around to watch the party.

Taking six of their claymores, Webb screwed a grenade fuse into both of the fuse wells on each of the mines. He slipped the mines, faceup, into the rucksack and laid them on top of the rest of the pile. After placing each loaded rucksack, he slipped his hands inside and positioned the mine so that its weight pressed down on the grenade fuse spoons. After carefully pulling the fuse pins, he fastened the rucksack's top flap down.

When the rucksacks on the top of the pile were picked up, the spoons would fly off the grenade fuses and detonate the claymores. There were enough plastic explosives in each mine to set off the rest of them by sympathetic detonation and the back blast. With a craftman's satisfaction he set the last rucksack in place, armed the claymore inside and slowly backed away to admire his creation. All he had to do now was to make sure one of the Nungs didn't bump into them in the dark tonight and blow them all sky-high.

When they had done everything they could to prepare themselves for the rescue, Santelli crawled off under a shrub to try to sleep. If the captain's plan worked, they'd be on the move all night. If it didn't work, however, then at least he'd be well rested before he died. Either way there was nothing else he could do right now, so he might as well try to sleep.

AS SOON AS HE HAD BRIEFED Santelli on his plan, Reese put in a call to Pierce back at Ban Phoc. "Dusty Strider Five, this is Strider Six. Over."

The sergeant must have been sitting right by the radio. "Strider Six, this is Five. Go."

"This is Six. Be advised that we're halted three klicks away from our objective. One Zero reports that he's cut off, so we're going to try to get him out tonight. I'll be out of communication starting at 0100. If this works, we'll be heading back a little over an hour later with One Zero in tow. Over."

"This is Five. Good copy. Be advised that Rocky Lariat's higher has done an about-face on this mission. As of two hours ago, you're completely sanctioned. How copy? Over."

Reese couldn't keep the grin off his face. He also couldn't imagine what in hell had led to such a turn of events. "Roger, copy. Anything further? Over."

"This is Strider Five," Pierce answered. "Negative further. Over."

"This is Six, roger. Stick by the radio. I'll be back to you as soon as I can. Over."

"Strider Five, standing by. Out."

Reese gave the handset back to the RTO and went to where he was bedding down for the night. He had told Torres he wanted half of the men to try to sleep while the other half stood guard, but almost everyone was wide awake. Exhausted as they were, they were too wired to relax. A few tried to eat something, but most did little more than nibble at their rations.

Reese choked down a couple of cans of C-rations without even noticing what he ate. After washing the tasteless food down with warm water from his canteen, he stuffed the empty cans back into his rucksack, wrapped his poncho liner around him and tried to get comfortable.

Usually he could sleep anywhere anytime, but he wasn't able to drop off right away tonight. His eyes automatically scanned the dark jungle below their ridge, looking for the enemy he knew was there. A few hours later, when the moon came up, it would be easier for them to watch the approaches as well as to move through the jungle themselves. In the pitch-black now, however, he strained his ears, listening for sounds of movement through the jungle below.

Reese's only concern right now was for Santelli and the rest of his men. Too much was riding on the raid tonight. If even the smallest thing went wrong, very few of them would live to see the morning.

He went over his plan again and again in his mind, trying to find the weak points in it, but he could find nothing that could be improved upon without having to make a recon of the objective. Considering that he knew nothing about the enemy's positions around Santelli, the plan was in the hands of the gods of war now. He willed himself to relax and finally drifted off into a light sleep.

24

Camp A-410, Ban Phoc

Dick Clifford went into the back room of the bunker for another cup of Pierce's industrial-strength coffee before returning to his radio watch. His stomach was already rebelling under the onslaught of the caffeine, but he couldn't stop drinking the vile stuff now. He had to stay awake until Reese called back to tell him if the night rescue attempt had been successful.

Pierce and Hank Wheeler had been scheduled for the night watch in the bunker, but both of them were sacked out on the bunks in the back room with the coffeepot. When the team sergeant had learned that Clifford planned to stay up all night, he promptly went to sleep.

Clifford didn't understand how in hell the two Special Forces men could sleep at a time like this. He was so keyed up that he couldn't have slept if his own life had depended on it. Never having spent time in the field, he hadn't learned the one thing all veteran soldiers knew by heart: never pass up a chance to catch a little shut-eye.

He shook his head and walked back out to the big room and headed over to the large-scale topographical map of the Parrot's Beak that Reese had tacked on the wall. Slowly sipping hot black coffee, he carefully studied the terrain around Santelli's position. Reading a map was no substitute for actually seeing the lay of the land in person, he knew, but it was the closest he would ever get to the action. He didn't regret the way he fought his personal war; at the same time he rather envied men like Reese who fought their war in a way he would never know.

Clifford was reasonably sure he would do well under fire. He knew he would never have the chance to test his courage that way. While he didn't want to live the life Reese did, he would have liked to have one chance to prove to himself what he was made of.

He glanced down at his watch again. Reese should be calling in soon to report he was moving out. The CIA man strode across the room to the radio. He leaned back in the folding metal chair, cradling the plastic coffee cup between his hands, forcing himself to keep from glancing at his watch every thirty seconds. He didn't see how in hell the team's radiomen could stand the monotony of pulling the night watch all the time. It would have driven him stark raving mad within a week.

He picked up a battered week-old copy of *Stars and Stripes* and thumbed through the pages without seeing the words. Throwing the paper down, he got back on his feet and paced up and down the confines of the small room, stretching and swinging his arms. What in hell was Reese doing? Why hadn't he called?

REESE STARTED awake when he felt a hand over his mouth. In the moonlight he saw one of the Nungs crouched beside him. The striker put a finger to his lips. The Special Forces officer brought his arm up close to his face and looked at his watch. The luminous dial read 1:35 a.m. He nodded to the Nung and sat up.

In the silvery light the jungle below looked like a dream landscape of vivid light and dark shadows. The rescue team would be able to move more quickly because they could see where they were going; but it was also light enough that if they weren't real careful, the enemy could also see them coming. The final approach to the NVA's lines was going to be a real bitch. Of course, no one had ever said this thing was going to be easy.

Wrapping his poncho liner around himself for warmth, Reese quietly secured his weapons and walked to the center of the patrol's star perimeter. Waiting for him were Torres, Vao and five of the Nungs. The moonlight revealed that all of them had renewed the sweat-streaked camouflage greasepaint on their faces and hands and had stripped their gear down to the basics: one full canteen, their weapons, knives and ammunition.

In a whisper Reese went over the plan one last time before making a quick call to tell Ban Phoc they were on their way. An obviously nervous Clifford took the call and wished him luck. The men split into their two groups, and Reese led his team silently down the side of the ridge into the jungle below. The black and green stripes of their cammies and face paint melted into the light and dark of the jungle's harsh shadows thrown by the moon. As long as they stayed out of the direct moonlight, they were almost invisible from just a few feet away.

Torres and his three Nungs followed close behind them. Even under the best of conditions, navigating at night was always difficult, and this wasn't even close to the best conditions. Reese was keeping close to the shadows, and if Torres lost track of them now, he'd never find them again in this terrain.

As silently as ghosts, the six men hurried to their rendezvous with Santelli.

LIKE ONE of the night shadows, Reese quietly crept up on the first of the enemy positions in the ring around Santelli's small hill, the silenced Ruger pistol in his hand. The four-power telescopic sight had been mounted on it so that he could be sure to get the necessary first-shot kills. Even though it wasn't a Starlite scope, the telescope's optics would intensify the light of the moon and stars and allow him to see his targets more clearly.

The Ruger's magazines were loaded with .22 Long Rifle hollowpoint ammunition that would open up to .30-caliber size upon impact. The success of this operation depended on Reese getting the rounds into the brains of his targets on the first shot to paralyze their nervous systems. A hit anywhere else might cause them to cry out, so he needed to make head shots in either the temple or the upper face.

Following close behind him, Vao held the naked blade of a K-bar knife in his right hand. The fighting knife had been presented to him by one of his earlier SF commanders, and over the years it had bled the life out of more than one careless Communist soldier.

The other two Nungs, their fingers on the triggers of their M-16s, were close on Vao's heels. On the initial hits they were backup in case Reese and Vao were discovered and had to run for it. Other than that they would stay well back under cover and let the two men make their silent kills by themselves.

Reese's first objective was a machine gun position fifty feet in front of him. The North Vietnamese usually manned their guns with three men and, peering through the brush, he saw the ruby glow of two cigarettes at the NVA position. A third man might be sleeping somewhere nearby. If he was, Vao would have to take him out with his knife.

Reese was pleased to see that the NVA felt comfortable enough to light up at night. That meant they weren't expecting visitors.

He ducked back and checked the faintly glowing numbers on his watch dial. In half an hour Torres and his team were scheduled to open up on the enemy positions on either side of the small hill. It was also time for him to make his move.

The Special Forces officer touched Vao's arm. When the Nung warrior looked at him, Reese held up two fingers, made smoking gestures and then pointed to himself. Vao nodded. Reese then held up one finger, making a sleeping gesture by placing his folded hands against his tilted face and then shrugged. Vao nodded again. Next Reese slashed swiftly across his arm with one finger. Vao grinned and nodded. Reese finished his silent orders by tapping his watch and holding up two fingers. The captain was going to shoot in two minutes.

The Nung was as silent as death as he started to crawl up to the machine gun position. The blade of his K-bar had a matt-black finish, and a mere quarter inch of the bare, sharpened edge showed bright metal.

One of the NVA guards turned around to flick his cigarette butt away and saw the brief flash of reflected light from the knife. He leaned forward, raised his AK and squinted into the uncertain darkness.

Peering through the pistol scope, Reese saw the NVA nudge his partner. The second man raised his weapon, as well. Reese knew that, somehow, they had spotted Vao. Holding the Ruger steady with both hands, the captain sighted in on the head of the NVA nearest the Nung.

The Ruger popped and the .22-caliber rounds slammed into the NVA's temple right above his ear. He grunted as he collapsed. His buddy called out in alarm and reached for him just as Reese shifted his point of aim and fired two more shots. The second man fell over the body of the first.

Instantly Vao leaped to his feet, ran the last few steps to the machine gun pit and jumped inside, his knife ready. Even though his eyes were adapted to the darkness, the bottom of the pit was pitch-black in the shadow. He knelt and, extending his left hand, cautiously felt around. A vague shape stirred at his feet and he lunged for it.

Clamping his hand over the NVA's mouth, Vao pressed the point of his knife against the junction of the struggling man's neck and shoulder. When he was certain of the blade's placement, he slammed it in to the hilt and gave it a vicious twist, opening both the NVA's carotid artery and his jugular vein.

The North Vietnamese was unconscious in less than five seconds. He was dead in less than sixty.

Reeking from the hot blood that had sprayed on him, Vao ripped the ammunition belt from the machine gun and dropped it outside the foxhole. Had he not been afraid of making a loud, metallic noise that would carry on the night air, he would have removed the bolt from the weapon and thrown it away, as well.

Scrambling back out of the pit, Vao huddled in the dark, waiting for Reese. The officer suddenly appeared in front of him. Vao held up three fingers and then closed them one by one against the palm of his hand. All three NVA were dead. Reese glanced down at his watch. The kill had taken less than two minutes.

The other two Nungs of his team quickly joined them by the machine gun pit. Reese sent them out to the left flank while he motioned Vao to follow him to the right. He wanted to take out at least one more position on each side of the machine gun pit for insurance.

The two North Vietnamese in the next position on the right were asleep and, while Reese steadied his pistol on the side of a tree trunk and sighted in on them, Vao crept up to their foxhole. The knife flashed twice.

When Vao silently rejoined him, Reese could smell the piercing metallic reek of fresh blood on the cool night air. The other two Nungs came back smelling the same.

Now that the other position was taken care of, Reese left Vao and the two Nungs at the machine gun pit to guard the open hole in the enemy line. Keeping to the shadows, he slowly made his way up the side of Santelli's ridge line.

This was where the operation could get tricky. He had told Santelli which way he was coming in, but there was no way they could exchange signals without giving themselves away. He could only hope the young LT had made damn sure all of his strikers knew he was coming. One nervous finger on the trigger and it would all be over.

He was only a little over halfway up the hill when he heard a faint noise in front of him. Halting instantly, he crouched low to the ground, his finger tensed on the trigger of the Ruger.

"Captain?" someone whispered from a few feet in front of him.

"Yeah," he answered softly in relief, relaxing the pressure on the trigger.

"It's Santelli, sir."

Reese got to his feet and followed the lieutenant to the top of the hill. Santelli's people were drawn into a small circle at the edge of their old perimeter. Like Reese's team, they were pared down to their bare essentials of weapons and ammunition. In the center of the hill he could see a stack of rucksacks in the moonlight.

"Welcome to the party, Captain," Kowalski whispered.

Reese grinned, the moonlight reflecting off his teeth. "Get ready," he said quietly, glancing down at his watch. "It won't be long now. As soon as Torres opens up, we'll get the hell out of here. Old Vao and two strikers are waiting for us at the bottom of the hill."

Suddenly the stillness of the night exploded. Streams of dull red tracer fire lanced from the jungle on the other side of the ridge, and the darkness was shattered by the flash of grenade explosions in the middle of the enemy positions. Torres and his men were right on time.

Caught off guard, the enemy quickly returned fire. Over the light chatter of the Nungs' M-16s Reese could hear the harsher bark of AKs, the rattle of heavy machine guns and the shouts of the NVA officers as they frantically tried to rally their troops.

"Let's go," Reese said quietly.

With Reese taking the lead to guide them, the Nung sterile team started down the side of the hill first. If they ran into any opposition, the sound of their AKs firing would confuse the NVA into thinking they were firing on their own people. Warily Santelli and his other men followed behind them in single file, their fingers on their triggers.

On the other side of the hill behind them the NVA had brought their mortars into play. The hollow, ringing sound as the rounds left the tubes echoed through the trees. The fleeing men crouched even lower until they heard the mortar rounds explode in the jungle on the other side of the hill.

At the bottom of the hill Vao and the two Nungs suddenly appeared from the shadows, took the point position and quickly led them away.

The fleeing men had gone less than a klick when a thunderous explosion shook the jungle and a flash lit up the night. Obviously the enemy had sent someone up the hill to check on Santelli, and some curious NVA had triggered Webb's booby trap.

Now the enemy knew for sure that the recon team had slipped through their fingers. Reese just hoped to hell that Torres and his people had been able to break away in time.

"Let's move it out," he said urgently. If the NVA has anything on the ball, they'll be scouring the vicinity for them ASAP. Keeping a close watch on their rear, the small column pushed on through the night.

25

April 20, Camp A-410, Ban Phoc

In the command bunker Clifford stared dumbly at the quiet radio console in front of him. His night-long vigil had completely exhausted him physically and mentally. His stomach was a pool of burning acid, his butt ached from the hours he'd sat in the torturous folding metal chair and he was having trouble focusing his mind on anything. He looked up blearily when Sergeant Pierce walked in from the back room.

Pierce saw that the CIA man was beat down to his socks. "Why don't you go try to get some sleep, sir?" he suggested, carefully pulling his fatigue jacket over the bandage on his shoulder. "I can take over the radio watch now."

Clifford shook his head heavily. "I've got to call the colonel and let him know I've lost communication with them."

"Why don't you give them a little more time, sir? It's still not first light outside, and they've probably turned off their radios. We do that at night so we won't give our position away if someone tries to call us. Sound travels quite far at night. Why don't you give them till dawn at least?"

Clifford staggered to his feet and grabbed his coffee cup from the table. Halfway to the coffeepot, he grimaced and turned around. "How do you stand this shit, Sarge?"

"Oh, the coffee's not so bad once you get used to it, sir."

"No." Clifford shook his head violently. "The waiting, the uncertainty. Sitting night after night in this shit box, drinking too much of that goddamn coffee and waiting to hear if someone's gotten themselves wasted." He shook his head again. "What a fucking way to live."

Pierce smiled. "It's not all that bad, either, sir. You get used to it, too, after a while."

"Not if I can fucking help it." Clifford was still trying to shake his head clear. "From now on I'm keeping my young ass in Tan Son Nhut where I belong."

The radio suddenly burst into life. "Rocky Lariat, Rocky Lariat, this is Dusty Strider Six. Over."

Clifford sprang to the radio microphone. "This is Lariat. Send it."

"This is Strider Six," Reese radioed. "Be advised we've joined up with the Strider One Zero element and are back at our Romeo Oscar November. We'll be leaving this location in three zero. Over."

"This is Lariat. What's your status? Over."

"This is Six. One Zero has your package and we hope to deliver it by dark. Over."

Clifford sighed with relief. The BDA films would get Colonel Marshall off his ass, but he still wished he had more information about the men he'd sent on the mission.

"Lariat, roger, copy. Anything further? Over."

"This is Strider Six. Negative. Out."

Clifford put the handset down and went over to the map. "Do you think he can get out by nightfall?"

Pierce joined him at the map. "I think so. It's going to be a real hump, though." He paused for a moment. "And it's going to depend a lot on Charlie. The captain's got almost a full platoon in there with him now, and it's real hard to keep that many people hidden in the woods."

Clifford stared at the map for a few more seconds before turning away. "I'm going to get some sleep now. Call me if anything happens."

"No sweat, sir."

Pierce watched the CIA man slowly climb the stairs leading out of the bunker and smiled to himself. Clifford wasn't really a bad guy at heart. Maybe if he stayed around the camp for a few more weeks, he might figure out what this war was all about.

THE FIRST TENDRILS of dawn were just stretching across the sky when Reese passed the handset back to the Nung RTO. Torres and his men had been waiting for him when his column had closed in on the patrol base, and now that he finally had all his people back together Reese gave them a brief rest break. They apparently were safe where they were as long as they didn't stay too long. The troops needed the time to redistribute the remaining equipment and ammunition between themselves and grab a hurried meal before they moved out again.

He went over to where he'd left his rucksack and rummaged inside to find something to eat. He was spooning the last of a can of C-ration peaches into his mouth when Santelli walked up. In the early daylight the lieutenant was showing the strain of his mission and the long night march. His dark eyes were bloodshot and his unshaven face looked haggard. He took his bush hat off and rubbed the back of his neck.

"Have a seat," Reese said, patting the ground beside him. "You look beat. You had anything to eat?"

"I had a LRRP bar," Santelli answered, dropping to a crouch beside his CO. "Look, sir, I really didn't get a chance to thank you for saving our asses last night. I thought for sure those fuckers were going to do a Custer number on us up there."

Reese placed his hand on the lieutenant's shoulder. "I couldn't let them waste you, LT," he said with a smile. "It takes a long time to get an officer replacement, and I need you to run the camp for me."

"I think I'm about ready for a little of that right now." Santelli's smile was weary. "This running around in the woods kind of gets to you after a while."

"Unfortunately," Reese sighed, slipping into his rucksack straps and getting to his feet, "we've still got a lot of ground to cover before we're home free, so let's get 'em back on their feet and moving."

"Yes, sir," Santelli said, standing. "And thanks again."

"No sweat, GI."

Three hours later Kowalski hurried up the jungle trail to Reese. "Captain," he panted, "we've got us a problem again."

"Let me guess," Reese said wearily. "We've got NVA coming up on our ass again."

The sergeant knelt by the captain's side and pulled out his map. "The drag team says there's at least a company of them coming on fast."

"How long do you think we have?"

"Half hour or less."

Reese bent down and looked at Kowalski's map. With as many men as he had now the only way they could make good time had been to keep to the established trails instead of trying to break jungle. They had covered a lot of ground this morning, but they had been making a trail that even a blind man could follow. He had been taking a risk moving that way, but most of the men had been on the march for almost twelve hours straight. Breaking jungle would have quickly worn them out completely.

It had been a good try. Now the men were almost at the end of their endurance. Even keeping to the established trails, there was no way they could outrun a fresh enemy force moving up behind them.

Reese made a sudden command decision. He was tired of running. As far as he was concerned, it would be better to stop and fight now rather than let themselves be run to ground like frightened rabbits chased by a pack of dogs.

"You feel up to giving them a little grief?" Reese asked casually as he scanned the map and the terrain around them.

Kowalski shrugged. "We might as well give it a try, Captain. I don't see that it's going to get a hell of a lot better anytime in the near future, so we'd better do it now while we still can."

"Okay," Reese said, his finger tapping the map. "It looks like there might be some kind of clearing a couple hundred yards farther on. Take the point on up there, check it out for an ambush site and get back to me. I'll get the rest of them moving." When Kowalski left, Reese called Santelli over. "We've got to break contact with those fuckers," the captain explained. "I sent Kowalski up ahead to recon an ambush site."

Santelli glanced around at the Nungs. Most of them were too tired even to keep a good watch on their rear. Another hour or two on the run and they'd be too exhausted to fight. "I wish we didn't have to do this, sir. But you're right. We can't keep running much longer."

"If we do a good enough job on these guys," Reese said, "we can rest for a couple of hours afterward."

"I sure as hell hope so, sir."

"Let's get on it. The sooner we get it done, the sooner we can take a break."

When Reese reached the edge of the small clearing, he found Kowalski waiting for him. "What do you think, sir?" the NCO asked, his eyes sweeping the area.

Reese surveyed it critically. The opening in the jungle was about two hundred yards deep by a hundred wide. The bush and grass was sparse, not enough to give good cover, but the jungle on the opposite side was thick and perfect to hide an ambushing force. The trail led right through the middle, and as fast as the pursuing NVA were moving, they would probably keep to the trail rather than fan out to the flanks. Particularly if it appeared to them that their quarry hadn't left the beaten path.

The Special Forces officer turned back to Kowalski. "This should do nicely, Sarge. Take them on down the trail, but don't let them stop till they get to the trees on the other side. I don't want any tracks leading off the trail."

"Yes, sir."

"When you're well back into the trees, fan them out on both sides of the tree line. Get good firing positions and cover your flanks, but keep them well back and make sure they're out of sight from the clearing." Reese motioned Webb over to him. "Find out how many claymores we have left, Sarge, and set them up at the tree line covering our trail."

"Yes, sir."

"LT," Reese said, turning to Santelli, "did you leave your Ruger back on that hill?"

The lieutenant patted the bulge inside his tiger-striped jacket. "Never fucking happen, sir."

Reese smiled. "Good. Follow me. You and I are going to announce this party."

While Reese and Santelli walked back into the tree line at the far end of the clearing, Webb took the only two claymores he could find and set them up on the sides of the trail some twenty yards out, aimed at a killing zone centered on the trail. After camouflaging the mines with long grass, he trailed the firing wires back into the edge of the trees and found a position from which he had good observation of the clearing.

Fifty yards back into the jungle, Reese found a good ambush position and explained his plan to Santelli. The lieutenant grinned broadly. "That ought to surprise those little fuckers," the junior officer said.

"That's the general idea, LT," Reese said, grinning back.

As soon as everyone was in position, Reese dropped his rucksack and settled back behind his tree to wait. After checking the Ruger pistol and the magazine in his CAR-15, he broke open a LRRP ration and added water to it. He couldn't remember when he'd last had a full meal, and he was suddenly so hungry that he started spooning the food into his mouth before it had a chance to soak up the water. He forced himself to stop after a couple of bites. Eating a half-done LRRP would give anyone cramps when it expanded in the stomach, and that was the last thing in the world he needed right now.

He took a long swig from his canteen, swirled the water around in his mouth and swallowed it. The water was warm, flat and tasted of plastic. Pulling his bottle of salt tablets from his rucksack, he downed a couple and followed them with more stale water. By this time the ration was rehydrated enough to eat. He stuffed the greasy rice-and-pork mixture into his mouth as fast as he could, swallowing without chewing.

In a few short minutes the food and salt revived him. He almost felt like a new man; all he needed now was a shower and a good night's sleep and he'd be one hundred percent. In the meantime there was still the little matter of a company of North Vietnamese biting at their heels. If the drag team was right, he wouldn't have long to wait for them.

A few minutes later the Nung nearest him signaled and dropped back down into cover. Their guests were coming.

Reese got to his feet and stood behind the tree, the scoped Ruger in his hand. A few feet away Lam Noc and another Nung from the sterile team crouched under the leaves and grass, their AKs poised. Across the trail Santelli waited with his own silenced Ruger.

Through the leaves Reese watched the NVA point man cautiously enter the tree line. The man was good, the American had to give him that. He carefully checked both sides of the trail and the ground in front of him as he passed under the cover of the trees at the edge of the clearing. The question was, was he good enough to spot the ambush?

The point's backup man, the slack, wasn't as alert as the point man was. Reese smiled: the guy was walking along with his eyes to the ground as if he were on a Sunday stroll. That would make Santelli's job much easier.

As soon as the point man got within fifty yards of his tree, Reese took a two-handed grip on the Ruger and, bracing his forearm against the tree trunk, stuck the end of the barrel through the leaves. He wanted to sight in on the man's temple, right above his ear, but the soldier was wearing an oversize apple-green NVA pith helmet that covered the target point. Reese didn't want to risk the chance that he would strike the helmet, deflecting the small-caliber bullet, so he shifted his sight picture. Shooting the corner of the man's eye was more difficult because of the thickness of the skull around the eye socket, but it was all he had. Reese held the sight picture steady as the point man walked closer, still holding his fire. He wanted his target to get deeper under the cover of the trees.

The point man was only twenty yards away when he suddenly stopped and turned to look into the jungle, as if he'd seen something. Reese's finger tightened on the trigger as he slid his sight picture over to center on the MVA's eye and fired.

The enemy's head snapped forward, and he was dead before he had even started to fall. The slack barely had time to register what had happened to his partner before Santelli planted two rounds into the side of his head. He, too, fell without a sound.

Lam Noc and the other Nung commandos sprang from cover and raced out to the trail. Grabbing the dead NVA soldiers under the arms, they hastily dragged the bodies back into the brush. Lam dashed back out, snatched up the point man's pith helmet and clapped it on his own head.

With the second Nung hanging back to cover him, Lam Noc slowly walked back out to the edge of the clearing, his AK held at port arms. Raising his right arm, he motioned the NVA forward. As soon as the enemy's lead element stepped out onto the trail, he calmly turned and went back into the trees as if he were taking up the point position again.

The NVA company started across the clearing at a slow trot. They were on the alert, but not overly so. Their point man had signaled that the way ahead was clear.

26

Parrot's Beak, Cambodia

Hunkered down at the edge of the tree line, Webb watched tensely as the enemy lead element came across the clearing toward him. These guys were hard hats, NVA regulars, which was bad news. They were well equipped with rocket launchers and squad machine guns, and they looked fresh. If this little scheme of the captain's didn't work, the good guys were going to find themselves in a world of pain real fast. The Mike Force Nung strikers were light infantry. They weren't equipped to stand and slug it out toe-to-toe with well-armed North Vietnamese regulars.

Suddenly feeling exposed, the demo man crouched even lower, the firing devices for the claymores in his hands. When the NVA were only twenty-five yards from the trees, he squeezed the firing handles on the clackers, scrunching his eyes shut as he did. The thundering blasts of the two antipersonnel mines slashed a wide swath through the enemy formation, dropping over a dozen of them with the deadly flying pellets.

The explosion was still echoing through the trees when the Nungs opened up on the rest of them with everything they had, drowning out the cries of the wounded in a storm of small-arms fire.

The stunned NVA troops frantically dived for cover, but Reese had chosen his battlefield well. There was little protection in the clearing from the relentless fire. A few tried to charge the Nung positions in the tree line and were cut down before they could run more than a few steps.

The enemy soldiers in the center of the formation broke and ran for cover at the opposite edge of the clearing. The second they popped their heads up, someone fired at them. A deadly hail of 40 mm HE grenades rained down on them as the Nung M-79 gunners fired as fast as they could stuff the fat cartridges into the breeches of their shotgunlike grenade launchers.

For the first sixty seconds Reese's men had everything their own way. Then things changed.

By the time Reese and Santelli had run back up to the Nung positions at the edge of the tree line, the NVA soldiers had organized themselves and were returning stiff counterambush fire. AK and heavy machine gun fire from the far side of the clearing raked the foliage, but far more dangerous was the rain of rocket-propelled grenades from the RPG launchers. Although they had been designed as an antitank rocket, the 82 mm RPG rounds made a deadly antipersonnel weapon, as well. On impact the rocket warheads sprayed the trees with shrapnel. Without fighting holes to protect them from the frag the Nungs could only lie where they were and take it.

Ducking behind a tree to escape the blast from one of the rocket rounds, Santelli snatched an M-79 and a bandolier of ammunition from one of the Nungs. Snapping the weapon open with a practiced flick of the wrist, he stuffed an HE round into the breech and snapped it shut. Flipping up the front sight and adjusting it for range, he carefully sighted in on the backblast of a North Vietnamese RPG gunner on the far side of the clearing and squeezed the trigger.

His eyes followed the HE round on its slow trajectory through the air and was rewarded with a secondary explosion when the 40 mm grenade set off a pile of RPG rockets. "Get the RPGs!" he shouted to the other M-79 gunners.

The Nungs shifted their fire to the far edge of the clearing and the rain of RPG rounds faded. Santelli snapped off two more shots and handed the launcher back to the striker. The enemy small-arms fire, however, was still heavy, and even with the protection of the tree line, the Nungs were taking casualties.

From his position where the trail entered the trees, Reese saw one of the strikers come up on one knee to sight in on his target. A burst of AK fire spun him around, and he slumped to the ground, shot through the head. Regardless of their casualties, however, it looked like the battle was starting to go their way. NVA bodies littered the clearing and the enemy fire seemed to be slacking off a little. If their ammunition held out, they might win this one.

Shouting encouragement, Reese took careful aim and triggered off a long burst of 5.56 mm from his CAR-15. The range was a little too long for accurate shooting with the submachine gun, but he had to do something useful.

The enemy company commander knew he was in trouble. The Mike Force had him cold. Shouting at his men on the edge of the clearing to keep up the volume of fire, he ordered his sergeant to pull some of his troops back and try to get around through the trees on the Yankees' left flank. By twos and threes North Vietnamese soldiers disengaged and made their way around the end of the clearing.

Vao and his men were on the far left flank of the firefight. So far they hadn't been hard-pressed; most of the fighting had been to their right where the trail cut through the clearing. The old Nung was directing fire when he spotted movement through the trees to his left.

Shouting a battle cry in the ancient Nung Chinese dialect, Vao leaped to his feet, the M-16 in his hands blazing fire as he charged directly for the enemy. When Vao cried out, the other strikers on his team left their positions and charged into the woods after him.

Now that they had been spotted the NVA flanking element opened up on the Nungs. An AK bullet caught Vao under the right collarbone. The old warrior staggered and fell forward onto the ground. He struggled to raise himself, but collapsed.

When their leader fell, the Nungs went crazy. Screaming, they charged through the trees, hurling grenades and firing their weapons from the hip. The other strikers heard their brothers and ran to join them. There was no stopping the Nungs, so the Americans followed them.

For a moment the North Vietnamese poured fire into their screaming attackers. When it seemed to have no effect, they broke and tried to run back around the edge of the clearing. Caught in a cross fire from the Nungs behind them and those still in the tree line, they were chopped to pieces.

The enemy commander decided to run, too. Pulling back his few remaining troops, they faded into the jungle behind them. The last running NVA fell as Kowalski emptied the last half of his CAR-15's magazine into him.

A stunned silence fell over the battlefield. For a few seconds the only sounds that could be heard were the moans of the wounded.

SANTELLI SLOWLY ROSE to his feet and looked around the clearing. Once more he had come through the battle without a scratch. The Nungs were already scouring the battlefield, dispatching the enemy wounded with shots to the head. There was no need for silence after a firefight of that size. Anyone within two miles knew exactly where they were.

Dropping the half-empty magazine from the bottom of his K, Santelli automatically slapped a fresh one into place before moving out into the open. That was his last full magazine and he had already stripped the 9 mm rounds from his Hi-Power pistol magazines to use in his submachine gun. One more firefight, even a small one, and he would be completely out of ammunition. It was time to pick up an undamaged AK-47 and a full magazine carrier from one of the enemy dead.

He was choosing a weapon from the dozens that littered the clearing when he heard Kowalski call to him. "LT, over here! Vao's down!"

The lieutenant hurried back under the trees.

"It looks pretty bad, sir," Kowalski said.

Kneeling at Vao's side, Santelli ripped open the Nung's blood-soaked cammie jacket. The puckered entry wound high on his chest bubbled frothy blood: the bullet had entered his lung. Santelli placed the palm of his hand over the wound to seal it while he lifted Vao to a sitting position to check the exit wound. He felt jagged pieces of shoulder blade protruding from his back. That was bad and good. They meant that the bullet was no longer lodged in his body, but his lung was pierced and there was a serious danger of it collapsing before they could get him to a field hospital.

Vao's eyes were glazed with pain. "I told Sergeant Pierce that I heard the tiger call my name."

"Don't talk," Santelli ordered him sharply. "You've been shot in the lung and I've got to seal the holes."

Kowalski ripped open a field dressing and handed the foil-lined wrapper to Santelli. The lieutenant slapped the foil side against the entry wound and held it in place. "I need another one for the back," he snapped.

The sergeant quickly handed another dressing to him. After sealing the exit wound, Santelli placed the field dressing pad over the entry wound and secured the tag ends of the ties as tightly as he could around Vao's chest. The second dressing was placed over the exit wound and tied in place.

Santelli leaned over the Nung. "Cough as hard as you can. You've got to reinflate your lung."

The greatest danger of a sucking chest wound was that it allowed outside air into the chest cavity, diminishing the lungs' ability to inflate. If a man couldn't fill his lungs, he died.

Vao tried unsuccessfully to draw a deep breath.

Santelli raised the Nung to his feet. "Cough, goddamn you!"

This time the Nung was able to draw in enough air to cough weakly. A froth of blood appeared at the corner of his mouth.

"Cough again!"

The Nung coughed more strongly this time, spraying blood on Santelli. This time he was able to breathe, and he sucked the air deep into his lungs.

Santelli sat him back down, plugged a bag of blood expander into his arm and called for a litter. Through one of the interpreters he told the Nungs carrying him that if the old soldier started coughing again, they should stop and get him on his feet so that he wouldn't drown in his own blood. Vao joined the other casualties while Santelli went to find Reese.

"We've got eight casualties," Santelli told him. "Three dead and another five wounded. Two of them are litter cases, including old Vao. But he's the only one of them in serious danger."

"How's he doing?" Reese asked.

Santelli slowly shook his head. "I don't know. He's got a sucking chest wound. If we could get a Dust-off in here, we could save him. I don't know how long he can hang on without it."

"There's no way in hell they're going to give us a Medevac this far into Cambodia," Reese said grimly. "We're just going to have to keep a close eye on him and try to get him the hell out of here as fast as we can."

"Vao's a good man, sir," Santelli said. "I'd hate to lose him."

"Me, too," Reese said, remembering the old warrior during the night rescue.

He looked over to where the Nung medics were working on their casualties and wrapping limp bodies in ponchos. "If we can," he said quietly, "I want to bring the dead out with us, too."

"The Nungs can handle it," Santelli said. "They hate to leave their brothers behind."

"I know."

Kowalski walked up, wiping the half-dried blood from his hands on his cammie pants. "We're about ready to move out again, sir."

Reese had wanted to give the men a break, but with Vao and the other casualties they had to press on. Every extra minute they spent in Cambodia meant a minute longer before they could get medical attention.

"Good. As soon as you're ready, take the point."

Carrying the litters with the casualties in the middle of the formation, the men moved out again, this time more slowly.

By afternoon Reese's column was moving at a snail's pace and even the younger Nungs were exhausted. In only another two hours or so they would be out of the Parrot's Beak and back on their home turf. Then the choppers would come and take them back to Ban Phoc. It was almost over, and all they had to do was keep putting one jungle boot in front of the other, no matter how slowly.

Reese was in the middle of the formation with Torres when the point element suddenly halted and went to ground. While the exhausted Nungs spread out in the bush, grateful for the halt no matter how long or short it was going to be, Reese hurried to the front of the column. Kowalski was lying on his belly, his map opened in front of him. Reese slipped down beside him, the unspoken question on his face. The sergeant pointed down into the plain below them.

Reese looked and saw a large North Vietnamese encampment, at least two companies, spread out under the sparse vegetation. Thin tendrils of smoke rose from their cook fires, and he could see the enemy resting under makeshift shelters, their weapons close at hand.

"Fuck!" Reese muttered softly, his jaw clenched.

The NVA were camped right in the middle of their escape route, and there were just too damn many of them spread out in the valley to make a detour.

"What are we going to do now, sir?" Kowalski asked quietly. Even the hard-charging veteran sergeant was showing the strain of the past three days. He had been on point since the ambush and was exhausted from watching for the enemy.

"Don't worry, Ski," Reese said, getting to his feet. "I'm going back to talk to that SOG guy. It's about fucking time he lent us a hand with this shit."

"I sure as hell hope he can, sir," Kowalski agreed wearily. "We've come a long fucking way only to have it end so damn close to home."

Reese clapped him on the shoulder. "It's not over yet, Sarge, not till the fat lady sings."

Kowalski smiled weakly. "I just hope to hell that fat bitch has a sore throat today."

27

Cambodia - South Vietnam Border

Reese quickly called the Americans together for a conference on their latest emergency.

"Okay, here's the picture," he said, spreading the map out on the ground. "And we've got us a real problem this time. We're here—" his finger stabbed a point on the map "—and the border's over there, less than an hour away. But, except for the way we came in, we've got NVA all around us."

He looked up for a moment, his eyes moving from one man to the next. "The way I see it we only have two choices. We can wait till nightfall and try to sneak past them or we can backtrack now and try to find another way to get around these guys. We've got our wounded, though, and it'll be a bitch to move them through the hills on our flanks. On top of that it'll take too much time. We need to get them out of here as fast as we can. So, as far as I'm concerned, both options suck heavily."

"Is there any way we can get a lift in here to pick us up?" Santelli asked hopefully.

Reese shook his head slowly. "I really doubt it. Even if SOG would okay it, it's too risky for the slick drivers. If they get shot down inside Cambodia, we'll never get them out. And there are just too damn many of us to go out in one lift."

"This sounds like a job for Superman," Webb muttered. "He can fly by and bomb the shit out of them for us." The proper application of high explosives was always the demo man's answer to life's little problems.

"Actually, that's exactly what I was thinking of," Reese said with a wicked grin. "But with a little help from the Zoomies instead of Superman. I'm going to see if I can get SOG clearance to call a Tac Air strike right on top of their asses. That should ruin their whole fucking day."

"That's not a bad idea," Santelli agreed. "The only problem is that we're still a klick or so inside the border. Do you think the flyboys will risk jumping the fence?"

"That's a chance we'll just have to take." Reese looked grim. "But if I get the right FAC, maybe I can talk him into doing a little creative map reading with me and we can pull this thing off. It's worth a try at least."

"We sure as hell don't have anything to lose, sir," Santelli agreed. "Let's give it a try."

Reese made several notations on his map, marking the location of the center of his unit and the extent of the enemy's positions. He looked up at Santelli. "Go on up with Kowalski and keep an eye on 'em from there while I duck back and try to get through to somebody who can give us a hand with this."

While Santelli went forward, Reese crawled back to where he'd left Torres. "Tony," he called softly, "let's have the radio."

Torres emerged from his concealed position, crawled over to him and gave him the handset.

"Switch it over to the B-40 push," Reese said. As soon as the frequency was set, the captain keyed the mike. "Dry Lightning, Dry Lightning, this is Strider Six, Strider Six. Over."

"This is Dry Lightning," came the reply from the powerful radio station at the B-team headquarters in Can Tho. "Send your traffic. Over."

"This is Strider Six. Let me talk to Lightning Three Alpha. Over."

There was a short pause while the radio operator went to find Three Alpha, the air-ground operations officer. "Six, this is Three Alpha," answered the B-40 staff officer responsible for arranging tactical air strikes in support of Mike Force ground operations. "Go ahead."

"This is Strider Six. I've got a problem here and could use a little priority Tac Air. Over."

"Roger, Strider. Send it."

Giving a target location exactly one klick west of where the NVA were actually located, Reese filled in the air-ground ops officer on his situation. "This can be cleared through Rocky Lariat for confirmation," he added.

"This is Lightning Three Alpha. Good copy, Strider Six. I have your target at 613429. Let me clear this through Rocky Lariat and then I'll check with the blue suiters to see what they have available today. I'll get back to you on that ASAP. Over."

"This is Strider Six. Roger, we'll be waiting. Out." Reese had a big grin on his face when he handed the handset back to the RTO. The only good thing about SOG knowing he was in Cambodia was that maybe Clifford could get them a little help this time and finally get their asses out of this mess.

If he didn't come through, more of his people were going to die.

A little less than an hour later a voice came in over the radio. "Dusty Strider Six, Dusty Strider Six, this is Mac the Fac, the Blue Bird of Happiness, on your push. Over."

Reese looked up into the sky, but he couldn't see the small spotter plane of the Air Force forward air controller. He must have been keeping station well out of sight so as not to give the North Vietnamese any warning of what was soon coming their way.

"Mac, this is Six," Reese radioed back. "I hear you loud and clear. How about me? Over."

"This is Mac," the air controller answered. "I've got you Ham and Limas. Look, I've got a bunch of thirsty birds up here just loitering around in the sky burning gas, so where's my target? Over."

"This is Six, roger. Your target is the troops in the woods in front of us at 603429. My center mass is nine hundred yards due east and my flanks are out a hundred yards on either side. Make your runs north to south and you can't miss 'em. The only thing we've seen in the way of triple A is the usual small-arms stuff. Nothing major. Over."

"This is Mac, roger. My poop sheet says your target is supposed to be at 613. The numbers you just gave me put you right over the border in No-No land. What's the story? Over."

"This is Six," Reese answered. "Look, Mac, we've got NVA all over us down here, we've got wounded and we're having a little trouble reading the map. How copy? Over."

There was a short pause while the FAC made up his mind about risking his flight to attack a target inside Cambodia. As Reese had suspected, once the flyboys were on the scene, they didn't want to go home with their ordnance still hanging under their wings. Since they'd been dragged away from their air-conditioned club to fly the mission, they might as well make it worthwhile.

"Roger, Six," Mac radioed. "I'm having a little trouble reading my map, too, but I've got you spotted now. Like the man in the song says, 'Get ready 'cause here it comes.' Seven-fifties, nape, rockets, the whole nine yards. You keep your heads down now, you hear?"

"Roger. I'll pop smoke on my flanks, so you'll know who's who down here, but get it going. Over."

"Blue Bird FAC, roger. Out."

Reese and Torres hurried back to rejoin Kowalski and Santelli so they could watch the show and direct the strike. From the ridge line they would have a ringside seat for one of the greatest free shows in all of

Vietnam. Warning all of his people to keep their heads down, Reese had the smoke grenades popped.

As soon as the first tendrils of colored smoke drifted above the trees, the NVA saw it, too. Reese could hear their officers shouting orders as the North Vietnamese scrambled for their weapons. If the jets didn't arrive in a few minutes, they were going to be up to their asses in bad guys again. Already he could hear the thunking sound of mortar rounds as they were shot out of their tubes, heading in their direction.

Even though Reese was scanning the sky for the planes, he almost missed seeing the dark bat wing shapes of the six B-57 Night Intruder Canberra bombers swooping toward the jungle. Normally the twin jet B-57 Canberra bombers stalked the night skies over the DMZ and the border regions, interdicting North Vietnamese supply traffic moving into the South along the Ho Chi Minh Trail. Today Mac the Fac had been able to get six of them from the Eighth Bombing Squadron at Phan Rang to come down south and play around in the Parrot's Beak for a little change of scenery.

It sounded as if the world were coming apart when the 750-pound bombs left the rotary bomb bays of the diving Night Intruders to come crashing down in the middle of the NVA positions. The thundering high-explosive blasts ripped the valley's thin vegetation to splinters, dug deep, smoking craters in the ground and flung men into the air like broken, bleeding dolls. Pulling out of their steep dives, the six Canberra jet attack bombers gracefully banked high in the sky at the end of the valley and bore down on their targets again.

Stunned, the North Vietnamese quickly recovered and ran for the three antiaircraft gun emplacements dug in around their perimeter. Whipping the camouflage nets away from the guns, they frantically cranked the traverse and elevation wheels on them, trying to bring their weapons to bear on their attackers.

Through his field glasses Reese now saw the antiaircraft guns and reached for the radio mike. "Mac, this is Six. Over."

"This is Mac. Go."

"This is Six. Better warn your boys that they have brought out some triple A I didn't spot before. Most of it looks like 37 mm. Over."

"Roger, I've got them spotted," the FAC answered. "We're going after them right now."

One of the antiaircraft guns, the deadly twin-mount 37 mm Russian-built automatic cannon, fired off a few hurriedly aimed shots at the three jets. The glowing orange tracers of the shells sped harmlessly past the speeding Canberras. The other two NVA gun crews had reached their weapons just in time to receive the full fury of the renewed attack from the sky.

Each Canberra bomber carried four 20 mm cannons mounted in its wings, and the hard points on their outer wing panels had been loaded down with five-inch high-velocity high-explosive rockets that day. The cannon barrels belched flame and the rockets ignited with puffs of dirty white smoke to lance down from under the Canberras' broad wings.

The 20 mm HE cannon shells and the heavy rockets slammed into the 37 mm gun emplacements, flinging shredded bodies and pieces of blasted antiaircraft guns high into the air. The few enemy gunners who survived the onslaught were burned to cinders in the second wave of the attack as three Canberras playing follow-the-leader delivered their five-hundred-pound napalm tanks right on top of the antiaircraft gun emplacements. Angry black and red flames boiled up into the sky. The stench of napalm and burned bodies mingled with the sharp, metallic smell of the explosives.

With the antiaircraft threat blown to smoking ruins, the B-57s were now free to continue their runs at their leisure. The first flight of three jets made several more low bomb runs, dropping a pair of 750-pounders on each run. The other three jets circled the enemy and attacked targets of opportunity, blasting anything that moved with their formidable armament.

From their hiding place Reese and his men watched as the B-57s turned the NVA camp into smoking rubble. It looked to them as if the attack was right on target, but it was difficult to see clearly because of the clouds of smoke and dust thrown up by the bomb and rocket explosions.

"Strider Six, this is Mac," came the voice on Torres's radio. "How are we looking down there? Over."

Reese took the handset. "This is Six," he answered. "It looks good to me so far, Mac, but the smoke's obscuring the target."

He suddenly had an idea. "Say, can you do some spotting from the air for me? Over."

"Roger, what do you need? Over."

"We need a clear path to the west," he answered, watching the Canberras sweep low again over the enemy positions, the 20 mm cannons in their wings blazing flame. "If you spot something, let me know. We've got to get the hell out of here as soon as you're done. Over."

"This is Mac, roger. Let me finish this and I should be able to help you. Out."

Across the narrow valley the Canberras made one final pass over what was left of the NVA camp. They dropped all of their remaining ordnance, mounted swiftly into the sky and banked away, heading northward again. Their job was over and there was cold beer waiting for them back at the bar of the Phan Rang Air Force Officers' Club. A guy could work up a real thirst bombing the shit out of Charlie.

A few minutes later the forward air controller was back on the radio to Reese. "Strider Six, this is Mac the Fac. It looks like if you take a bearing of 277, you should be able to sneak past what's left of them down there. Right now I don't think they can find their ass with both hands and a radar set. Over."

Reese chuckled. "Roger, 277. Thanks, Mac. I owe you a cold one. Over."

"I'm making a note of that. You can pay me the next time you get to Tango Sierra November. Just ask for Mac the Fac. Out." High in the smoke-stained sky the small gray Cessna 0-2 wagged its wings as it banked away to the southwest.

28

Just Inside South Vietnam

Extracting Reese and the Mike Force would have been almost anticlimactic had it not been for the bodies of the Nung strikers they carried with them. Once the unit was a klick and a half safely back inside South Vietnam, Reese called a halt and formed a small defensive perimeter in a grassy clearing. As far as he knew, they hadn't been followed, but this was no time to slack off. He took off his bush hat and let the breeze dry the sweat from his short-cropped brown hair as he looked around the plain. They had made it. It had cost the lives of several of the Nung strikers and was probably going to cost him his commission, but he had gotten Santelli's people out. Now they could all go home.

The weary Nungs rested while Reese got on the radio to Pierce to arrange for the lift to take them back to Ban Phoc. "Dusty Strider, Dusty Strider," he radioed. "This is Strider Six. Over."

"This is Strider Five. Go."

"This is Six. We're at the Papa Zulu. Over."

"Five, roger. The birds have been standing by for the past hour and will be en route ASAP. Echo Tango Alpha two zero mikes. Over."

"Six, we'll be waiting. Out."

Since Reese's mission was fully sanctioned now, there had been no need for the sergeant to use underground connections to get the helicopters he needed. Clifford had arranged to have one of SOG's regular flight-support units to come in to get them.

As soon as the call was made, Reese slipped out of his rucksack and went to check on his wounded. The three who could walk were bearing their pain with Oriental stoicism. They were all young and saw their wounds as badges of honor. The Nung with the shattered thighbone on the litter next to Vao had been put out with morphine. He didn't know it yet, but his days as a warrior were over. The medics would be lucky to save his leg.

Vao hadn't been offered morphine, since it would only have further impaired his breathing. He was bearing up as only an old soldier who had been wounded before was able to. His face was sallow but composed and he was breathing easily. Reese knelt by his litter. "How are you doing, Vao?"

The old Nung smiled weakly. "I have been better, *Dai Uy*. But this old man will not die today. The Cong will hear from me yet again."

Reese smiled. From what he had seen of the old Nung, it would take a five-hundred-pound bomb to kill him. "The choppers are inbound. And they'll have you in a hospital in no time now."

Vao looked concerned. "*Dai Uy*, I have been in your hospitals before. Do not let them keep me too long, or I will die from the food."

Reese grinned. "I'll see that they feed you right," he promised. "I'll have our own cook bring you your meals by chopper."

Vao looked relieved. "Thank you, *Dai Uy*. An old man like me can die if he does not eat good food."

"Don't worry," Reese reassured him. "I won't let them starve you to death."

The old Nung closed his eyes, and Reese stood up to let him rest. Going back to where he'd stashed his rucksack, he sat down and leaned against it. Pulling his hat down over his eyes, he willed his tired muscles to relax one by one, letting the tension drain out of his body as he felt the exhaustion overtake him. The two days had taken a lot out of him. His mind was still racing. Even with the choppers coming for them, he knew it wasn't over yet, not by a long shot.

"The slicks are inbound, sir." Torres hurried up to Reese with a radio handset in his hand. "And they've got Dust-off with them. Also, I've got someone on the horn who says he has to talk to you ASAP."

"Who is it?"

"Rocky Lariat."

Reese recognized Clifford's call sign. "Fuck him. He can wait."

Torres grinned. "I'll be more than glad to tell him that for you, sir."

In the distance Reese heard the familiar beat of the Hueys' rotors. He reached for the smoke grenade on his assault harness, pulled the pin and tossed it out in front of him. Thick green smoke billowed into the air.

"Saddle up!" he shouted.

A BONE-WEARY MIKE REESE stepped out of the Huey slick to find Dick Clifford waiting for him at the helipad. Slinging his CAR-15 over his shoulder, the Special Forces officer reached into his fatigue jacket pocket and brought out Santelli's film cans. "Here's your BDA," he said, tossing them to the CIA man.

Clifford pocketed the film canisters without looking at them. "Thanks," he said, his voice flat and expressionless. "Colonel Marshall wants to see you back in Saigon ASAP."

Reese's eyes flicked over to the slick and the poncho-wrapped bodies being off-loaded. "That makes two of us," he said softly.

"How soon can you be ready?" Clifford asked, following Reese's glance.

"Let me get cleaned up, change clothes and talk to Santelli and Pierce first."

"An hour, then?"

"Yeah, that should do it."

"Reese?"

"Yeah?"

"I'm really sorry about this, man." The CIA man sounded sincere. "How many people did you lose?"

Reese looked directly into Clifford's eyes. "Three dead and several more WIA."

"Any of the U.S.?"

Reese shook his head. "No, this time they're all Nung."

"I'm still very sorry."

"So am I," Reese said as he turned to go. "They were damn good people."

Clifford silently watched the Green Beret walk off. He knew what Marshall would do to Reese. It was too bad. The war needed more junior officers like Reese, but that wasn't the way the game was played in the politics of the Vietnam War. Reese was just a little too independent, and that scared the shit out of too many people in high places, particularly people like Colonel Marshall.

The CIA man went back down inside the command bunker to arrange for a chopper to take him and Reese back to SOG headquarters. When that was done, he went back outside and walked down to the helipad with his bag. Self-conscious, he wanted to get completely out of the way of the Special Forces people while they saw to their dead and wounded.

REESE DIDN'T HAVE much to say on the flight to Saigon. He sat back, closed his eyes and tried to rest. Even though he'd had time to grab a quick shower and shave, he was still drained. And he wanted to be at his best when he faced Marshall.

When the chopper landed at the Hotel Three pad at Tan Son Nhut, a jeep was waiting for them with MACV-SOG markings on its front bumper. Reese climbed into the back seat while Clifford gave the driver instructions. It was a short ride over to the low concrete building that housed the secret MACV-SOG headquarters.

The jeep pulled up in front of the building and the men got out. Clifford led Reese through the MP security checkpoints before taking him up to the second floor and Marshall's office. They stopped in front of the colonel's door and Clifford knocked twice.

"Enter."

Letting Clifford go in first, Reese marched into the room and halted the regulation three feet in front of Marshall's desk and brought his hand up in a snappy salute. "Captain Michael Reese reporting as ordered, sir."

Marshall returned his salute with a vague wave of his hand. "You're in a heap of trouble, son," the colonel said, leaning back in his chair. "What do you have to say for yourself?"

Reese maintained his position of attention, his eyes focused on a spot on the wall six inches above Marshall's head. "Nothing, sir."

"Nothing?" Marshall leaned forward. "What the hell do you mean, nothing?"

Reese was silent.

"Listen, Captain," Marshall snapped, "you're about three steps away from deep shit, and I want to know what this is all about."

Reese locked eyes with Marshall. He had decided that if the colonel was going to throw his ass in jail, then he was going to have to work for it. Reese wasn't going to volunteer for the hangman. "I don't know what the colonel's talking about."

Marshall's eyes narrowed. "You know damn good and well what I'm talking about, Reese. Just who in hell do you think you are to try to pull something like that?"

"What do you mean?" Reese tried his best to sound innocent. "Going to the aid of one of my units that had been cut off? That's the job of any commander with half a pair of balls." He paused slightly before adding, "sir."

The colonel's face hardened. "I don't have to listen to that kind of smartmouth shit from any junior officer."

"Maybe General Abrams will have some thoughts on that topic, sir."

"Are you threatening me?"

"No, sir," Reese said, walking the fine line between insubordination and standing up for himself. "But may I remind the colonel that I'm not an assigned member of this command. I'm assigned to the Fifth Group U.S. Special Forces. And, sir, in my organization officers are expected to do everything in their power to preserve the lives of the men under their command. If there's some kind of MACV-SOG regulation that prevents commanders from going to the aid of their troops when they're cut off, then I'm not aware of it, sir. Perhaps I was not properly briefed."

Seeing that he was getting nowhere, Marshall pointed over to the chair where Clifford sat immobile. "I also understand you threatened the life of one of my staff."

"No, sir," Reese replied calmly, his eyes still focused above the colonel's head. "I merely took the necessary steps to ensure that Mr. Clifford wouldn't interfere with the conduct of my duties as I saw them."

"By threatening to have him killed!"

"No, sir." Reese fought back a grin. "I didn't plan to have him killed. I told my strikers only to wound him, not to kill him."

Marshall glared at him. "That alone is worth a general court-martial."

Here it was, the heavy guns, but two could play that little game.

Reese looked the colonel straight in the eye and called his bluff. "I'll be glad to explain my actions to a general court, sir. Particularly to any court-martial that's convened here in Saigon."

Reese knew there was absolutely no chance Marshall would risk exposing Santelli's Cambodia mission by putting him in front of a court-martial. Military courts were open to the public and the press. All it would take would be for one reporter to get even a faint sniff of what had happened and it would be all over for Marshall as well as half of MACV-SOG's operations. Also, if he went before a court, Reese would be entitled to a defense and part of that defense would mean putting Marshall on the witness stand to explain why he had ordered the recon mission in the first place. And second, he would have to explain why he hadn't provided an adequate backup for Santelli's mission.

The colonel looked at him for a long, hard moment. "You think you're pretty fucking smart, don't you, Reese?"

"No, sir," Reese kept his eyes locked straight ahead. "I don't. I'm simply a man who wants to go back to his unit and get on with fighting the war. I didn't ask to take part in this operation, sir, and I must say I don't care for the way it was planned or controlled." He lowered his eyes and looked the colonel straight in the face. "And I'm prepared to explain my position to a court-martial board, sir."

There was dead silence in the room for several long seconds. The tension was thick.

Marshall finally spoke. "Captain, I'm sending you back to your unit. But be advised I'm going to keep a very close eye on you, and I don't want to see your young ass in here again."

Reese kept his face blank. "That makes two of us, sir."

Marshall glared at him for a long moment. "You're dismissed."

Reese rendered him a snappy salute and, doing an about-face, marched out of the room. Clifford followed him out silently, closed the door and stopped in the hall. "Can we talk in my office?" he asked as he blotted the sweat from his forehead with a handkerchief.

Reese shrugged. "Sure, why not?"

He followed the CIA man into a small office off the main hall. Clifford held the door open for Reese and then closed it behind him. "Look," he started for the umpteenth time, "I'm sorry about that in there."

"What?" Reese grinned. "You mean the colonel's ass-chewing? Shit, man. I've had my young ass chewed by experts, and that man's a fucking amateur!"

Clifford looked alarmed and glanced around the room as if he were looking for hidden bugs.

Reese laughed as he slid into the folding metal chair beside Clifford's desk. "Relax. Marshall's much too busy picking the frag out of his ass to worry about listening in on you right now."

"What do you mean?"

"You saw the look on his face when I told him to go ahead and court-martial me." Reese laughed. "He looked like I'd handed him a live grenade. That's the one thing he couldn't allow to happen under any circumstances. And since I'm not really part of your sorry little band here, there wasn't a hell of a lot more he could do to me. He had to let me go." Reese massaged the back of his neck. "Jesus, I'm glad that's over with, though. Getting a colonel pissed off at you isn't what you'd call a good career move."

"I tried to cover for you," Clifford explained. "But your sergeant told me to let him know what had happened."

"That's what he told me," Reese replied. "And it worked in our favor just like Pierce thought it would. We'd have never gotten that Tac Air support in time if it hadn't been for the SOG clearance."

Suddenly Clifford understood, and he sat down heavily in his desk chair, blinking. "You knew all the time that Marshall couldn't do anything to you, didn't you?"

The Special Forces officer smiled slowly. "Well, not really. But I was hoping the fact that we were only op-con to SOG would help me if he tried to get too deep in my shit. When all he could think of was to threaten me with a court-martial, I knew he had to be bluffing. He was holding an empty hand.''

"Well, I'll be damned," Clifford said softly.

Reese slowly pulled himself to his feet and walked over to the door. "I'm going to take off now. I've enjoyed just about as much of this SOG shit as I can stand."

"I'll see you around," Clifford replied.

"Don't take this personally," Reese said with a smile, "but I sure as hell hope not."

29

Tan Son Nhut, Saigon

Once he stepped outside the MACV-SOG Headquarters building, Reese stopped, took a deep breath and looked around the sprawling base. Tan Son Nhut was said to be the busiest airport in the world, and he could well believe it. Every few seconds another plane took off from or landed on the crowded runway. Everything from the tiny olive drab 0-1 Bird Dogs to the big brightly colored civilian Boeing 707s competed for the limited airspace over Saigon.

Tan Son Nhut was so big that it had the population of a small American town. Most of the people were blue suiters who ran the base and looked after the planes, but Army support troops were stationed there as well as Vietnamese and American civilians. These thousands of people spent their working days at Tan Son Nhut without any idea of what was going on right next door inside the MACV-SOG building. As far as Reese was concerned, they were a hell of a lot better off not knowing.

He had learned what the spooks were doing the hard way, and he was lucky to have gotten out of their clutches halfway intact. He had brought his people back from Cambodia and had still managed to hold on to his captain's bars at the same time. Against the odds he had managed to pull it off. Now he could get back to his real job—running a Mike Force company. That called for a big celebration tonight.

Digging out his wallet, he found the business card he'd collected from the reporter he'd met in the Continental Palace. With it in hand he marched across the base to the PX and the phone booths outside the main door. After the usual delay the Vietnamese operator connected him with Laura Winthrop's extension at the United Press office.

"Laura Winthrop," she answered.

"Hi, this is Mike Reese."

The reporter thought for a moment. "Oh, yes, the Green Beret I talked to in the Palace."

"That's the one." Reese smiled to himself. "Look, I've got to stay in town for the evening and I wondered if I could buy you some dinner?"

There was a pause on the line.

"Come on," Reese prompted her. "I know it's short notice, but we can go dutch if you like and talk about who's winning the war."

Laura laughed. "Okay, Mike, you're on. I'll meet you in the rooftop restaurant at the Caravel at seven."

Reese smiled again. "Great, see you at seven."

He took a cab to the Continental Palace again and booked a room for the night. He might be meeting Laura at the Caravel for dinner, but there was no way he was going to try to spend the night there. The place was full of REMFs and asshole reporters, partying as if the end of the world were coming in the morning. He had stayed there once before, and it was impossible to get a decent night's sleep with those guys yelling and chasing their whores up and down the halls at all hours.

Since he hadn't expected to be on the town tonight, he hadn't brought a change of uniform. The one he was wearing was going to have to do for his dinner date. He could, however, wash off the sweat from his session in the colonel's office.

After a long, hot shower he placed a wake-up call with the front desk and lay down on the bed. The past few days were quickly catching up with him, and he wanted to be at his best when he met Laura. He fell asleep instantly.

THE PHONE RANG AT SIX. Reese had been in a deep sleep, dreaming he was still in the Cambodian woods. He woke to find himself in a cold sweat. After quickly showering again, he dressed and descended the broad stairs to the lobby. Out in front of the hotel Reese found one of the swarms of shoeshine boys and gave the kid five hundred piasters to put a quick shine on his jungle boots. It was better than nothing.

It was still early, so he decided to walk to the Caravel instead of taking a cab. With the sun down Saigon was just starting to come alive. By nightfall the streets would be crowded with horny GIs looking for a good time and the Vietnamese who made their living seeing that they got it. It was a buyer's market. Every little hole-in-the-wall bar Reese passed had their greeters standing out in front, trying to entice him inside for a drink with one of their lovely girls. Knowing how the "Saigon Tea" system worked, Reese passed them by.

In between the bars teenage boys came up to him and offered him their sisters' services for a short time or a quick blow job in the next alley. When they saw Reese wasn't interested in acquiring a quick case of the clap, the young salesmen changed gears. They offered him pornographic photos, counterfeit Seiko watches, packs of Marlboros stuffed with machine-rolled joints and little plastic bags full of heroin and hashish. At least the Tet Offensive hadn't changed that part of Saigon; it was still the biggest sin city in all of Southeast Asia.

He finally broke free of the sidewalk salesmen and arrived at the Caravel's rooftop restaurant. He got a table as far away from the stage as possible and nursed a cold German beer while he looked out over the city. Although he didn't like the crowd at the Caravel, he had to admit that it was the only place he knew in-country where you could get a decent German beer. Not only did they stock Löwenbräu, but they had Beck's and St. Pauli Girl, as well. And with the all-American clientele that crowded the bar, the beer was always cold.

As he watched the traffic on the streets below, it occurred to him that he should have put in a land line call back to the camp to let Santelli and Pierce know he wasn't spending the night in Camp LBJ, Long Binh Jail. With Pierce's underground connections, perhaps the sergeant already knew. He'd give them a call, though, when he got back to the hotel, just to put their minds at rest.

While Reese waited for his dinner date a Filipino girl band took to the stage and started their act. Their first song was a loud rendition of Creedence Clearwater Revival's "Proud Mary," sung with that particular flat intonation typical of singers unable to speak real English but who were adept at mouthing the proper sounds. What the lead singer lacked in linguistics, however, she made up for with her crotch-length, thin, purple miniskirt, sleek thighs and white Nancy Sinatra boots.

Reese sipped his beer and focused on the bottom of the singer's miniskirt while she butchered the song.

"I see you've made yourself right at home," Laura said with a laugh.

Reese snapped his eyes back and quickly stood. "Sorry 'bout that. I didn't see you come up."

Laura glanced over at the singer. "That's pretty obvious."

The reporter was wearing a thin white summer dress that hugged her slender body. And, from the way it clung to her, he knew she was wearing very little else. Her long blond mane framed her face and fell freely down her back. She was definitely the best-looking woman he'd seen in many years, stateside or in-country.

"She's a little skinny, don't you think?" Laura asked.

"What?"

"The singer, she's too skinny."

"I guess," Reese shrugged. "I hadn't really noticed."

"That's not what it looked like to me when I came in," she teased as he pulled the chair out for her to sit down.

"Actually, I was thinking about good German beer. Can I get you a Löwenbräu?"

She laughed. "Sure you were. And, yes, I'd love a beer. It's been a hard day."

"What are you working on?" Reese asked to get her off the subject of the all-girl band.

"Oh, nothing much." She tossed her head, flipping her hair over her shoulder. "Just a little piece about the effect of the bombing halt on North Vietnamese traffic along the Ho Chi Minh Trail."

"Sounds like an interesting story," he said, suddenly intrigued. "What's your angle?"

When she leaned her elbows on the table, her full breasts strained against the thin fabric of the dress. Reese had to focus on her face to keep from staring at them.

"MACV's been feeding us a lot of bullshit about how much the supply traffic has been increasing. But we're not buying it. Hanoi promised us they'd curtail their resupply operations in the south if Johnson would stop bombing the North."

"And you believe Hanoi?" Reese asked tensely.

Laura laughed. "Only a little more than I believe the Five O'Clock Follies at MACV." Like most reporters, Laura considered the daily afternoon press conference at the MACV Public Information Office a whitewash session.

Reese relaxed a little. If there was anything he didn't need right now, it was to get hooked up with a reporter who was parroting the Hanoi line. He had already gotten off to a bad start on this tour, and something like that would sink him if the word got around.

"Both sides are lying to us," she said bluntly. "Anyone with half a brain can see that."

"I'm glad to hear you realize that. Too many of your compadres think the North Vietnamese are the truth-tellers in this thing."

"Well, I'm not one of them," she stated flatly.

"I'm glad to hear that, too. Who was it who said that truth is the first casualty of war?"

Laura looked pensive for a moment, then shrugged. "No idea."

The waiter arrived to take their orders and ended that line of conversation. After they ordered steak dinners and another round of Löwenbräu, Laura leaned forward again. "Tell me a little about yourself."

Reese laughed. "Always the reporter?"

"Not really. It's just that I don't know anything about you other than the fact that you're a Green Beret and you've been over here before."

Reese pulled the famous hat out of his uniform pant pocket. "That's a green beret. I'm a Special Forces officer."

She laughed. "I've heard that before. So tell me, why did you want to get into the Special Forces?"

"Well," he said, "it's a long, long story."

"I'd love to hear it."

"Actually, it's not that much of a story," he admitted. "It goes back to Kennedy's 'Ask Not' speech. I was in college, in Army ROTC when I heard it, and it impressed me. Then, when he authorized the Special Forces, I figured that if they were good enough for the President, they were good enough for me, too."

"Where did you go to school?"

"Univerity of Washington, a political science major with a Russian language minor."

"So you speak Russian?"

He grinned. *"Da."*

"That's not much use here, is it?"

"You never can tell, I might run into a Russian adviser to the NVA."

"What do you want to do when this is over?"

Reese hesitated. "I don't know," he said carefully. "I really haven't given it that much thought. Maybe go back to graduate school."

The arrival of their dinners gave Reese an excuse to stop answering her questions about him. They both had a good appetite, and the food was the closest thing to a real American meal in Vietnam. When the waiter cleared the empty plates away, Reese ordered an after-dinner brandy and coffee for himself and a gin and tonic for her.

While they made small talk Reese suddenly thought of a way he could cause a few headaches for Dick Clifford—kind of a payback. "Say," he said, "on your Cambodian story, if you can protect your source, I can give you a tip."

Now Laura was all business. "We always protect our sources," she said, eyes sparkling. "Freedom of the press and all that."

"Okay. Have you ever heard of an outfit called the Studies and Observations Group?"

She frowned. "I think I've heard of them. Aren't they some kind of weather-forecasting thing? Or a tactical studies think tank?"

Reese bit back a laugh. Keeping a straight face, he said, "Well, I guess that's part of what they do. I don't really know all that much about them. But if you really want to talk to someone who does know a lot about the North Vietnamese traffic on the Ho Chi Minh Trail, try to get through to a guy named Dick Clifford at the Studies and Observation Group."

"What does he do there?"

"Oh, he's a civilian employee."

Laura leaned forward, her face intent. "Why are you telling me this?"

Reese smiled and raised his brandy glass. "Well, you might say I just want to pay you back for the pleasure of your company over dinner."

Laura cocked her head to one side, looking skeptical. "Or maybe you're just fucking with me."

He grinned broadly. "That's not a bad idea. But I'm not lying to you."

Laura laughed. "Not so fast, GI. This is our first date. Give it a little while longer."

He leaned back and took a sip of his brandy. "I'm willing to wait," he said quietly.

Laura studied him for a long moment. Reese wasn't drop-dead handsome, but there was something about him that interested her, something she could see in his eyes, an attitude. "Maybe you won't have to wait that long. How about a nightcap in my apartment?"

Reese was stunned. He had certainly given more than a casual thought to getting Laura in the sack, but he hadn't thought it would happen this quickly, or at her invitation. "Sure," he gulped.

She smiled a knowing smile. For all of his Green Beret swagger, young Mike Reese was just one more American male. She grabbed her purse and stood. "My roommate's on assignment this week, so we'll have the place to ourselves tonight."

30

Cholon District, Saigon

It was a short ride in a yellow-and-blue Renault taxi to Laura's apartment. She lived in a huge French colonial villa on a side street at the edge of the Cholon district. The news service Laura worked for picked up the tab for the house as well as providing a small security force to guard the compound. The old Nung on guard at the front gate raised his hand in a French-style salute when he saw the captain's bars on Reese's green beret.

"Ni hao, co ba," Reese greeted him.

The guard grinned. *"Ni hao, Dai Uy."*

"I didn't know you spoke Chinese," Laura said, turning to him.

Reese smiled. "I don't really, but I've learned enough to say hello. I have Nungs in my unit, and it helps to know a few social niceties."

"I'm impressed."

He laughed. "Don't be. I know the same things in German, Spanish and Vietnamese, too. Yes, no, thank you and how to order a beer."

The main room of the villa had been converted into a dayroom for the reporters. Several couches and overstuffed chairs were clustered around a big TV set and a pool table. Tonight the room was empty.

"You want something to eat?" she asked, pausing at the foot of the stairs leading to the second floor. "We have a half-French cook who makes a dynamite noodle soup. Fresh vegetables, shrimp and not too many peppers."

"No thanks," he said. "I'm stuffed."

He followed her upstairs, keeping his eyes on the gentle sway of her hips as she climbed. He was a little taken aback by her sexual aggressiveness. But whatever her motives were he was more than ready to go along with the program. It had been a long time since he'd gone to bed with a woman. During the nine months he'd been at Fort Benning without Judy, there had only been a couple of occasions when he'd picked up someone at a party.

"Here we are," she said, opening the door. "Home, sweet home."

The warm smells of perfume and powder that underlay a faint scent of female hit him like a hammer. It had been a long time since he'd smelled anything that good, and it made his gut tighten.

She walked across the living room, opened the windows onto the balcony and offered him a chair outside. "What would you like to drink? I've got Scotch, brandy..."

"Brandy's fine," he said, taking a chair.

She came back with a bottle, two glasses and an ice bucket. "I hope Remy's okay," she said as she poured him a glass full of the dark amber alcohol. "Ice?"

"No thanks."

He sipped his drink and felt the warm glow of the brandy. She slid into the chair next to him and pulled her long legs up under her. "At least we can talk here without having to shout over the band."

Reese laughed. "If they're loud enough, you won't notice that they don't really know the words to the songs."

For a moment they both looked out over the streets of Saigon, not quite knowing what else to say. Even with the post-Tet curfew, there was still a lot of traffic on the street below. The city was always more alive at night than it was during the day, and not even the South Vietnamese police, the White Mice, could keep the fun-loving Saigonese in their houses after dark.

Reese slowly sipped his brandy, studying her profile as she studied the busy street below. "Do you ever wonder what this place would be like without the war?" she asked suddenly.

He laughed. "There'd be a lot fewer Americans here, that's for damn sure!"

"I like Saigon. I want to come back here when this is all over and maybe write a book."

"What I did in the war?"

She turned to him. "No, something more on the order of what the war did to Saigon, a novel of people caught up in the war."

"You want to be a writer?"

She laughed. "It's almost a cliché, isn't it? Every reporter thinks he or she is going to write the great American novel."

"I thought Hemingway had already done that."

She smiled. "Don't get me started on him, the revered writer of modern fairy tales."

"Have you read *For Whom the Bell Tolls?*"

"Oh, yes," she replied. "The classic story of a man and a woman in love during a war. 'I felt the earth move,'" she quoted, laughing. "I've even seen the movie several times, but Gary Cooper's just not my type."

"What is your type?"

She looked at him over the rim of her glass. "Oh . . . someone a little younger, maybe a little more handsome. Someone who's not so damn noble and devoted to the cause. Robert should have tried to escape with Maria at the end instead of sacrificing himself."

"I was always told that a woman likes a man who's willing to lay down his life for her."

She shook her head. "I don't buy that kind of bullshit fairy tale. If my man dies for me, I won't have him around when I want him."

Reese laughed. "I like the way you think."

"A woman has to be practical," she replied. "White knights these days are in real short supply. If you find one, you don't want him running off and doing stupid things like getting himself killed."

"The voice of a modern American woman."

"You have something against modern women?"

"Not at all," Reese defended himself. "In fact, I rather like them."

Laura studied him, a serious look on her face. "You want to go in?" She suddenly shivered. "It's getting a little chilly out here."

"Sure." Reese got to his feet.

"Give me your glass," she said when she stepped back into the room. "I'll get you a refill."

She was gone a long time before she came back. Reese was standing at the window, looking out onto the street, when she rejoined him. "Thanks."

Laura had a faint smile on her face as she put her glass down on the end table and reached behind her. Unbuttoning her dress, she shrugged out of it and let it slither to the floor. She was wearing nothing under it.

Reese's breath caught in his throat. The light reflected from the street touched her full breasts with a golden glow and hid the juncture of her thighs in shadow. It was that shadowed area that drew him to her. He could almost smell her musky scent on the cool night air.

He put his glass down and dropped to his knees in front of her, pressing his face into her firm but soft belly and wrapping his arms around her hips.

"The bed's more comfortable," she said softly.

Reese got back on his feet, and she took his hand and led him in. Her scent was stronger in the bedroom, and his blood raced as she turned on the small lamp on the night table before climbing into bed and pulling the sheet up over herself.

He sat on the edge of the bed and started unlacing his jungle boots. Kicking them off, he stood and reached for his belt buckle while she lay with her back against the wall, watching him. She couldn't help smiling when she noticed that it made him a bit nervous to have her staring at him. Dropping his clothes, he got under the sheet and rolled over onto his side to face her.

He tried hard not to stare when she pulled the sheet away from their bodies. She was stunningly beautiful. Suddenly he felt a bit hesitant, like a kid in a candy shop with a twenty-dollar bill. He didn't quite know where to start. Reaching out, he placed a hand on her belly and moved closer to her.

She was soft and warm. Her tanned skin was a perfect, silky, golden match for her long blond hair. He nuzzled his face into the hollow of her neck. God, she smelled good. He brought his hand up to the fullness of her breasts and felt her nipples harden under his touch. He also felt himself come erect and press against the softness of her thigh.

She felt him, too, and her hand crept down between their bodies to fasten around him. Parting her long legs, she wrapped them around his thigh, pressing herself against the hard muscles of his leg as her fingers caressed him.

They were both ready—more than ready.

He rolled over on top of her, and she pulled her legs up to better accommodate him. Kneeling above her, he paused for a second, but she drew him inside her impatiently.

She was hot, slick softness as he sank into her. He didn't last any time at all. A few deep strokes brought him to an explosive orgasm. She held him tightly against her as he shuddered and shook with the force of his climax. As he lay in her arms, fighting to catch his breath, he realized he hadn't lost his erection.

She was aware of it, too, and started thrusting her hips against him. He answered her thrust slowly at first, then with quickly building force. Soon they were both frantically clutching each other as he rode her. Their climaxes hit them at the same time, and he bit back a cry as he exploded inside her again.

When it was over this time, he relaxed. Pulling out of her, he lay beside her and went back to exploring the curves and hollows of her lush body. She reached for a cigarette and offered him one, which he declined. He was too busy.

When she butted her smoke, she reached down between his legs and quickly brought him erect again with light, teasing strokes. Finally she reached over and pulled him on top of her again.

This time he hammered himself into her, riding her as hard as he could, thrusting deeply into her. She started her climax before he was even halfway there, moaning deep in her throat as her fingers dug into his back. He raised himself on his arms and, thrusting as deeply into her as he could, hammered himself against her, bringing his own climax again. When he felt it start to come, he collapsed on top of her, shuddering and shaking.

Reese rolled over on his back, panting. He was surprised at how winded he was. He could hump through the boonies for days on end, yet he was badly out of shape for bedroom athletics. He made a note to get into better shape for this particular activity. Maybe she could be his regular training partner.

He pulled the sheet up to cover them and to soak up the sweat. The room smelled of sex, brandy and cigarette smoke. It had been a long time since he'd smelled that particular combination, and he hadn't realized just how much he'd missed it. He breathed deeply.

At his side Laura drifted off into a deep sleep. As soon as her breathing lengthened, Reese slipped away and grabbed a cigarette from her pack on the night table. Usually he didn't smoke, but there was nothing like a cigarette and a drink after sex. He recovered his brandy glass and sipped as he watched her in the faint glow from the street lights. Christ, what a woman!

He butted his smoke, drained the last of the brandy and got back into bed. She murmured softly and snuggled against him, and he dropped off to sleep instantly.

THE NEXT MORNING Reese was back on the Hotel Three chopper pad at Tan Son Nhut at 0900 hours, waiting for the chopper to take him back to Ban Phoc.

When he had awakened in Laura's apartment, she'd had to rush off on an assignment. After a quick breakfast of coffee and cold rolls, she'd hurried off, promising to get in touch with him later. He still didn't know what to think about the night before. He did know, however, that he wanted to see her again. More specifically, he wanted to sleep with her again. He had never met anyone like her in his entire life, and he wasn't about to let her get away from him if there was anything he could possibly do to prevent it.

From the day he had married Judy, she'd always treated sex as something to get over with as soon as possible before it messed up her hair. Laura, on the other hand, acted as if she actually enjoyed it. He'd heard there were women who really did like sex, but with the exception of a couple of drunken party girls he'd never come across one who did. He had figured it was just another part of American mythology, like Spanish fly. Now that he knew better, he liked the feeling of being satiated.

The only question in his mind was, did she enjoy sex with all her men as much as she had seemed to enjoy it with him? In fact, how many other men did she have in her life? He didn't see how someone as good-looking as she was could live the life of a nun. Particularly not in a place like Vietnam, where good-looking round-eyed women were in such short supply and horny American men were around every corner. Considering how quickly she'd invited him into her bed, he seriously doubted she was even trying to live like a nun. But even if she had men lined up six deep at her door, he would just have to work his way up to the front of the line. He wasn't about to back off now.

However, he did need to sign that divorce petition Judy had sent him. He had been putting it off for a number of reasons, and now he could finally do it. The time had come for him to admit he had made a serious mistake with her and start over again with someone new.

The whump-whump of approaching Huey rotors snapped him back to the business at hand. No matter what happened between him and Laura, he still had a Mike Force company to run. A man didn't survive long in the jungle if he had his mind on women.

31

May 3, Camp A-410, Ban Phoc

A refreshed Mike Reese returned from his RON in Saigon to a camp that hadn't even begun to recover from the losses they'd suffered on the Cambodian mission. There were still six Nungs dead, several more wounded, two of them seriously, and two of his A-team were on the sick list. The first thing Reese had to do was get the camp back in fighting trim again.

Jack Santelli met him on the landing pad with a clipboard in hand. "I'm sure glad to see you back, sir," the lieutenant said. "I was afraid Pierce and I were going to have to smuggle you a hacksaw blade in a carton of smokes."

Reese grinned. "It was touch and go for a while," he admitted. "And I was getting a little worried myself. But when Marshall and I were done, I don't know who was in the worst shape—him or me."

Santelli laughed. "I would have liked to have sat in on that session."

"It was bloody," Reese admitted. "I was lucky to get out of it with my ass intact."

"At least you're not going to finish out your tour in Camp LBJ."

"You got that shit right," Reese said as he started walking to the command bunker. "Okay, what's the status of the camp?"

"Well, sir," Santelli said, thumbing through his papers, "as you know, we buried six strikers yesterday and we still have another eight in the hospital, including old Vao. We've got an ammo resupply coming in this afternoon and they're finally filling our due-outs on the claymores for the perimeter with this shipment. As soon as we recruit replacements for the Nungs we lost, we should be in pretty good shape."

"How are Pierce and Wilson doing?"

"Silk's going to be out of it for another week or so with that leg wound, but the Indian's up and running. He's out working on the north wall today. He didn't like some of the fighting positions and wanted to rebuild them."

Reese shook his head. "He's getting too old for that kind of shit. He ought to be taking it easy for a few days till that shoulder heals."

Santelli laughed. "You tell him that, Captain. He was up at first light and hard at it right after breakfast."

"You tell him I want him to knock off today and rest up. If you have to, tell him that's an order from me. I want him on light duty for the next couple of days."

"I'll be glad to," Santelli said.

"And since it looks like you've got everything well under control, I'm going to crash in the team house for a couple of hours. I didn't get a hell of a lot of sleep last night."

Santelli looked at his CO appraisingly; he'd thought Reese looked a little too refreshed after only one night away. He must have gotten lucky. "Sure thing, sir." The lieutenant grinned. "I can't think of anything happening today that I can't handle."

"Call me if you need me."

EARLY THE NEXT MORNING Reese flew to B-40 headquarters at Can Tho to make a full report on the Cambodia fiasco to Major Jim Nolan, the B-team commander.

"You know, Reese," Nolan said, leaning back in his chair when Reese finished his report, "you're about the luckiest son of a bitch I ever saw."

"Yes, sir," Reese agreed. "I know. It could have been a hell of a lot worse. We'd have really been in a world of pain if we hadn't gotten that air strike when we did. We were on our last legs when that FAC showed up."

"Other than the replacement strikers, what do you need to get Ban Phoc back up and running again?"

"Mostly time, sir," Reese replied. "Both my operations sergeant and one of my medics are walking wounded. I can give the medic some slack time, but I need Sergeant Pierce back on his feet before we go into any major operations."

"You want me to give you a replacement for him?"

"Good God, no, sir!" Reese said. "That guy is worth a hundred run-of-the-mill NCOs, even hard-core SF types. I definitely want to keep him. I just have to give him a little time to heal up."

Nolan quickly scanned the operations schedule on his desk. "You're in luck. Since you just took over, I had your company down for light duty as it was and I can extend that for another week. Except for local security patrols, you're on stand-down till the tenth."

"Thanks, sir."

"Just get them back on their feet as soon as you can," Nolan cautioned. "That buildup you saw in the Parrot's Beak means we're probably going to be in for interesting times in the very near future."

"That's not what SOG thinks," Reese commented.

Nolan smiled. "SOG has their way of looking at things and I have mine. It just so happens that I agree with your estimate of the situation. I've been talking to some of the Road Runners, and they're reporting the same things you saw. Someone's going to get their dicks knocked stiff before too much longer. Charlie doesn't drag that much stuff down from the North unless he plans to use it."

"That's the same way I look at it, sir," Reese agreed. "I just hope they're not going hunting for Special Forces camps."

"I think Saigon and some of the bigger installations are in for it again," Nolan said. "Hitting the Mike Force camps would only hold them up and expose them to too much firepower. We may be on the shitty end of the stick for a lot of things, but we've still got some pretty powerful friends. Right now, for instance, I've got two spookys sitting on the ramp at Binh Thuy whenever I need them."

"That's good to know," Reese said. "Spookys saved my ass a couple of times, and it's always nice to know he's on call."

Nolan stood and extended his hand. "Glad to have you back. Give me a call if you need anything."

Reese shook his hand. "I'll keep you informed, sir."

THE NEXT DAY old Vao showed up at the main gate to the camp on the back of a 50 cc Honda motorbike. His chest bandages showed traces of blood and he wore hospital slippers with his tiger-striped pants. By all rights he should have been flat on his back in a hospital bed, but somehow the old warrior was back where he belonged—with his troops.

Vao's early return from the hospital was a perfect excuse for Reese to throw a company party. He knew the Nungs would get drunk, anyway, to celebrate their leader's return, so he might as well bow to the inevitable and declare it an official party. That way he could dip into the unit slush fund to finance it.

Also, he felt he could use the slack time to get to know some of his own A-team members a little better. In the rush of the past few days he hadn't had much chance to get to know his men. One of the things that made the Special Forces A-teams so effective was that the men were closer than was usual in an infantry line unit. When Reese went on operations with them again, he wanted to feel he knew his people better.

While he was at it, he could invite Butler and his Black Knights down at the same time. He and the

Nungs owed them one, and he didn't like to be in anyone's debt.

Since Reese had ordered Sergeant Pierce onto light duty, he delegated to him and his network the task of preparing everything for the party. One of the first orders of business was to buy a water buffalo calf for the main course. When they came back with the animal, Reese was glad he wasn't running a Montagnard CIDG company. He had never quite gotten used to watching the big, docile animals being hacked to death with machetes as the festive beginning for a Yard feast. The Nungs would simply shoot the animal in the head and be done with it.

When Reese called to invite Rett Butler and his men, the pilot started to grumble about having to fly that far just to get drunk. Reese replied that he understood if he couldn't make it; he was sure he could find someone else to drink his share of Jack Daniel's for him. At that Butler warned Reese he'd better not run out of JD before he got there.

THE PARTY STARTED OFF with a bang. Late the next afternoon two slicks jammed with Butler's pilots made a high-speed pass over the camp low enough to rattle the tin sheets on the roofs of the barracks. Circling, the two choppers flared out and came in for a landing.

Butler stepped out of the cockpit of the lead slick. He was dressed in a clean, pressed flight suit with the colorful Black Knights patch on the right breast and a black silk ascot at his throat. Spit-shined flight boots, a nickle-plated .357 Magnum in a custom shoulder holster and a thin cigar in the side of his mouth completed his costume.

"As I live and breathe," Reese greeted him, "if it isn't Rett Butler and his infamous band of merry bastards."

"So this is Bum Fuck," Butler said as he slowly looked around the camp. "And I'd always thought it was in Ethiopia."

"That's Bum Fuck East," Reese corrected him. "This is Bum Fuck Far East."

"That explains it." The pilot grinned around his cigar. "I sure as hell hope your hospitality is better than your godforsaken surroundings. And, since I know you Green Beanie types pride yourselves on living a barely civilized existence, I brought along a couple of items to add a little class to what would surely be a dreary affair otherwise."

He turned around. "Ladies?"

An Army nurse in snugly tailored jungle fatigues and two Red Cross girls in light blue dresses stepped down from the back of the slick.

Butler smiled. "May I present Lieutenant Susan Holland, Miss Cindy Andrews and Miss Pamela Patterson. Ladies, this is our host for the evening, Mad Mike Reese, the fearless leader of this band of brutal mercenaries, uncouth barbarians and social misfits."

Reese bowed. "I'm honored."

"Oh," Pamela gushed, a wide toothy smile on her American cheerleader face, "this is so neat. A real Green Beret camp. I've never been to a real Green Beret camp before.'' She looked past Reese, scanning the grounds. ''Where's the tiger you feed the VC to?''

''Tiger?'' Reese asked, raising an eyebrow at Butler.

The pilot took her arm. ''Pam, please don't talk to him about that. He's a little sensitive about it blowing his image as a liberator of the oppressed masses.''

The Red Cross girl turned to the pilot. ''But you told me they fed their VC prisoners to their tiger. I want to see the tiger.''

Butler shrugged. ''That must have been at a different SF camp.''

''Oh.'' Pamela sounded disappointed, very disappointed.

''I'm sorry we don't have a tiger,'' Reese said with a big grin. ''But would you settle for a real, live, liver-eating Nung warrior instead?''

Pam looked up inquiringly at the pilot, her bright blue eyes shining.

''I'll explain later,'' he said.

''Ladies,'' Reese said, ''if you'll follow me, I'll see that you get something to drink.''

''I hope you have something to eat, as well,'' the nurse said. ''I'm starved.''

''How do you like water buffalo?''

The nurse smiled. ''I just got off a long shift and I'm hungry enough to eat the ass end of an elephant.''

Reese grinned. ''I'll talk to the cook and see what he can round up for you.''

''Wiseass.''

As soon as the girls had been introduced to the other A-team members and had been given something to drink, Reese took Butler off to the side. "What's this shit about telling that Doughnut Dolly I had a man-eating tiger in the camp?"

Butler grinned and glanced over to where Pam was talking to Santelli. "What can I say, man? Tigers turn her on. They're her favorite animal. You know, I told her that story and she started biting me." He absent-mindedly rubbed his crotch. "That one's a real man-eater for sure."

"I'll bet she is!"

Susan walked up to them with a drink in her hand. "Where's that water buffalo you were talking about?" she asked Reese.

"I don't think it's quite done yet," he answered, running his eyes up and down her slim frame. She sure as hell looked better in jungle fatigues than any other woman he'd ever seen. "But can I interest you in some round-eye hors d'oeuvres until the beast is ready? Maybe a barbecued shrimp or two?"

"I thought you Green Berets only ate native food— snakes, monkeys, water buffaloes, that sort of thing."

Reese smiled. "Actually, monkey is overrated. Give me a nice juicy cobra anytime. Sautéed in a light *nuoc mam* sauce and then broiled over a fire of rice straw."

Susan shuddered and Butler laughed. "I told you these guys were barbarians."

"At least they don't water the drinks the way you cheap bastards did the last time you had us over for a party," she shot back.

"Hey!" Butler sounded offended. "Wait a minute. You hit us right before payday and we were flat broke!"

Reese looked over and saw Kent, the interpreter, walking toward him, waving him to the tables. "Ladies!" he called out. "Dinner's served!"

The feast was a typical Nung celebration. The Americans of the A-team and their guests sat at the head table and the Nungs sat in descending order, according to their rank and status in the camp. Still in his bandages, Old Vao sat on one side of Reese and Kent on the other. The girls sat next to the two Nungs, with the nurse on Reese's right.

The Nungs began the festivities by proposing several toasts to their American advisers. A Nung would stand up, raise his glass and make a short speech. Kent would translate and then the Americans had to down their drinks in response. The glasses were immediately refilled with whatever they were drinking and the toasts went on.

After the fourth toast Susan Holland leaned toward Reese. "Did you invite us out here to get us drunk, or are you really going to serve dinner?" Her voice was plaintive.

Reese laughed. "Dinner's coming," he said. "Believe me. We just have to get through a few traditional Chinese formalities first."

She glanced down at her glass. "A few more of these traditional formalities of yours and I'm going to be in the bag." She looked back up at him. "But I've got to warn you. I'm a mean drunk."

Reese laughed. "I'll tell the guys to watch their step around you," he promised. "I don't want you beating up on them."

"And I thought you guys were real men."

After a final toast to the women, the Nungs got down to the serious business of eating. As with all Oriental feasts, the food was brought in as separate courses. The first was one of Reese's favorites—shrimp with black mushrooms and bamboo shoots. Halfway through her bowl of the dish, Susan looked over at Reese. "Not bad, Captain, but I'm still waiting for the water buffalo."

"It's coming," he assured her. "Right after the roast monkey and the sautéed snake."

32

May 5, Camp A-410, Ban Phoc

By the time the nine-course meal was over, several of the pilots and Cindy, the Red Cross girl, were quite drunk. They had gotten caught up in the spirit of the party and had started toasting their hosts between courses. As they soon learned, a little of the high-octane mixture the Nungs filled their glasses with went a long way.

Susan Holland had watched herself, however. Though slightly flushed, she was still completely rational when she walked away from the table. "That wasn't bad, Captain." She smiled. "But you do need to tell your chef to add a little more garlic to the steamed monkey brains and cashew entrée. It was a little on the bland side tonight."

He grinned. "How did you like the cobra flambé?"

"I've never had better."

"Can I get you a drink?"

"How about something civilized this time instead of that killer whiskey and Coke the Nungs were passing around? Butler was right about you people being barbarians." She grimaced. "Diluting Chivas Regal with Coke!"

He laughed. "Actually it was Pepsi. But would you care for a brandy? My private stock of Remy Martin?"

She looked at him with an appraising look in her green eyes. "My opinion of you just went up ten points, Captain. My daddy always said you could tell a lot about a man by what he drinks."

"The same goes for women, you know."

"I thought the only thing you guys worried about was how much a woman drank, not what?"

"Not me," he replied. "I've always gone for class."

"And that's why you invited Rett Butler and his band of bastards to this affair?" She shook her head disbelievingly. "To add a touch of class?"

Reese laughed. "I needed someone to make my guys look good in comparison."

She smiled. "You did that."

"I take it you've been around the major before?"

She involuntarily dropped her gaze. "I've been to a couple of their parties. Why?"

"What in hell's his real name?"

"Roman Early Thompson Butler," she answered. "Something real down home, Deep South like that. It's an old family name."

"No wonder he goes by Rett."

"Where's that brandy you promised me?"

"On the way," he answered.

When Reese headed to the bar at the other end of the mess hall, he noticed that several of the Nungs, including most of his interpreter staff, were gathered near the hors d'oeuvres table next to the bar. Peering over their shoulders, he saw Pam seated on one of the folding metal chairs, chatting with the interpreters. Her legs were folded up under her, and the short skirt of her blue dress was hiked up in what could only be called a carelessly provocative posture that featured the tightest pair of tiger skin-patterned bikini panties he'd ever seen. She looked half-drunk but still sober enough to enjoy all the attention she was getting. Every now and then she would spread her creamy thighs a little wider to give the Nungs an even better look.

The Nungs were completely mesmerized. It looked like Butler was dead right about tigers being Pam's favorite animal. He shook his head slowly as he turned away. Butler was probably right about the Red Cross girl being a man-eater, too; if Kent wasn't real careful, it looked as if he'd find out tonight.

When Reese got back with Susan's drink, the nurse was engaged in animated conversation with a slightly drunk Jack Santelli. "Captain," he said when he focused in on Reese, "Susan and I were just talking about you."

"You'd better go rescue Kent," Reese told him. "He's about to be devoured by a man-eating tiger masquerading as a pair of bikini panties."

When Santelli looked at him blankly, Reese gestured with his head toward the mob surrounding the Red Cross girl.

"Right away, sir."

Susan had an amused look in her eyes when Reese handed her the drink. "Aren't you sending an innocent to his fate?"

Reese smiled. "Jack's a big boy. He can handle himself."

"How about you? Are you a big boy, too?"

"I know my way around."

"I'll bet you do."

Butler had designated two duty pilots to stay completely sober so that they could fly everybody home. Just before ten o'clock one of them stood on a chair and shouted, "Major Butler, it's time to go, sir!" He tapped his watch.

The pilot had joined the Pam watchers and ignored the man.

"Rett!" the designated flyer shouted again. "We've got to get the hell out of here!"

"Okay, okay," Butler growled, finally acknowledging him. "Don't get overanxious."

Butler downed the rest of his drink and held his hand out to Pam. She let him lead her away from her admirers.

"Can I walk you to your ride?" Reese asked Susan.

"Thought you'd never ask."

On the way down to the slicks Pam walked beside Butler, chatting a mile a minute about the Nungs.

"Say," Butler asked her, slipping his arm around her waist, "how'd you like to join the mile-high club?"

Several of the other pilots snickered, but Butler kept a poker player's face. "It's a real exclusive pilot's club. Not too many girls get invited to join."

"Oh!" she said enthusiastically. "That sounds like fun!"

"It is, believe me."

At the choppers Susan extended her hand. "Stop by and see me if you're ever in Nha Trang," she told Reese. "I'll buy you a cup of mess hall coffee."

He shook her hand. "That's a deal."

Butler turned and put his hand out to Reese. "Great party, Captain. Sorry to eat and run, but we've got an early call in the morning."

"Glad you could make it."

"It was the least you could do after that monkey fuck you put us through. You owed us."

Reese laughed. "Next time I'll ask someone else."

"Do that, please," Butler said as he climbed into the rear compartment of the slick, and reached down and helped Pam into the back with him. "I don't think we could stand another one of those."

"Have a good flight back," Reese called out to the pilot.

"I will!" Butler shouted back. "Believe me, I will!"

THE RINGING PHONE in Dick Clifford's BOQ room at the Brinks Hotel brought him out of a sound sleep. He fumbled for the receiver and brought it up to his ear. "Yeah?"

"Sorry to bother you," the voice on the other end of the line said, "but I thought you'd like to hear this one."

"Who the fuck is this?" Clifford growled as he fumbled for the light by his bed.

"For Christ's sake, Clifford, get the fucking banana out of your ear! This is Goodman in the situation room."

Now Clifford recognized the voice of his fellow CIA man and MACV-SOG operations specialist. "This had better be good," he warned, glancing at his watch. "It's four o'clock in the fucking morning."

"You're going to love it," Goodman promised. "Charlie's attacking again. He's shelling cities all up and down the country, and at least ten battalions are trying to cut off Saigon. Shit, man, we've even got enemy in the wire out here at Tan Son Nhut. MACV's already calling it the Second Tet Offensive."

Clifford sat upright in bed. "I'll be a son of a bitch," he said softly. He had been right all along. "Have you called Marshall yet?"

Goodman laughed. "Nope, I was saving that little chore for you. I thought you'd enjoy doing that yourself."

Clifford grinned. "Thanks, buddy. I owe you a big one."

After hanging up the phone, he pulled on his pants and lit a smoke before dialing the colonel's number. There was some justice in this fucked-up war, after all. The unfortunate thing was that men were dying tonight to prove he had been right all along.

It took six rings before Marshall picked up the phone. "Colonel Marshall."

"Sir, this is Dick Clifford. I've just received word from the situation room that the NVA have launched another massive attack against the city. They're assaulting the defenses at Tan Son Nhut right now."

There was dead silence on the other end of the line.

"Sir, did you hear me? Charlie's in—"

"I heard you, goddamn it," Marshall growled. "I heard you."

Clifford smiled. Now maybe the old bastard would take his intelligence reports a little more seriously. He could hear muffled coughing on the other end of the line and the click of a lighter as the colonel lit up.

"Do you think you can get over to the situation room?" the colonel asked.

"Yes, sir." Clifford would get there or die trying. He had missed getting in on the Tet Offensive until noon of the third day, and he was damned if he was going to miss out on this one, too. "I'll be there in half an hour."

"I'll get there as fast as I can," Marshall said. "But if you get there before I do, start working up an order of battle estimate on what we're dealing with here."

"Yes, sir."

"But for God's sakes, Clifford, keep it to yourself till I can go over it."

"Yes, sir."

Clifford had a broad grin plastered all over his face when the colonel hung up. Now he had to make his way through the fighting in town and get to the SOG building. But, after sticking it to Marshall, he felt as if he were ten feet tall and covered with hair. He wasn't worried at all about a few thousand enemy soldiers; he'd make it through to the SOG building if it killed him.

He quickly dressed in dark clothing and strapped on his shoulder holster with its powerful .357 Colt Python. Digging into the back of his closet, he brought out the 9 mm Danish Madsen Model 50 submachine gun he kept there as a last-ditch defense piece if the hotel was ever attacked. Like most of the CIA's Madsens, this one had no serial numbers stamped on it anywhere and had originally been ordered for black ops use. Like all too many of them, it had been sidetracked into use as a personal weapon. With its cyclic rate of over five hundred rounds per minute, you could get real personal, real quick.

Stuffing a pair of loaded magazines for the burp gun into his back pocket, he scooped up all the cigarette packages he could find, stuffed them into his front pockets and headed out into the hall of the Brinks BOQ.

Outside the hotel the security guards were hunkered down behind the sandbag-and-barbed-wire barricades that flanked the entrance. He could hear gunfire and explosions from the direction of Tan Son Nhut, and it sounded serious. Even more serious than Tet.

"You can't go out there, sir," one of the MPs said when he saw Clifford start for the street.

The CIA man slid the bolt back on the Madsen to chamber a round and looked out onto the darkened street. "Duty calls, Sarge."

THE WAILING OF THE CAMP siren brought Reese straight out of bed. He glanced at the luminous dial of his watch, saw that it was slightly after four in the morning and wondered what in the fuck was going on now. It was too late for an attack on the camp, and he didn't hear any gunfire. Struggling into his pants and boots, he ran for the command bunker.

Flying down the stairs into the bunker, he found that Sergeant Pierce had beat him there. "What's going on?"

Pierce handed him a clipboard with a radio alert message. "Saigon and several other cities have been hit by mortar and rocket attacks. MACV says that at least ten battalions have encircled Saigon and are assaulting Tan Son Nhut."

Reese quickly read the message form. "Assholes!" he exclaimed. "We told them it was coming."

"B-40's called a red alert," the operations sergeant said. "I've got the people in their holes."

"Good," Reese said, turning to the big wall map. "Now we'll finally see what those little bastards are up to."

Santelli came stumbling down the stairs, his M-16 in his hands. Reese saw that he was still slightly drunk and decided the night air would do him good. "Jack," he told the lieutenant, "they're hitting Saigon and we're on full alert. Get out there and make sure everyone's on their toes."

"I'll be damned," Santelli said. "I can't wait to hear what that SOG colonel has to say about this!"

MOST OF THE PREDAWN attacks were only mortar and rocket strikes at American installations and some of the larger Vietnamese cities, but some American units came under heavy attack that morning. At Dong Ha in Quang Tri Province, eight thousand troops of the

320th NVA Division assaulted the supply base. Five thousand Marines and South Vietnamese ended up fighting a bloody three-day battle before forcing the North Vietnamese back across the DMZ with heavy losses.

The Kham Duc Special Forces camp in Southern I Corps was hit by two regiments of NVA Regulars, trapping over a thousand Allied troops inside the perimeter. Air power came to their rescue. Army and Marine gunships and Air Force fighter bombers bombed and strafed the enemy positions to blunt the attack, sometimes dropping napalm within twenty yards of the perimeter. During the aerial onslaught, Air Force C-130 Herky Birds flew in to evacuate the CIDG defenders and their dependents. Most of the defenders were rescued, but at a cost of eight of the supporting aircraft, including a C-130 that went down with 150 CIDG troops and others on board.

The most serious fighting, however, was centered around Saigon. Elements of the Twenty-fifth Infantry Division and Air Cav units immediately responded to the attack and softened the NVA assault on Tan Son Nhut and the Bien Hoa Bridge. A two-day lull in the fighting followed only to erupt again into furious combat in the Chinese district of Cholon and the area around the Phu Tho Racetrack.

As the days wore on, A-410 stayed on full alert and waited to see if the NVA were going to pull back from Saigon and withdraw into Cambodia as they had done after Tet. If they did, Reese's Mike Force company would be sent against them as blocking forces while

Airmobile Infantry units were moved into position to pursue them.

For Reese, waiting was worse than fighting. When he heard about the fighting in the Cholon district of Saigon, he worried about Laura's safety. As far as he could find out, her villa was on the edge of the fighting, but he hadn't been able to get through to her news agency to see if she was all right. As had happened during Tet, the phone lines had been cut. He hoped to hell she was out in the countryside somewhere on a story. Like everyone else, he would just have to wait to find out.

33

May 11, Camp A-410, Ban Phoc

For the next several days the battle raged in and around Saigon. When the sudden attack was stalled by the strong American and South Vietnamese resistance, the NVA dug in in the Cholon district, the Phu Tho Racetrack and the Y Bridge and prepared to fight and die there if necessary. As the Allies rushed more troop units in to dig them out, the North Vietnamese called for their own reinforcements to come to their aid.

At midday on the eleventh a two-battalion regiment of NVA regulars crossed the Cambodian border south of the Parrot's Beak. These were fresh troops out of North Vietnam, and they were well armed with crew-served weapons up to and including 120 mm heavy mortars. Once safely inside South Vietnam the only thing that stood in the path of their forty-mile dash to reinforce their embattled comrades in Saigon was the small Special Forces camp A-410 at Ban Phoc.

Right after dark that evening the NVA regiment came upon the camp. Rather than leave the Mike Force unit intact with the possible opportunity to harass their rear, the North Vietnamese commander decided to take the camp out instead. It would delay them for a few hours, but it would be an easy first blooding for the troops of the relatively new, combat-inexperienced regiment.

Within minutes of receiving their firing orders, the enemy set up their 120 mm heavy mortars while the infantry units moved in closer and prepared to take up their assault positions under the cover of a rain of well-aimed mortar rounds. From there they would swarm out and storm the wire when the barrage lifted.

THE NVA MORTAR TEAMS had been given detailed intelligence information about the layout of Ban Phoc gathered by the VC camp watchers that every American installation seemed to have hanging around just out of sight. The first of the mortar rounds hit dead center on the camp's command bunker. Mike Reese was inside writing out the routine messages that had to be sent to B-40 that night when two of the thirty-four-pound HE rounds struck almost simultaneously on the flat roof right above the radio console. The first round blasted away most of the sandbag cover on the top of the roof and the second one detonated on the inner layer of PSP that formed the bunker's ceiling, sending razor-sharp frag slicing down into the interior.

Sergeant Pierce had heard the distinctive metallic thunks of the mortar rounds leaving their tubes and was racing for the command bunker when they hit. He saw the roof cave in with the explosions. As another 120 mm round hit the corner, blowing away the roof completely, he threw himself flat on the ground. The inside of the bunker was now exposed.

He knew the night duty crew was trapped in the wreckage. But he also knew the mortar barrage would be followed by a ground attack. When the rain of mortar rounds subsided, he reluctantly got to his feet and raced for the fighting positions in his sector. There was no point in rescuing the men in the bunker if the NVA breached their perimeter. Dead or alive, they would have to look after themselves for a while. He had to direct the fight from his sector of the line.

The relentless rain of heavy mortar rounds smashed much of the camp's defenses as well as the command bunker in the five-minute barrage. One of the 106 gun pits took a direct hit, blasting the recoilless into useless scrap metal. A 120 had caught one of the .50-caliber crews in the open and taken them all out with one blast. Even the 81s weren't returning counterbattery fire. As suddenly as it had started, the rain of mortar shells ended with a last white phosphorous round directly in the center of the camp.

As soon as the mortar barrage lifted, waves of screaming NVA infantry rushed the last hundred yards to storm the camp's perimeter. Before the defenders had time to recover, they found themselves fighting for their lives as a full battalion of North Vietnamese regulars hurled themselves against the barbed wire and punji-stake defenses.

The dark olive NVA uniforms looked black in the flickering light of the fires, the muzzles of the AKs blazing bright orange flame. The blinding flash of bangalore torpedoes and the flash of the green tracers as the assault teams blew holes in the camp's wire defenses lit up the night.

Pierce reached his fighting hole just in time to hit the clackers for the claymores in his sector. The deadly antipersonnel mines did their butcher's work, blowing big gaps in the enemy's ranks. But there were far more screaming NVA than there were claymores.

With the claymores gone, Pierce started throwing hand grenades. Off to his right, Pierce heard Larry Webb's battle cry ring out over the storm of small-arms fire. Knowing that the demo man was holding down his end of the sector made Pierce feel better.

One of the camp's 81 mm mortars was still in action, the Nung crew sending rounds out of the tube as fast as they could drop them. Most of the shells they fired were charge-zero HE, and the Nungs were trying to bring them in as close to the wire as they could. But interspersed with the HE were illumination rounds, parachute flares that showed Pierce a hellish scene in their flickering light.

The NVA were throwing themselves wildly on the barbed wire, smashing it down so that their comrades could run over top of them. Mangled bodies hung there, nothing slowing the tide. The Nungs were burning through their magazines on full automatic as the enemy exchanged a hail of AK fire in their direction.

From the corner of his eye he saw a Nung take a full burst in the chest and fall forward into his hole. His partner leaned over him and took the next hit himself. Pierce took out the NVA who killed them and ducked down behind his sandbags to change magazines. When he came up again, he saw that several of the Nung positions up and down the line were empty.

The NVA were charging the holes in the line. As a result, Nungs had to fire in the direction of their comrades to hit the enemy. Too few defenders were left to hold the outer perimeter. It was time to fall back to the inner perimeter.

"Pull back!" Pierce shouted between half-magazine bursts. "Pull back!"

IN THE TRENCHES of the inner perimeter Jack Santelli was finally getting to live out one of his military fantasies. He had always wondered what it would be like to fight a desperate balls-to-the-wall battle like the Alamo or Custer's Last Stand. He decided he didn't care for it one damn bit. If they couldn't hold their present positions, there was no place for them to go but into body bags. The camp would be overrun.

The ferocity of the NVA assault had forced him and his Nung platoon back and out into his fighting hole on the outer perimeter by the main gate. He and Kowalski had been able to pull most of the strikers back to the inner defensive line where they were still trying to turn the enemy back. Despite their efforts they were making very little headway. For every NVA they killed, several more jumped up to take his place.

One of the biggest problems was that they were fighting without direction from their team leader. The land lines back to the command bunker had been knocked out. Santelli had no way of knowing what was going on in the other sectors of the camp, and he couldn't call for reinforcements. He also had no way of knowing if Reese or Pierce were still alive. He only knew that the command bunker had been smashed. If they could somehow turn back this attack, then he could spare the time to see about the men who had been trapped in the bunker. Until then he had bad guys to kill.

Santelli slapped another magazine into the bottom of his M-16 and shot the bolt forward to chamber a round. Flicking the selector switch down to full automatic, he triggered off a short burst and was rewarded by a high-pitched scream from the shadows in front of him. He fired again. Snatching a grenade from the side of his ammo pouch, he pulled the pin and threw it as far as he could into the shadows. The flash of the explosion revealed more charging NVA. He fired off another burst.

FROM ITS SANDBAGGED position in the center of the star-shaped perimeter, one of the camp's two M-40A1 106 mm recoilless rifles belched fire again and again. The antipersonnel fléchette rounds it fired were all that were keeping the charging North Vietnamese at bay.

SFC Vic Hotchkiss was the duty NCO that night and had been returning from an inspection of the perimeter when the first of the mortar rounds fell. He had dived for cover into the first place he'd found—the gun pit for the recoilless rifle. As soon as the barrage had lifted, he'd started loading and firing the gun himself. One of the gun's Nung crew had soon shown up and taken over the loading duties so that the Green Beret could aim and fire faster.

The fléchette rounds were tearing great holes in the attacking NVA, but Hotchkiss was quickly running out of antipersonnel ammunition. "Load me!" he shouted to the Nung loading for him.

The sweating Nung swung open the breech of the 106, slammed another fléchette round into the firing chamber and locked the breechblock in place again. "Up!" he yelled.

Peering through the sight on the top of the barrel, Hotchkiss swung the rifle around to cover a new sector of the camp. He zeroed in on the front wave of the enemy charging the wire and pushed the firing button. The rear of the gun belched with flame from the backblast and, with a metallic clang, over a thousand finned steel darts the size of small nails exploded from the muzzle. The fléchettes swept through the ranks of screaming NVA storming the perimeter, tearing them to bloody shreds.

"Load!" Hotchkiss shouted hoarsely over the roar of the battle.

The Nung slammed the last of the rounds into the gun. "No have any more fléchette." he shouted. "Only HE left."

"Fuck!" Hotchkiss cursed. He cursed the gun; he cursed not having any more fléchette ammo; he cursed the Air Force for not being overhead to give them a hand; and he cursed himself for not being out on a nice safe night ambush patrol in the bush tonight. He cursed everything he could think of except the Nung Mike Force troops dying in the trenches.

The Nungs had been forced back from the outer fighting positions by the overwhelming odds. Hotchkiss knew they would die in place before they ever thought of deserting the inner positions. The Nungs weren't superhuman—they would run if they could— but there was no place for them to run now and they knew it. All they could do was fight their enemies and die in the tradition of the Nung warriors. And there was little that Hotchkiss could do to help them now that the last of the fléchette rounds was gone.

"Load HE!" he shouted. Firing the plastic explosive antitank rounds that close in was almost as dangerous to the friendlies as it was to the NVA. Hotchkiss decided that it was better than doing nothing. They had to have more fire support than just the single 81 that was still in action.

The Nung loader had turned around to grab one of the HE rounds when Hotchkiss caught a glimpse of a North Vietnamese aiming his RPG rocket launcher at their position. "RPG! Get down!" he yelled as he threw himself behind the sandbag blast wall.

The Nung turned around just in time to catch the full force of the antitank rocket round as it hit the side of the breech of the 106.

Deafened by the explosion, his ears ringing, Hotchkiss looked up. The recoilless rifle had been smashed and thrown against the side of the gun pit. The Nung's body was draped over the rear of the gun. His chest had been ripped open.

The Green Beret staggered to his feet. Blood ran from his ears and nose as he stumbled across the open ground to the mortar-blasted command bunker. The barrage and RPG hits had collapsed most of the roof and torn a big hole in one wall. But maybe there was still a slight chance that the radios were working.

Burst sandbags and broken timbers blocked the entrance. Hotchkiss tore into the wreckage at the damaged corner of the structure, enlarged the opening and crawled into the dark interior. He stumbled across something on the floor and thumbed his lighter to life. By the flickering flame he saw two bodies. The first was one of the young Nungs, probably the duty runner. The second was Hank Wheeler, the radioman on duty that night.

A flashlight lay in the rubble of the floor, and he snapped it on before the lighter burned his fingers. He checked the Nung; the man was dead. Then he rolled Wheeler over onto his back. The radioman had been hit in the head and was unconscious. Hotchkiss quickly tied a field bandage around his head wound. Until the attack was over that was all he could do for him.

Someone moaned from the other end of the room. Hotchkiss grabbed the flashlight and went to investigate. Captain Reese had been halfway between the commo room and their duty sleeping quarters in the back when the wall had fallen in on him. Hotchkiss shoved the sandbags off Reese and found that the captain was still breathing. He could see no wounds on him, so he grabbed Reese's legs and dragged him into the clear.

When the cool air hit his face, the officer moaned and his eyes fluttered open.

"You okay?" Hotchkiss asked, heaving a roof timber out of the way.

"Yeah, just help me get up."

Hotchkiss helped his commander to his feet. "Jesus," Reese said, putting a hand out to steady himself, "what happened?"

"You got hit in the first barrage. The Nung's dead and Wheeler got hit in the head."

"How are we doing out there?" Reese asked.

"We're still holding the inner perimeter, but they took out both the 106s, and only one of the 81s is still going. We've got to get us some air support quick or we're fucking finished."

Reese looked over at the bank of commo gear half buried in sandbags and roof timbers. From the look of the smashed radios there was no point in even trying to use them to call for help. "How about the Prick-77 in the tower?" he asked Hotchkiss.

The sergeant stopped abruptly. He hadn't even thought of the small tactical radio they kept in the tower to talk with the patrols returning to the camp. "I think the tower's down, sir, but the radio might have survived. I'll go see if I can find it."

Reese grabbed an M-16 from the ready rack and pulled back on the charging handle to chamber a round. "Go!" he said. "I'll try to cover you from here."

34

Camp A-410, Ban Phoc

Hotchkiss snatched up an M-16 and raced up and out of the bunker. The battle still raged furiously. The perimeter had been breached in several places and by now the NVA were assaulting the inner defenses. The camp's last .50-caliber heavy machine gun was all that was keeping the enemy from overrunning the very heart of the camp. The machine gun's barrel was smoking with the sustained fire, and Hotchkiss knew it would burn out before long.

The NVA's RPG rocket launchers were bracketing the gun pit. In some places the enemy had pressed ahead through the wire of the outer perimeter, and the Nungs in the inner ring of the trenches were fighting them hand-to-hand.

In the flickering light of the fires and mortar flares, he saw a Nung, already bleeding from several wounds, leap out of the trench. Screaming, he launched himself into the midst of a group of North Vietnamese who were storming through a break in the concertina. A blinding explosion told Hotchkiss that the Nung had had live grenades in his hands.

The Nung's sacrifice had stopped that particular assault, but there were just too damn many of them to turn back. If they didn't get some fire support ASAP, they couldn't hold them off much longer.

The spindly wooden observation tower was lying flat on the ground. Hotchkiss vaguely remembered seeing one of the legs take a mortar hit during the initial barrage. The platform that had been on top of the tower seemed to be fairly intact, however, as he crawled up to it. He scrambled over the sandbag wall and dropped into what had been the inside of the covered platform. The radio should have been right inside.

A burst of AK hit the other side of the sandbags, splattering dirt in his face. He scrambled back out over the other side of the platform, keeping both of the sandbag walls between him and the enemy.

If it wasn't inside, where was the fucking radio?

Looking around frantically, he glimpsed a glitter of light. It was the plastic tip of the whip antenna, sticking out from under a sheet of roofing tin. He crawled over and pulled the radio to him by its slender antenna. Switching it on, he held the handset to his ear and heard the welcoming hiss of the squelch. When he pressed the push-to-talk switch, the hiss stopped.

Clutching the precious box to his chest, he raced back across the open ground to the demolished command bunker. Reese and two of the Nungs, both of them wounded, had widened the hole in the corner of the bunker and were doing their best to hold off the enemy from there.

Safely inside the walls of the bunker again, Hotchkiss extended the whip antenna of the radio as high as he could without exposing himself to enemy fire. He keyed the mike and shouted into the handset several times without success.

"I can't reach them, sir!" he shouted to Reese over the gunfire. "The antenna isn't long enough to reach 'em from down here."

"The main antennae are down," Reese yelled back. "Try plugging it into the ground plane antenna. And call Hillsboro first—they'll be able to pick us up."

Hotchkiss ripped the ends of the ground plane antenna loose from the useless main radios. A ground plane antenna was simply a long length of two strands of commo wire buried in the ground and aimed in the direction of a particular receiving station. Most Special Forces camps had a ground plane antenna laid in to use as a backup in case their main antennae were knocked out of action.

Hotchkiss didn't have the slightest idea how the radio waves from the buried wire could reach even their intended destination, but somehow they did. And they had better work this time, or they were all dead.

He quickly attached the bare end of the wires to the external antenna leads on the Prick-77 and keyed the handset again. "Hillsboro Control, Hillsboro Control," he called the Air Force Flying Tactical Air Control Center orbiting high above the western edge of South Vietnam. "This is Dusty Strider, Dusty Strider. Over!"

Hillsboro was a C-121 Super Constellation rigged as a flying communications center that was on-station twenty-four hours a day, monitoring radio traffic from the Special Forces camps and recon teams and passing on their requests for Tac Air support. Making contact with Hillsboro had saved the lives of more than one Green Beret.

"Dusty Strider, this is Hillsboro Control," came the faint voice on the speaker. "I read you very weak but steady. Send your traffic. Over."

"This is Dusty Strider," Hotchkiss answered. "This is a Blue Star call. Can you patch me through to Spooky Control at Binh Thuy? Over."

"Roger, wait one."

"Dusty Strider," came a new voice over the handset, "this is Spooky Control. Go."

"This is Strider at the Ban Phoc Special Forces camp. We're up to our asses in bad guys. Can you get something out here to give us a hand instantly? Over."

"Roger Strider, I've got a Spooky on-station I can divert to your location, Echo Tango Alpha fifteen minutes. Can you hold out that long? Over."

"This is Strider. Whether we're alive or not, tell him to kick the shit outta this place. We've got at least a battalion of hard hats cornered here. Over."

Hotchkiss could hear the Air Force radio operator chuckle. "Roger, Strider, I'll get him coming your way. His call sign is Spooky Eight Three. Over."

"This is Dusty Strider, roger. Thanks a lot. Out."

Hotchkiss put the radio handset down and grabbed his M-16 again. If Spooky could get here in time, they might have a chance. If he didn't this was as good a place to die as any other. Joining Reese and the two Nungs, he carefully aimed the rifle through the hole in the bunker wall and squeezed off a shot.

SIX THOUSAND FEET high in the sky Captain Mick Dugan, the AC-47 Spooky gunship pilot, banked his twin-engined, converted-transport plane to the left. The Fourth Air Commando Squadron pilot was getting close to the beleaguered Special Forces camp. "Dusty Strider, Dusty Strider, this is Spooky Eight Three on your push. Over."

"This is Strider," Hotchkiss answered after a second. "Go ahead."

The pilot could hear the gunfire in the background. Somebody down there was in deep shit. Of course, that was the only reason anyone ever called on Spooky's services. They had their ass in a crack and needed someone to bring some serious smoke down on the bad guys for them. As the pilot's business card read, "When you hurt enough to need the very best, call Spooky."

"Strider, this is Spooky Eight Three," Dugan radioed. "I'll be over your location in zero two, ready to go to work. Where do you want me to put it? Over."

"This is Strider. Anything outside the fence is fair game," Hotchkiss answered. "We've pulled back to the inner defenses, and there's a couple hundred of them out there. You can't miss. Over."

Dugan chuckled to himself as he keyed the mike. One Charlie or a hundred; it really didn't matter to him. Once Spooky got on their asses it was all over.

"Roger, Strider, I've got you in sight now. We'll be starting our flare run shortly. Over."

As soon as the first of the high-intensity magnesium flares popped over Ban Phoc, the Spooky pilot could clearly see what the problem was. The small star-shaped camp on the top of the low hill looked as if it were swarming with dark-colored ants.

He flew past the camp until the center of it was passing under his portside engine cowling. He checked his airspeed and then kicked the plane over into a hard left-hand pylon turn and looked to his left side window. Mounted in the middle of the window was a Navy Mark 20, mod-4 gunsight salvaged out of an A-1E Skyraider. He tightened his turn until the main gate of the camp's barbed wire perimeter was centered in the cross hairs. With his right thumb he pressed a switch mounted on the control wheel.

From what had once been the cargo compartment in the rear of the transformed transport plane, a deep-throated, whining drone sounded as two of the mini-guns opened up. The feared Sky Dragon was speaking again.

To the men on the ground the miniguns sounded like heavy canvas being violently ripped apart. Twin fingers of red flame flashed from the plane's left side. Only one round in every five in the minigun ammo belts was a tracer, with the guns firing so fast that twenty tracers left the barrels every second. The thick fingers of red flame raced down to touch the ground right outside the perimeter wire.

Twenty yards in front of the wire an NVA assault platoon was charging the camp's main gate when the finger of flame swept over them. In less than an instant what had been two dozen men was a scattered pile of bleeding, ragged dog meat. The fingers of flame had also touched the satchel charges they were carrying and detonated them, adding to the carnage. Very few of the enemy survived.

The twin fingers of flame winked out as abruptly as they had appeared. They flashed again a second later and a little farther down along the outer perimeter. Again the deep, ripping sound filled the air.

The surviving defenders held their fire and ducked well behind the sandbags. While Spooky spoke, no man wanted to get in the way.

After the second burst of fire, the NVA broke and tried to run from the dragon in the sky. Their attempts to escape Spooky's wrath were in vain. Very few of them made it over the several hundred yards to the nearest cover. In the brief silences between the minigun bursts a low moaning sound was heard, the sound of dozens of wounded men all screaming at the same time. Some of the defenders clapped their hands over their ears to block out the new and chilling sound.

Overhead, Dugan kept the flares going as he orbited the camp, keeping the gunship in a tight left-hand bank. When the North Vietnamese broke and ran, he opened up his orbit a little to bring the guns to bear on the fleeing groups of men.

From his vantage point high in the night sky, Dugan didn't see the panicked, running NVA troops as men. He didn't have to hear them scream, smell their blood or carry their bodies away later; they were just easy targets for his guns. As far as he was concerned, this was by far the best shooting and target practice he'd had in a long time. He calmly lined up his sight again and pressed the firing button.

As abruptly as it had begun, the heavy ripping sound from the gunship cut off. The handset of Hotchkiss's Prick-77 radio spoke in the sudden stillness. "Dusty Strider, this is Spooky Eight Three. Over."

"This is Strider," the sergeant answered. "Go."

"This is Eight Three. I'm bingo ammo. I'll stay on-station and drop flares for you until I run out of them, too. The fast movers have been called, and they'll be here before too long and lay some soft bombs for you in the tree line in case your visitors decide to come back. The strike commander will be Maverick Lead on this push. Over."

"Roger, Spooky. We'll be waiting for him. Thanks. We owe you a big one. Over."

"No sweat, Strider," the pilot replied. "You can catch me in the bar at Binh Thuy and thank me with a couple of rum and Cokes. Just ask for Mick Dugan. The bartender will know where to find me."

Reese and Hotchkiss stepped out of the blasted command bunker and looked around the smoking ruins of the camp. The acrid smell of cordite and the coppery, metallic stench of fresh blood mixed with smoke from the fires started by the mortar attack.

In the flickering light of the flares Reese saw at least two hundred NVA scattered on the ground outside the camp and hanging in the wire. From inside the perimeter Nung sharpshooters were putting the wounded out of their misery with carefully aimed shots. Although that wasn't exactly in the spirit of the Geneva Convention, Reese didn't stop them from doing it. This was no time to be screwing around guarding prisoners.

Inside the camp litter parties were moving quickly through the trenches, recovering the wounded and taking them to the makeshift dispensary in the ruins of the mess hall. Some of the able-bodied Nungs were already stringing new rolls of concertina wire to cover the gaps that had been blown in the perimeter. Others were running from one fighting position in the trenches to the next, distributing ammunition and recovering damaged weapons. Even with the whole place a mess, Ban Phoc had survived and they could still fight if they had to.

Lieutenant Santelli and Sergeant Pierce staggered up to the ruins of the command bunker. "Glad to see you made it, sir," Pierce said with relief. "I was beginning to worry about you."

"How's the rest of the team?" Reese asked.

"I've accounted for everyone but Wheeler," Pierce answered. "Wasn't he in the bunker with you?"

"He got hit in the head," Hotchkiss replied. "But he's still alive."

"Thanks for the Spooky, Captain," Santelli said, wiping his hands on his pants. "She sure as hell saved our asses."

"Hotchkiss did that," Reese said. "And he's also got some fast movers coming in soon to lay some cluster bombs in the woods for us. That should keep 'em away from here for the rest of the night."

"I sure as hell hope so." Pierce sounded weary. "I've enjoyed about as much of this shit as I can stand."

35

May 12, Camp A-410, Ban Phoc

A filthy, sweaty, smoke-stained Mike Reese stood by
the wreckage of the command bunker and surveyed his
camp. The fires had all been put out; only thin tendrils
of smoke still drifted up into the cool morning air. The
air was filled with the stench of war: the sour smell of
half-dried blood, the sharp, metallic smell of high explosives, the faint, rotting smell of torn and blasted
bodies already decomposing in the sun. By noon the
reek would be overpowering.

Much of the smell came from the bodies of the NVA
dead that littered the camp. Outside the wire they lay
in piles where Spooky's miniguns had cut them down.
If the gunship had been just a few minutes later, it
would have been mostly Nung and American bodies in
those piles. As it was, considering the ferocity of the
attack and the overwhelming odds that had been
thrown against them, their own casualties hadn't been
that great.

Wheeler was in pretty bad shape and had already
been evacuated. Fortunately the rest of the team had
suffered only minor wounds and were still available for
light duty. The Nungs, however, had been hit hard.
And coming as the attack did on the tail of the Cambodian mission, A-410's combat strength was way

down. While Ban Phoc could still defend itself if necessary, it would be some time before they were back up to full combat effectiveness.

Lying on the ground by the entrance to the bunker was the sign proudly announcing that Ban Phoc was Camp Bum Fuck, Home of A-410, The Mushroom Detachment. Before the attack the sign had been a good joke, letting visitors know how the A-team felt about being stuck way the hell out on the fringe of the action. Now they could no longer say they were being kept in the dark and fed bullshit like mushrooms.

Even with the destruction, life at Ban Phoc went on. The Nung cooks were sifting through the rubble of the mess hall, trying to salvage enough pots to cook breakfast on small fires. Somehow one of the shower tanks had survived unpunctured, and the Nungs were lining up to wash off the grime and blood of combat. Others were busily filling sandbags to rebuild the outer fighting positions in case Charlie decided to offer an encore. As soon as Reese had replacements for his heavy weapons and radios, they'd be back in business.

Torres walked up to Reese with their last operating PRC-77 radio on his back. "B-40's on the horn, sir. They want a status report on our facilities."

Reese shook his head. "Jesus H. Christ! Tell 'em the whole fucking place is a shambles! Tell 'em to look up the standard Mike Force camp TO&E and send us one each of everything, including a new campsite. It'll take us a month just to clean this place up and another month to rebuild it back to what it was."

"I'll tell 'em we're still doing a survey of the damage, sir," Torres said calmly.

"Yeah, that's fine." Reese suddenly sounded weary. "How long did they say it would take for the Dust-offs to get here?" There were still some men with minor wounds who needed to be checked out in a proper medical facility.

Torres glanced down at his watch. "Fifteen minutes or so, Captain, maybe twenty."

"We got a total friendly body count yet?"

"No, sir. I'll get on that right now."

"I'll need to know as soon as possible so I can call it in." Reese took a long, slow look around the camp. "We still have to hold this place and we're going to need some CIDG reinforcements."

BY MAY 13, cut off from further reinforcements, the remnants of the NVA units in the Saigon area were forced to withdraw. What the papers had started to term mini-Tet was over. Again the campaign had been a crushing military defeat for the North Vietnamese. While not as bad as the beating the NVA had taken in the Tet Offensive, it had been costly to them nonetheless. Over five thousand enemy dead littered the rubble in Saigon and Cholon. There was no way of counting those wounded or killed in the countryside.

Another 154 American and some 326 South Vietnamese troops had also lost their lives in the attack. Worse than that, fifty thousand more Vietnamese civilian refugees had been added to the already crowded cities. The press was going crazy again, pointing fingers of blame and wailing doom and gloom as they had done after the Tet Offensive. Reporting that the North

Vietnamese had gotten their asses kicked once again didn't sell newspapers back in the States.

In MACV-SOG Headquarters in Tan Son Nhut, Colonel Marshall was going over the after-action reports. He had to draft an answer to a query from General Westmoreland's office as to why SOG hadn't had better intelligence about the enemy buildup.

It was no big deal. Simply another old "cover your ass" exercise like the one he'd gone through after the sudden eruption of the Tet Offensive in February. Marshall knew what to say to keep Westmoreland off his ass, but he also knew that this time he shared some of the blame for the surprise. He still wasn't quite ready to admit that Clifford had been one hundred percent correct in his prediction. But he was willing to pay a little closer attention to the CIA man's intelligence estimates in the future.

Right now he had to say something that would let MACV Headquarters think he had the situation well under control and was taking effective steps to prevent a third surprise attack from happening. For all his bitching, Marshall sincerely liked his job and didn't want to get "kicked upstairs" along with Westy and his staff.

One measure he could implement quickly was to increase the recon team activities along the Cambodian border area. That would mean expanding the RT program, which would be relatively easy. There were always men to volunteer for the behind-the-line dangers of SOG recon team duty. The part that wouldn't be so easy would be finding another Hatchet Force unit to use as the backup force for the new RTs. He would have to request that another Mike Force company be released from Fifth Group to handle that task.

Marshall thought of the cocky, smart-mouthed young Special Forces captain Clifford had sent into the Parrot's Beak. What was his name? Reese, Mike Reese, commanding the A-410 camp at Ban Phoc.

He and his unit had proven they could operate effectively across the border on Clifford's mission, as they would have to do as a Hatchet Force. It would be easy enough to transfer them to SOG control, pull them out of their Delta camp and send them up close to the border somewhere to back up the RTs. Hatchet Force was rough duty, but someone had to do it, and Reese had nominated himself by shooting his mouth off.

The colonel smiled slowly. Now he would see just how good this guy really was. He reached for his phone to call Clifford into his office. He wanted to get going on this ASAP.

Clifford approved of the colonel's plans to field more RTs. In fact, he had been after him to do exactly that for several months now. It was always amazing to see how many of the ideas he proposed came back to him sooner or later with someone else's brand stamped on them.

"And," the colonel concluded, "if we field more RTs, then we'll need another Hatchet Force unit to back them up." He paused briefly. "And I've found a Mike Force company that's perfect for that assignment."

"Who's that, sir?" Clifford asked.

Marshall almost smiled. "Company A-410 at Ban Phoc."

"Mike Reese is really going to love this, sir," Clifford responded.

"I don't care what that young captain likes," Marshall growled. "I need more troops on the Cambodian border to support the new RTs, and his company fits the bill perfectly. They're Nungs and they've got a lot of combat experience under their belts. I want you to brief him first thing tomorrow morning and get his young ass in gear. I want their new camp operational in two weeks."

Clifford whistled silently. Two weeks was a very short time to carve a CIDG fighting camp out of the raw jungle. "Will he have the engineer support he'll need to get it built that fast?"

Marshall sat back in his chair. "He'll have every goddamn thing he could possibly want. I'm giving you orders for Fifth Group and the Eighteenth Engineer Brigade to spare no effort to get that camp built. I want it built on time, and I'm not going to listen to any bullshit excuses about shortages of either matériel or manpower. This has absolute top priority, and I'll even send the Sea Bees up there to build it if the Army engineers can't hack it."

"Yes, sir."

Marshall scrawled his signature across the bottoms of several order forms and handed them to Clifford. "Get moving on this right now. I want daily reports on their progress. And I want to be kept informed about any delay that occurs, no matter how short. You got that?"

Clifford got to his feet. "Yes, sir. I'll get right on it."

"I'm not going to get caught with another surprise attack like this last monkey fuck."

Clifford bit his tongue. He decided that discretion was the better part of valor; he still had to work with the old bastard.

Marshall watched Clifford close the door on his way out. Then he chuckled. He would give anything to see the look on Reese's face when Clifford gave him the good news.

REESE WAS GRIM-JAWED when he stepped out of the chopper at the Ban Phoc pad and saw a sweat-stained Sergeant Pierce waiting for him. "What's up, Captain?" Pierce asked, mopping his forehead.

Reese and Pierce had been busy supervising the rebuilding of the camp when the team leader had been called to go to B-40 earlier that morning for an urgent classified briefing. He had been gone most of the day, and Pierce was curious.

"Someday I'm going to have to learn to keep my big fucking mouth shut," Reese muttered.

"What happened?" Pierce looked concerned. At this point the last thing they needed was more problems.

"You remember Colonel Marshall?"

"I'm not likely to forget him," Pierce said. "What did that old bastard want this time?"

"Well…" Reese hesitated, trying to find a way to tell the operations sergeant that he had put the whole team in the shit because he had pissed off the SOG colonel. "It looks like he didn't forget me, either."

Now Pierce looked at Reese anxiously. He liked this new captain and looked forward to finishing out the rest of his tour with him. "What did he have to say?"

"Well, there's good news and bad news."

"Give me the good news first."

"We don't have to finish rebuilding the camp."

"Why not?"

"It looks like Marshall has decided he needs to have another Hatchet Force unit to back up some new RTs he's putting in the field, and he picked us for the job."

"Sweet bleeding Jesus," Pierce breathed.

"That's real close to what I said when Clifford gave me the good news," Reese said. "Except that I forgot about the bleeding part."

"What are we supposed to do first?"

"Let's get the team together and I'll go over it," Reese answered as he headed for the command bunker. "But the first thing we're going to do is move to a new AO. We're going north to Three Corps as part of CCC."

SOG's cross-border operations were controlled by three command and control units: Command and Control North at Da Nang, Command and Control South at Ban Me Thout and Command and Control Central based at Kontoum.

"Where are we going?" Pierce asked.

"A little place on the border called Dak Sang—ever heard of it?"

"Can't say I have, sir. But that don't mean shit. There's a lot of places in Vietnam I've never heard of."

"Anyway, it's on the border south of Ban Me Thout."

"This is getting better and better all the time," Pierce said, his face brightening. "A Hatchet Force unit in a border camp."

"And we're going to have to build the camp ourselves," Reese added.

Pierce groaned.

"But," Reese continued, "Clifford says that Marshall's promised us all the support in the world, including the Sea Bees if we need them."

Pierce spit on the ground. "You know what they say, Captain. 'Promise in one hand and shit in the other and see which gets full the fastest.' I've got a feeling this is going to be a real bitch."

Reese laughed and clapped the sergeant on the shoulder. "Come on, Sarge, lighten up. This is a great way for you to finish your career. Your last chance to go down in the history books!"

Pierce looked at him. "Or a great chance to get fitted for a body bag like those poor bastards who got caught by those enemy tanks at Lang Vei. Those fuckin' border camps don't do much for your life expectancy, sir."

"It all counts toward twenty, Sarge."

Pierce nodded. "Yes, sir. But if you don't make it to your twenty, then none of it counts."

Reese looked over at his team sergeant. "You'll make it, Sergeant Pierce," he said seriously.

"But what the fuck, sir." Pierce grinned. "It could be a hell of a lot worse."

"How's that?"

He straightened the green beret on his head. "We could be stuck in the goddamn First Air Cav!"

The Hatchet Force—out to strike the killing blow against a deadly enemy—the NVA.

HATCHET

BLACK MISSION

Knox Gordon

Far from the highly publicized helicopter war televised on the evening news rages the secret war. Fought in neutral Laos and Cambodia, these clandestine "black" missions are carried out by the men of the Special Forces: an elite action group specializing in guerrilla warfare tactics, ready to deploy at a moment's notice.

In the air and on the ground, behind the desks and in the jungles... the action-packed series of the Vietnam War.

Take
4 explosive books
plus a
mystery bonus
FREE

Mail to: Gold Eagle Reader Service
3010 Walden Ave.,
P.O. Box 1394
Buffalo, NY 14240-1394

YEAH! Rush me 4 FREE Gold Eagle novels and my FREE mystery gift. Then send me 4 brand-new novels every other month as they come off the presses. Bill me at the low price of just $12.80* for each shipment—a saving of 15% off the suggested retail price! There is NO extra charge for postage and handling! There is no minimum number of books I must buy. I can always cancel at anytime simply by returning a shipment at your cost or by returning any shipping statement marked ''cancel.'' Even if I never buy another book from Gold Eagle, the 4 free books and surprise gift are mine to keep forever.   164 BPM BP91

_____

Name   (PLEASE PRINT)

_____

Address   Apt. No.

_____

City   State   Zip

_____

Signature (if under 18, parent or guardian must sign)

*Terms and prices subject to change without notice. Sales tax applicable in NY. This offer is limited to one order per household and not valid to present subscribers. Offer not available in Canada.

© 1991 GOLD EAGLE   4E-A2DR